In response, she went on her toes and licked his bottom lip. V... ... provided ... ... over her mouth before pulling back once more.

"Tell me. Tell me you're done with him." It came out as a gruff command, and he was grateful for the raspy quality of his voice. Kept him from what he really felt like doing...

Begging.

He wanted to beg Jill to be his and only his.

His tongue trailed down the soft, smooth column of her neck as she tilted back with a soft sigh.

"Tell me," as she again, his lips moving back up her neck and coming to rest at a sensitive spot under her ear. "Tell me you're mine."

ACCLAIM FOR *FRISK ME*

"Layne launches the New York's Finest contemporary romance series with this stellar example of the genre. Ava and Luc's sparks are immediate, and the evolution of their relationship—which starts with little common ground except a dedication to singlehood—is stimulating and realistic. They negotiate their professional and romantic interactions with banter that's clever but not self-satisfied, and their moment of truth feels warm and real. Fans of slightly gritty contemporaries will adore this."

—*Publishers Weekly* (starred review)

"Layne is hands down the queen of witty dialogue and sexy scenes. *Frisk Me* was a sensual combo of both that left me dying for more."

—Rachel Van Dyken, #1 *New York Times* bestselling author

"4.5 stars!... The first in Layne's New York's Finest series is funny, delightfully steamy, and deeply touching, setting the bar quite high... A bustling, detailed setting and a stellar cast of supporting characters... provide the perfect backdrop for her characters and keep expectations high for the rest of this soon-to-be-a-hit series."

—*RT Book Reviews*

"*Frisk Me* is a terrific love story—equal parts sweet and hot. Layne is a master of both sexual tension and the soul-satisfying HEA."

—Serena Bell, *USA Today* bestselling author

"I just loved this new series from one of my favorite authors and can't wait to read Anthony's story."

—ScandaliciousBookReviews.com

"*Frisk Me* had a story and characters that evoked strong reactions from me and I look forward to the rest of the series. 4.5 stars!"

—Bookaholism.net

CUFF ME

LAUREN LAYNE

FOREVER

NEW YORK   BOSTON

Copyright © 2016 by Lauren Layne
Excerpt from *Frisk Me* is copyright © 2015 by Lauren Layne

Forever
Hachette Book Group
1290 Avenue of the Americas
New York, NY 10104

www.HachetteBookGroup.com

Printed in the United States of America

First Edition: March 2016
10 9 8 7 6 5 4 3 2 1

OPM

Forever is an imprint of Grand Central Publishing.
The Forever name and logo are trademarks of Hachette Book Group, Inc.

The Hachette Speakers Bureau provides a wide range of authors for speaking events. To find out more, go to www.hachettespeakersbureau.com or call (866) 376-6591.

The publisher is not responsible for websites (or their content) that are not owned by the publisher.

For Kristi Yanta, who's been more integral to my career than she'll ever know.

I wouldn't be where I am today without you!

ACKNOWLEDGMENTS

As always, a huge thank you to everyone who touched this manuscript and helped bring Jill and Vincent to life.

So much gratitude for my editor Lauren Plude, who helped me really get to the heart of the love story. And for Megha Parekh, for jumping in feet first with an unfamiliar project and loving it. Special shout out to Kristi Yanta for the best beta-read in the history of publishing.

Thank you to the endlessly patient production team: Susan Higgins for the copyedits and Tareth Mitch for careful attention to details.

For the cover designers, marketing and publicity team, and everyone who made sure the book was as fabulous on the outside as I'd like to think it is on the inside.

For my amazing assistant Lisa, you keep me sane and I adore you.

Friends, family...you know who you are, you know what you do. I'm endlessly grateful.

CUFF
ME

CHAPTER ONE

There's something wrong with a man that grins like that at a crime scene."

Detective Vincent Moretti glanced up from where he'd been studying the gunshot wound of the vic and glared at the officer who'd been shadowing him for the past three months.

"I wasn't grinning."

Detective Tyler Dansen never paused in scribbling in the black notebook he carried everywhere. "You were definitely grinning."

"Nope."

Dansen glanced up. "Fine. Maybe not grinning. But I'm one hundred percent sure I saw you smile."

"How about you be one hundred percent sure about who shot this guy instead?" Vincent said irritably.

Dansen returned his attention to his damn notebook, but he didn't look particularly chagrined by Vin's reprimand.

Oh, what Vin wouldn't give to go back to those early days when all he'd had to do was *look* at Dansen, and the kid practically dropped into a deferential bow.

Three months of spending every workday in each other's company had the newly minted detective acting nearly as impudent as Vincent's actual partner.

Nearly being an important distinction, because Vincent didn't think they made 'em sassier, more stubborn, or more annoying than Detective Jill Henley.

And he would know. They'd been partners for six long years, and their pairing up as partners was proof of God's sense of humor.

Jill Henley was Vincent's opposite in every way.

Jill was chipper, charming, and smiley.

Vincent was... none of those things.

Especially not the last one. Although, if he was being really honest with himself, Dansen may have been right about Vincent cracking a smile earlier.

It's not that Vin was immune to death. There was absolutely nothing humorous about a man lying cold in his own blood and guts, dead from a gunshot wound to the stomach.

But after six years as a homicide DT for the NYPD, one learned to compartmentalize. To let the brain occasionally go somewhere else other than death even as you were staring straight at it.

It was the only way to survive. Otherwise it was nothing but puking and nightmares.

And speaking of puking...

Vincent stood and gave Detective Dansen a once-over. "If you're gonna barf, do it outside," he said, just to needle the younger man.

Dansen threw his arms up in exasperation. "That was one time. One time! And I hear it happens to everyone on their first day."

"Didn't happen to me."

"That's because you're a machine," Dansen muttered under his breath.

Vincent didn't respond to this. It was nothing he hadn't heard before. *Robot. Machine. Automaton.*

He just didn't know what people expected him to do about it.

In the movies, there was always some reason for the semi-mechanical, unfeeling action hero.

Either a dead wife, an abusive past, or some other sort of jacked-up emotional history. But Vincent had always sort of figured he'd been born this way. Quiet. Reserved. Broody.

It's not that he didn't feel. Of course he did. He just didn't feel *out loud*.

He wasn't sure that he really knew how to, and wasn't sure he wanted to learn.

But in Dansen's defense on the puking thing, the kid's first crime scene as a homicide DT had been a rough one. A sixteen-year-old girl sliced to pieces and then tossed in the Dumpster behind a one-dollar-a-slice pizza joint in Queens.

Vincent's fists clenched at the memory.

It had taken them three days to find the guy who'd done that to her—a real sicko who'd claimed he'd done it because he was "bored."

That was one son of a bitch he hoped prison was *really* rough for.

"Let's move out," Vin growled at Dansen.

He headed toward the door of the hotel room where the body was found, and Dansen fell into step beside him, flipping through his notebook. "Okay, so here's what I'm thinking. The wife is the one who found the body and called it in, but—"

"She also shot him," Vincent said, impatiently punching at the Down button for the elevator.

Dansen huffed in exasperation. "I was getting to that."

"Get there faster," Vincent said as they stepped into the elevator.

"So can I—"

"Bring her in for questioning?" Vincent finished for him as he pulled out his cell phone. "Do it. And don't go easy on her. She'll slip up within minutes, all tangled up in her own guilt."

The younger man snapped his notebook shut. "It's really annoying when you do that. Finishing other people's sentences."

"K," Vincent said distractedly, already striding off the elevator.

The lobby was crawling with reporters, and Vincent glared at Dansen, who held up his hands in surrender. "Don't look at me. I didn't call them."

Vincent gritted his teeth. He *hated* hotel cases. There was always some bellhop or housekeeper who couldn't keep his or her damn mouth shut, and the result was a media circus that made the police work a thousand times more complicated than it needed to be.

Not that it really mattered in this particular case. There

wasn't a doubt in his mind that the wife had pulled the trigger. Vin would bet his pension on it. He'd been doing this too long not to see the signs immediately. The too-fast way of speaking. The awkwardly forced eye contact in an unconscious effort to minimize nervous blinking. Fidgeting hands.

The vic's wife had all of the above. This murder was practically the definition of open-and-shut case.

"You care if I leave you to finish this one up on your own?" he asked Dansen as they headed toward Vincent's unmarked patrol car.

Dansen skidded to a halt. "Seriously? You even have to ask? I've been begging you for *three months* to let me take point, and—"

"All right, calm down," Vincent said, jerking open the door of the driver's seat. He hesitated before getting in, realizing that there were things to be said.

He rested an arm on the roof of the car and glanced at Dansen, who was…

Smirking.

"Wipe that shit smile off your face," Vincent said without any real heat.

"You're gonna miss me," Dansen taunted.

Vin narrowed his eyes. "Don't push it, kid."

"Kid? I'm thirty-one."

"Exactly."

Dansen gave an incredulous laugh. "You're thirty-three. Two years' difference hardly makes you my senior."

Not in years maybe. But in experience…

It wasn't about who was youngest or oldest. It was about who was best.

And Vin was confident that was *him*.

Vincent was damn good at his job. It was why he'd been assigned a trainee during Jill's leave of absence despite the fact that his lack of people skills was as legendary as his ability to sniff out even the most clever of murderers.

In truth, Vincent had been dreading his three months with the near-rookie, but it had been less painful than expected. Dansen was a good cop. A little green, but when Dansen was assigned his new partner tomorrow, Vin had no doubts that the guy would be able to handle whatever came his way.

And then Vincent's life would finally get back to normal.

Not that these three months without Jill had been abnormal, precisely.

He still worked the same backbreaking schedule. Still saw death more days than not.

Still went to breakfast with his family after Mass every Sunday, and argued with his brothers and occasionally with his sister during said breakfast.

He still watched sports most evenings, still worked out most mornings.

So really, his life wasn't different without Jill at all.

Except that it was. Wildly, horribly different.

He glanced at his watch. Two hours until her plane landed. Three hours, maybe four until he'd see her again.

Not that he was counting.

"So you're good from here?" Vincent asked. "If you need anything, I'll be…"

"Yeah, yeah, I'll call ya. You never did tell me where you were going."

"Probably because it's none of your Goddamn business."

Dansen put a hand to his chest. "I've come to love these heart-to-hearts of ours. The way we count on each other. Confide in each other—"

"My cue to leave," Vincent grumbled.

He started to get in the car, when Dansen called his name again.

Vin shot him an impatient look and was surprised when the usually confident Dansen looked away briefly before meeting his eyes.

"Hey, I just wanted to say..." Dansen cleared his throat from across the hood of the car, and Vin tensed, knowing what was coming.

God, he hated shit like this.

"You can drop the detective," Vincent said roughly. "Just call me Moretti. Or Vin. Whatever."

Dansen's smile flashed white across his dark face. "Do you know how many cops dream of the day when they're given permission to call one of the members of the royal family by their first name?"

"Oh Jesus. Don't start that again."

For the most part, Dansen had done a remarkable job of not irritating Vincent to the extreme over the past three months. But Dansen's ridiculous hero worship of Vincent's last name grated on his nerves. Yet another reason he couldn't wait for Jill to get back.

Jill, who'd never cared that Vincent's father was the recently retired police commissioner. Or that his older brother was a captain. Or that his younger brother was the NYPD's most famous officer.

Or that his grandfather had been a cop and his mother had been a police dispatcher...

Okay, so maybe Vincent could *sort of* understand

where Dansen was coming from. The Morettis were kind of NYPD royalty.

And Vincent was proud to be a part of it. Proud to carry on the legacy.

He just got damn tired of the ass kissing.

"Seriously though, thanks," Dansen said. "Couldn't have asked for a better detective to show me the ropes. A nicer one, sure. A better-looking one, definitely. And you can be a real—"

"Asshole, I know," Vincent said.

Dansen held up a finger. "Not what I was going to say. I think that's the first time you've tried to finish my sentence and gotten it wrong."

"I'm never wrong," Vin said out of habit.

"Fine." Dansen rolled his eyes. "You're an asshole. Happy?"

Vin didn't bother responding, just lifted his hand in a final farewell to Dansen before the younger man could say whatever it was he'd wanted to say, and lowered himself into the car.

Vincent slid on his aviator sunglasses as he fastened his seat belt.

Vin kept his face perfectly blank until he'd pulled away from the curb and merged into traffic.

Only then, only out of sight of prying eyes, did he let a smile overtake his face. A smile that quickly became a grin as he headed toward his longtime barber for a very overdue haircut.

He told himself that his decision to get his hair cut after weeks of putting it off had absolutely nothing to do with the fact that he'd be seeing Jill in a few short hours.

Vincent had never really given two thoughts to what Jill Henley thought of his looks.

But then, he and Jill had never spent three months apart. He'd never had a chance to realize just how much he'd...missed her.

Not that he'd be telling *her* that.

CHAPTER TWO

One never really realized how much New York City got under your skin until you left it for a while.

It was like one minute New York was your adopted home—a little bit intense, a lot scary.

And the next, you were holding your breath as your plane landed, your entire body on edge with the anticipation of being *home* again.

Jill Henley smiled as the plane touched down, her eyes closing just for a moment at the realization that she'd be sleeping in her own bed tonight. Going back to her job tomorrow. Eating at her favorite gyros place tomorrow.

But none of that—not the city, nor her pillow-top bed, nor the really freaking amazing gyros—were as important as *who* awaited her.

The Morettis.

Jill loved her mother desperately—it was the reason

she'd spent the past three months in Florida taking care of her.

But the Moretti family had become every bit as much family to Jill as her own mom.

She couldn't wait to see them again.

All of them.

Okay, so maybe there was one Moretti in particular whom she was especially excited to see.

Not that the excitement was mutual.

As she walked through JFK toward baggage claim, she couldn't figure out for the life of her why she was even the *tiniest* bit disappointed about the fact that Vincent Moretti wouldn't be the one picking her up from the airport.

She hadn't even asked him. He might have said yes. Maybe. But it would have been done with a grunt and a grumble, and probably a lecture about how his work-load was double because his partner had "up and ditched him."

Besides, it made more sense for Elena to pick her up anyway.

Not only was Elena her best friend, but Elena was an attorney at a fancy-pants law firm, with access to a company car that was a hell of a lot nicer than Vin's car and didn't smell like old coffee.

Plus, Jill had news.

Big news.

The biggest.

The kind of news that female friends squealed over in the appropriate, gushing manner.

So why was she so nervous?

Jill bit her lip as she waited at baggage claim for the carousel to start dropping her flight's bags.

She pulled out her cell and texted Elena. At baggage claim.

Cool. Stuck in traffic on airport drive. Can't WAIT to see you. xoxo.

Jill smiled. She and Elena had texted frequently while Jill had been in Florida, but texts and phone calls weren't the same as a good, in-person gab session.

They needed wine and cookies and ice cream. Oh, and pasta. God, she'd missed pasta. The from-a-jar spaghetti sauce she'd made for her mom once a week couldn't compare with Maria Moretti's made-from-her-own-tomatoes sauce.

Ten minutes later, Jill had heaved her two enormous suitcases off the carousel just as Elena called her phone.

"Ugh, I'm so sorry. Just now pulling up. Where you at? I'll run in."

"Run, huh?" Jill asked as she wheeled her bags toward the door. "Tell me, how high are your heels today, four inches or five?"

"Okay, so I'll stride purposefully," Elena said. "Just tell me what carousel thingy you're at. I can have Cory circle around."

"Who the heck is Cory?"

"New driver. He's totally cute. Great butt."

Jill rolled her eyes. "He can totally hear you, huh?"

"*Totally*. Okay, now where are you for real? I'm coming in, but if I break a nail—"

"Door eight," Jill said, and she stepped outside. "While you were flirting with your driver, I already got my bags. Also, how freaking cold is it right now? It was not this cold last winter."

"It totally was; you've just been spending too much time on the beach. Okay, we're approaching. What are you wearing?"

Jill glanced down at her white long-sleeve tee and jeans with her puffy-coat vest.

"Minidress, *obviously*. It's lacy, super short. Maybe a little see-through, I can't be sure. My hair's styled in big ringlets, sort of beauty queen style—"

"I see you, you little liar. Also, didn't we agree that the Uggs were going buh-bye after last winter?"

A black car pulled up in front of Jill, the back window rolling down to reveal the stunning, if slightly haughty, features of Elena Moretti.

"Hello, darling," her best friend said.

Then the back door was open and they were doing the squealing, hoppy thing that seemed entirely necessary after a three-month separation.

Well, mostly it was Jill doing the jumping and squealing, while the far more sophisticated Elena let Jill all but maul her with hugs.

"Down, girl," Elena said with one last pet of Jill's ponytail.

Jill pulled back so she could study her best friend, grinning in relief when she saw Elena looked exactly as she had when Jill left. Her best friend was stunning. Tall, hourglass figure, long chestnut hair, blue eyes...total hottie.

Add in the girl-power suits and killer heels, and you had a bona fide man-eater on your hands.

Speaking of men, a guy, whom Jill assumed must be Cory, gave them an indulgent smile as he easily hoisted Jill's suitcases into the trunk, before coming around and holding the door for them expectantly.

"He *does* have a cute butt," Jill whispered as she climbed into the backseat after Elena.

"Right? Oh, and if it comes up, you're a potential client," Elena said before turning her vibrating phone to silent and dropping it into her Chanel bag. "Hence why I'm using company resources."

"Cool, got it. I can totally play this," Jill said, clicking her seat belt into place. She cleared her throat. "You can't handle the truth!"

The driver faltered slightly as he lowered himself into the driver's seat, and Elena rolled her eyes. "What was that?"

"Jack Nicholson, from... actually, I have no idea what that's from."

"It's from *A Few Good Men*, and that's not what I'm asking. I'm wondering why the heck you're shouting it out all crazy-like right now?"

"Well, Jack's character says that while he's on the witness stand. And you said I was supposed to be a client, so..."

Elena stared at her. "Babe, what is it you think I do all day?"

"Lawyer stuff?" Jill grinned widely.

"Right. And I'm sure all you do all day is drink coffee and eat doughnuts, right? Cop stuff?"

Jill gave a happy sigh. "God, I miss doughnuts. Florida doesn't know how to do them right, and Mom decided that going without sugar was going to be her 'thing' during her sixties."

Elena looked horrified. "No wine? That has sugar."

"Yeah, I think she conveniently ignores that."

"How is she?"

"Better now," Jill said. "Getting her mobility back and all that."

A broken collarbone and hip were a nasty combination for anyone, but it had been especially hard on Kerry Henley, who prided herself in being an active "young" sixty-year-old. One day she'd been running a 5K, and then next she'd missed a step carrying her laundry basket down the stairs and been almost completely laid up for months.

It had taken up all of Jill's personal time plus a couple months of unpaid leave to care for her, but Jill hadn't hesitated to make the temporary move to Florida.

Her boss had assured her that her job would be waiting for her when she got back, and three months of your life is the least you could do for a parent who'd given eighteen years to caring for you.

Jill's in particular deserved her devotion; Jill's dad had dropped dead of a heart attack at forty-one, leaving Kerry to raise a headstrong (read: bratty) daughter all by herself.

"I'm glad she's better. I love your mom. I wish she'd come up to New York more often."

"You wouldn't say that if you had to listen to her complain about the pigeons and the subway and the weather."

"Could be worse. Last Sunday, my mother actually started a sentence with, "You're not getting any younger, Elena.""

"I can beat that. *Mine* suggested freezing my eggs."

"You're right. You win. And speaking of your nether regions, I'm so overdue for an update on this Tom guy you've been seeing. Did you guys decide to do long distance? Or are you going to wait until you find out if he's any good at sexting before you cut him loose?"

Jill bit her lip, gathering courage for what she was about to say. For some reason, she'd always pictured this moment as feeling...different. She expected feeling giddy and breathless as she made The Big Announcement.

Instead she felt hesitant.

So Jill did what Jill Henley did whenever she felt anything less than sparkles and rainbows.

She faked it.

Jill pasted a smile on her face, took a deep breath, and shot her left hand out in front of Elena's face.

"What, are you—" Elena broke off, her cool fingers wrapping around Jill's wrist as her mouth dropped open. "No. Freaking. Way."

"Way."

Elena let out an uncharacteristic squeal. "You're getting married?!"

The words hit Jill with a little slap.

She was getting married.

It felt...funny.

Probably because she wasn't used to it yet.

Elena threw herself across the backseat, arms wrapped around Jill's neck as she kissed the side of Jill's head repeatedly.

"Congratulations, darling! When? Do I get to be maid of honor? I won't wear green, but you know that. How did it happen? How did it happen? Oh yeah, and why did you not tell me?"

Jill managed to extricate herself from Elena's grip, only to have her left hand held hostage as Elena studied the square-cut diamond with a scary level of scrutiny.

"He asked last night," Jill said, gazing fondly at the ring. "I thought it was our farewell dinner, and, well, he had other ideas."

"Hell yeah, he did," Elena said, ceasing studying the diamond so that she could instead study Jill.

"I wanted to call you last night," Jill said apologetically.

"I so did. But I thought if I could hold off just a few hours, and tell you in person..."

"Forgiven. Of course. I mean, the news is so much better with the ring, you know?"

Let's hope everyone feels that way. Jill sat in thought as Elena lifted her hand, studying the ring.

Because if she'd been nervous to tell Elena, it was nothing compared to her nerves over telling Vincent. Which made no sense. She and Vin weren't romantically involved. Had never even come close.

And he might be the most surly grouch on the planet, but he cared about her. Cared about her happiness.

He *would* be happy for her.

Wouldn't he?

"I'm thrilled, you know that, right?" Elena asked.

Jill smiled because she knew that tone. "But..."

Her friend bit her lip for a moment, looking uncharacteristically unsure of herself before taking a deep breath. "Okay, I'm just going to come right out and say it. This happened fast. You've known the guy three months. You're all the way sure?"

Jill twisted the ring. "I'm sure. I'm totally sure. You'll understand when you meet him, El. He's just...he's just...he's *perfect.*"

"Perfect, huh? You just got engaged, so I'm going to allow for the hyperbole. But tell me why I should let this guy marry my best friend."

Jill blew out a breath, wondering how to explain. "You know you meet another person and just *get* them? It was like that."

"Explain."

Explain.

How did one explain Tom Edward Porter and how when you met someone as perfectly *right* for you as Tom was for her, you couldn't afford to waste thought on things like soul mates or passion.

You just had to go for it.

"Okay, it's like this," Jill said, twisting so she could better face Elena. "When you were little, did you ever make your brothers play wedding with you? You know, make one of them pretend to be the groom?"

"Um, of course."

"Luc?" Jill asked curiously.

"Obviously. He's the nicest of the bunch, and the youngest, which made him easiest to coerce."

Jill nodded. Elena had four brothers, and with the exception of mostly easygoing Luc, she couldn't imagine any of them patiently letting their sister dress them up as groom to her bride.

Luc Moretti—the *bambino* as he was lovingly known— might have managed to stand still just long enough to say his pretend vows.

Anthony, the oldest, was far too serious. Marco was more laid-back, although from what Jill had heard, he'd also been the most rowdy of the kids. Then there was Vincent, and the thought of him humoring anyone, least of all his sister... no. Just no.

Jill felt a tightening in her chest at the thought of the Morettis. *God*, she'd missed them.

Elena snapped her fingers in Jill's face. "Your mind is wandering. Focus, Jilly."

"Right, okay... so back when we were little girls and imagining our perfect future husband... we were *totally* picturing Tom."

"So...you're marrying an eight-year-old's fantasy? That's not creepy *at all*."

Jill laughed, missing her friend's *no bullshit* candor. "No, okay, it's like...Tom is just *nice*. He's the sort of guy you dream about on Valentine's Day when you're depressed about being single, so you buy bridal magazines, and then spend the evening looking at goofy white dresses, drinking too much merlot, and wondering when exactly *he* would arrive on a white horse."

Or maybe that was just Jill's Valentine's Day, more often than not.

It didn't matter. Tom Porter was like something out of a dream. The only box he didn't tick off in the Prince Charming checklist was the white horse, but that was okay because his Audi convertible was even better.

In fact, he was *so* perfect, *so* charming, that the first time she saw him, it had taken Jill several seconds to register that he was real.

And then several more seconds to register that he was talking to her.

It's not that Jill thought of herself as unappealing. She knew she was cute, because people told her so. Note, never beautiful, or even pretty. Never gorgeous. *Certainly* never sexy. But cute. Sometimes adorable. Because that's just what *every* thirty-three-year-old woman wanted to hear.

And she got it; she was average height, flat as a board, with a too-pointy chin and jaw, eyes too big for her face, and blond hair that she wore in a pony more often than not in an attempt to disguise how flat it could be.

But Tom?

Tom made her feel *beautiful*. He made her feel like a

woman rather than a girl who seemed to inspire pats on the head from those around her.

Tom had picked her up at a bar. Cliché, yes, but made less skeevy by the fact that neither of them had walked into that swanky hotel bar with the intention of going home with a member of the opposite sex. And they hadn't.

Gone home with each other, that is. Not that first night at least.

It had been the end of Jill's first week in Florida. Her mom had just started coming to grips with the immobile reality of her near future and understandably had turned ornery, even toward Jill.

Not that Jill could blame her.

The prospect of months of not being able to walk or use an arm would have made Jill a bit stabby too. Still, by the end of that first week, both mother and daughter had needed a break.

Jill had waited until her mom's friend came over for a marathon viewing of some show Jill had never heard of, and Jill had gone straight for her favorite therapy of choice: wine.

She was halfway through her first glass of a rather bright and delicious sauvignon blanc at a swanky beach-side resort when *he'd* walked in.

It had been impossible to miss him. The bar was practically deserted, being early on a Monday evening, but even if the bar had been packed with wall-to-wall people, she would have noticed him.

For starters, he was tall.

Like, six-foot-plus, definitely.

Broad shouldered in that football quarterback kind

of way. His hair was dark blond and styled to look like a freaking Kennedy, all thick and rich-person like. Skin... perfect golden tan. Not the type of tan of a sun worshipper, or worse, a fake sun worshipper, just a guy who spent enough time outdoors to not look like a zombie.

Perfectly tailored suit? Check. White, friendly smile? Yup.

Politeness toward the bartender as he ordered his rye Manhattan? *Be still her heart.*

Later, he would tell Jill that she'd been staring, and she didn't bother to deny it.

In that moment when he'd picked up his drink and slid off his bar stool at the other end of the bar, it had never, not once, occurred to Jill that he'd be coming toward her.

Not until the bartender fluttered a cocktail napkin down onto the bar beside her own, just seconds before a large male hand placed his drink on it, did she realize what was happening.

This gorgeous, untouchable man was coming over to talk to her.

Luckily, there was one thing Jill did very well, and that was talk to strangers. It came with the job, what with questioning suspects and witnesses and family members all day long. Because God knew her partner was no good at that part.

But anyway, the gorgeous man in the navy suit later told her it was her unabashed staring that had amused him enough to make his way to her.

It was her unabashed friendliness that had made him stick around.

Everything after that...well, it had happened fast. Only a week after, he'd stuck out his hand and introduced himself as Tom, Tom Porter, in a sort of James Bondian way that made her giggle. They had been eating dinner at that very same hotel restaurant.

Only a week after *that*, dinner with Tom had become the norm rather than the exception.

The week after that?

They occasionally threw lunch into the mix, either her coming to meet him at some fancy place while her mom was in physical therapy, or him bringing fabulous picnic-style lunches to her mother's house, where he'd proceed to charm Jill's mom *almost* as thoroughly as he charmed Jill.

Five weeks into Jill's stay in Florida, Jill had stuck around for breakfast.

In his hotel room.

And then there'd been last night.

"Okay, okay, so he's a dreamboat," Elena said as the car crept slowly through rush hour traffic toward Manhattan. "How'd he pop the question? Champagne? Roses? Fancy restaurant with a water view?"

"Holy crap," Jill said with a laugh. "Were you *there*?"

"I know all," Elena said, extending her hands to the side as though she were some wise sage. "Did you see it coming at all?"

"Not even a little bit," Jill admitted.

Not even with the expensive champagne, or the two dozen roses, or the fact that the restaurant staff seemed to be going out of their way to give Jill and Tom privacy at the terrace table overlooking the ocean.

She'd simply thought it had just been a really fantastic good-bye.

Instead it had been a bit more of a *be mine forever and ever*.

And Jill had said yes.

She'd said yes almost the second he'd gone down on his knee, not because she'd been that sure—she'd been *pretty* sure...*sort* of sure—she'd said yes because in that moment, Jill had wanted what Tom Porter was offering her.

A companion. A partner. *Love.*

And that's what it came down to. Jill wanted to be loved. She wanted *to* love.

She loved her mother, obviously. And loved the memory of her father, God rest his soul.

And though she had no siblings of her own, the Morettis had filled that gap. And with the recent addition of Luc's girlfriend, Ava, and Anthony's new wife, Maggie, she had some amazing girlfriends to add to the mix.

And last, but never least, there was Vincent. Her partner. In some ways her best friend, although in a way that was different from her relationship with Elena.

But as much as Vincent sometimes seemed like two parts of the same whole, he'd always held a bit of himself back from her. From everyone.

He'd made no secret of the fact that he had no intentions of getting married, ever. Any fantasies Jill had had that her partner would one day wake up and *see* her were long gone.

Which left her a bit...lonely.

She wanted someone to come home to at the end of the long day who would just be there. Who'd pour her a glass of wine, maybe rub her feet and just listen.

Tom offered Jill what nobody else had offered her...ever.

Love. Commitment. A future.

And she knew that he loved her. Fast as their relationship

had developed, she could feel it. And she loved him too. At least she was pretty sure.

"Aww, you like him," Elena said teasingly, reaching out a finger and poking the dimple in Jill's left cheek.

"I want to be happy, El. I want the happily-ever-after with someone who wants it with me."

She met her friend's eyes and saw from the flash of regret on Elena's face that El understood what Jill wasn't saying out loud.

I can't wait for Vin forever.

"I'm assuming you haven't told him?"

Jill shook her head and looked down at her ring, still trying to get used to the sparkle on her finger. "No. Like I said, not really a phone conversation."

"He's going to be thrilled," Elena said with a small smile. "I mean, he won't show it, of course, because he's emotionally barren. But he cares about you, babe. He just wants you to be happy."

"I am happy," Jill said.

Elena nodded distractedly, and Jill's eyes narrowed. She knew her friend well, and something was definitely on Elena's mind.

"Spill it," Jill said.

Elena blew out a long breath. "Okay, so it was supposed to be a surprise, but given that huge rock on your finger and the enormity of the bomb you're about to drop, I just can't let you go in unprepared."

Jill frowned. "Go in where?"

"To Anthony and Maggie's place. There's kinda sorta a surprise party awaiting you."

Jill clapped her hands excitedly. "I love surprise parties! Especially when they're for me."

"I know you do, I just didn't know if you were planning to tell everyone all at once, or if you maybe first wanted to break the news to ... *individuals* first."

Jill rubbed her thumb on the underside of the platinum band as she contemplated. In truth, she hadn't really thought about how she was going to break the news to her partner. Hadn't really let her brain go there.

"He was unbearable while you were gone," Elena said quietly. "Even more so than usual."

Jill snorted. "Yeah. I'm sure the separation was pure agony. You know, I barely heard from him?" she said absently. "I was gone three months, and I'd say he returned about ten percent of my texts, maybe two percent of my phone calls."

Elena sighed. "So what's the plan? I can make an excuse, say you're not feeling well—"

Jill's head whipped around. "No! I'm dying to see everyone. And your mom's cooking..." She rubbed her belly.

"Okay, so what about the rock? You want to take it off for now, wait until you figure out how to tell everyone? Because you know it's going to take all of thirty seconds for Ava or Maggie to spot that bad boy, and then it's going to be all over."

Jill twisted the ring on her finger as she stared down at her cell phone. The cell that hadn't once buzzed with a message of any kind from her partner. No *welcome home*, no *hey* ... nothing.

She glanced up at Elena. "It's worth celebrating, right?"

Elena's mouth dropped open. "Um, I'm offended by the question. Of course it is."

Jill reached across and squeezed her friend. "Then I can't think of anyone I'd rather celebrate with more than your family."

"Hell yeah!" Elena said, reaching into her purse and pulling out her phone. "I'm totally telling my liquor guy to have a shit-ton of champagne delivered to Anth's place."

"I love that you have a liquor guy," Jill said with a smile. "I've missed this. I've missed you."

Elena smiled without looking up from her phone. "I've missed you too. We all have."

Jill's happiness slipped slightly, and she turned to look out at the slowly passing city.

She was sure that most of the Morettis had missed her, but she wasn't sure about all of them.

And she certainly wasn't sure about the one that mattered. The one that had *always* mattered.

CHAPTER THREE

By the time Vincent found a parking spot even remotely close to his older brother's apartment, he was a good thirty minutes late to Jill's surprise party.

Elena had already sent him a scolding text that he'd missed the surprise part.

So had his mother.

He hadn't heard from Jill, but then she wasn't the type to bust his balls about stuff like that. She liked to reserve that for work-related topics.

Still, he regretted being late. But as it turned out, thinking of a welcome home gift for one's partner is something that should not be left for the actual homecoming day.

After his haircut, Vin's plan had been to go out and get...*something* to welcome Jill home.

But what was supposed to be a basic, simple errand had

led to Vincent driving all over the Goddamn city, growing increasingly clueless on what was appropriate.

Flowers? No. Vin didn't *do* flowers. To say nothing of what his brothers would have done if Vincent had shown up with fucking roses.

Wine? Fitting. Jill loved wine. But seeing as the wine was already likely to be flowing freely at Anth's place, a little anticlimactic.

Jewelry? Fuck no.

Clothes. Even Vin knew that was a no-no. You get the wrong size, you're a dead man.

But damn it, he'd wanted to get *something*. Needed to. Needed to show her...

He'd gotten her a doughnut.

A maple bar, which as far as he was concerned was a sorry excuse for a doughnut. If it wasn't chocolate, he didn't bother. But the first day he and Jill had been paired up, and she'd talked his fucking ear off, that was the first thing she'd told him.

Hi, I'm Jill! I think we're going to be great partners, but before we can be best friends, we're going to have to know each other's favorite kind of doughnut. Mine's a maple bar...

Vincent smiled at the memory as he knocked at the door.

There was no answer, and he was about to let himself in, when it opened.

A wall of sound hit him. Typical Moretti family gathering volume: loud.

"Vin! I'm so glad you're here."

Vincent flashed a smile at his new sister-in-law. Maggie Walker—no, Maggie *Moretti*—was just about the sweetest woman on the planet, and far too good for Anthony.

She was dressed in a knee-length navy dress, her brown hair spilling over her shoulders, a warm smile in place, as always.

"Hi, dear," he said, kissing her cheek as he slipped in the front door.

Vincent turned to face her, reaching out a hand and resting it unapologetically against her slightly rounded belly. "How's my nephew?"

She smiled and glanced down. "Don't let Anth hear you say that. He's convinced it's a girl."

"Only because he knows a junior version of him will be an absolute nightmare."

Anthony Moretti appeared at his wife's side. "I heard that, brother dearest. And, actually, I'm a junior. So if we have a son and name him Anthony, he'd be the third."

Vin shook his head. "You sound like an asshole."

Anth shrugged. "We're Italian. I don't make the rules."

"Whatever. Everyone all here?"

"Seeing as the party started at six, yeah, everyone's here, " Anth said.

"See? Asshole," Vincent grumbled, starting to brush past his brother and head toward the kitchen where all the noise was coming from.

Where Jill was.

Anth grabbed his arm, and Vincent glanced up in surprise before shaking free. "What the hell, man? I'm thirty minutes late. Not a big deal."

Anth opened his mouth, but shut it again after glancing at Maggie.

Vin shot a glance over his shoulder at his sister-in-law, whose expression was troubled. "Am I missing something?"

Neither responded, and he shrugged. "Whatever."

He continued toward the kitchen, his eyes automatically scanning the room for Jill, even as he registered that the hand holding the bag with the doughnut was slightly sweaty.

You idiot. Should have left it in the car.

His eyes locked on the group of women in the corner, but before he could find Jill, who was several inches shorter than the rest of them, his younger brother stepped in front of him, blocking his field of vision.

"Champagne?" Luc asked.

Vincent accepted the glass, mostly to get it out of his face, before frowning at the fussy flute. "Is there no red opened?"

Luc clinked his glass against Vin's. "We're celebrating, douche bag."

Vin took a sip. It was actually pretty good. "What are we celebrating?"

There was the briefest of pauses before Luc responded, and Vin's instincts went on high alert. Now both brothers were acting strangely.

Not good.

"That Jill's home," Luc said.

Vincent's eyes narrowed. His brother's voice was too cheerful, even for Luc.

Testing his brother, he stepped to the side. Luc sidestepped with him, blocking Vin's view of the women.

Bingo. Vincent took another casual sip of the champagne. "So, you going to tell me what's going on, or are you and Anthony going to flip for it?"

"We already did flip for it," Luc grumbled. "I won, and yet I notice Big Brother's conveniently loitering with his hot wife by the front door."

"Great," Vin said, clamping his brother on the shoulder. "You can tell me later then. In the meantime, you cool if I go greet the guest of honor?"

"Vin."

"Jesus," he muttered, turning to find that Anthony had decided to join them, and both brothers were giving him a grim look. "Who died?"

Anth grabbed a handful of Vincent's leather jacket before dragging him backward away from the kitchen.

Vin shrugged free and glared. "I swear to God, will you two clowns just—"

"Jill's getting married."

It was Luc that blurted it out, and Vincent very slowly turned to stare at his younger brother. Luc's blue eyes gazed back at him, and there was no trace of his usual humor.

Vin slowly shifted his gaze to Anthony, whose look was equally somber. "I'm sorry, man."

Vincent shook his head. "What do you mean she's getting married? Who the fuck is she marrying?"

"That guy she was seeing in Florida."

"What guy?!" Vincent was practically shouting now. This didn't make sense. None of this made sense. Jill couldn't be getting fucking *married*. She'd have told him. She'd have . . .

"Well maybe if you'd made the time to talk to her, you might have known she was seeing someone," Anthony snapped.

"Hell, maybe if you'd made the time to talk to her, she wouldn't have been seeing *anyone*," Luc muttered into his champagne flute.

Vin's eyes narrowed on his brother. "What the hell is that supposed to mean?"

"You know exactly what it's supposed to mean, you dumb, cowardly—"

Anth cleared his throat before socking Vincent in the shoulder.

It was as much warning as Vin had before a small, warm body collided against his.

Jill.

He'd been picturing this moment in his head for weeks now, and the joy, he'd expected.

The pain... not so much.

Jill was getting married.

Her arms were around his neck, and he very slowly wrapped one arm around her back before letting his face find the crook of her neck.

He told himself it was just a natural position, but there was nothing natural about the way he wanted to linger. Or the way his lips accidentally brushed her neck, or the way he wanted to kiss her there. To...

Jill was getting married.

She pulled back slightly before putting her hands on either side of his face and giving his head a little shake. "Would you believe that I've missed your ugly face?"

Her smile was all warmth and friendliness and familiarity, and he resisted the urge to rub his chest, which physically ached.

Tell her you've missed her too. Tell her that you...

Vin thrust the now completely crumpled bag at her. "Here."

She blinked in surprise, looking completely puzzled as she hooked a finger into the opening of the white bag.

He felt the curious gaze of his family as everyone gathered around, but he ignored them. Only Jill mattered, and...

Damn it, man, a doughnut?!

She had a hard time pulling the bag apart, probably because he'd smushed the contents to death, and it was just…

Good God, it was like he was a fucking Neanderthal.

He was about to rip the bag out of her hand and make some lame excuse about having to be somewhere…anywhere, when Jill's startled blue eyes snapped up at his.

She looked stunned. And…happy?

Please let her be happy.

"How'd you know?" she asked, tilting her head.

He blinked. "What?"

"How'd you know that a maple bar was *all* I could think about when I was in Florida? Would you believe they can't make a decent one?"

"No such thing as a decent maple bar," he said gruffly. "They're disgusting."

She ignored him as she pulled the completely flattened doughnut out of the bag and took an enormous bite, smiling happily as she chewed. "Perfect."

"It's not going to be perfect when you ruin the dinner I spent all day preparing," Vin's grandma grumbled as she generously topped off her champagne glass.

"*You* spent all day preparing, did you? Was that before or after yoga, or your 'afternoon delight,'" Vin's mother said, outraged.

"Whoa, whoa," Luc said, moving between the two women before a fight could erupt. "Two things. No fighting about cooking. Remember? That's why we hosted this shindig at Anth's place. Second thing, afternoon delight. Thought we agreed that Nonna's geriatric sex life was off-limits for family dinner conversation?"

"Oh, Luca," Nonna said with a shake of her head. "You're telling me you and Ava never—"

Luc's girlfriend gently reached out and tipped Nonna's champagne glass up to her lips. "Let's not finish that sentence, hmm?"

Vincent barely heard any of this.

He was too busy watching the way Jill happily devoured her doughnut.

She was holding the sugary mess with her left hand.

Which was adorned with a brand-new diamond that was threatening to break the heart he didn't know he had.

CHAPTER FOUR

Jill was getting married.

Vin had repeated the thought to himself at least a dozen times in the thirty minutes since his brothers had dropped the bomb.

Jill was getting married.

Nope.

Still didn't feel like fact. It wasn't...right.

"She looks happy."

Vin flicked his eyes to the side, trying to figure out if his older brother was looking for a fight, but Anthony merely stood there with his usual unreadable expression. Plus, he was holding out a beer, so...

Vincent accepted the beer with a grunt.

"You don't," Anth said, shifting so he mimicked Vincent's posture of back to the wall. It was a place Vin found himself a lot. Off to the side. Out of the way. Watching.

"I don't what?" Vincent asked.

"Look happy," his brother said.

Vincent didn't respond as he took a sip of beer, not really bothered by the observation.

Anth was hardly one to talk about looking happy.

Anthony Moretti was the oldest of the Moretti siblings, older than Vincent by two years, and nearly as taciturn as Vincent himself.

Less so now though, Vincent had to admit. His brother had become a different man since meeting and falling for Maggie Walker. Vin couldn't blame him; Maggie was good people.

Still, even with his beautiful new wife and baby on the way, Anth wasn't exactly forthcoming with big toothy grins.

Of the five Moretti siblings, he and Anth were the most alike. Marc and Luc were more easily likable. Quick with a smile and a joke. Elena, as the only girl, was the family darling, and as quick with a smile as she was with a tantrum.

But Anth and Vincent were cut of the same cloth. Quiet, reserved, ambitious.

It was these similarities that prevented them from getting along.

That, and the fact that Anth had never been good about minding his own business. He was classic oldest sibling in all the worst ways. Bossy. Interfering. Condescending...

"Aren't you two cute, over here looking all sulky and pissed," came a too-cheerful voice from Vincent's right.

Both he and Anth turned to glare at Luc. Yet another thing Vin and Anth had in common: they were both quite adept at getting irritated with their youngest brother.

"Shut it, *bambino*," Vin said. Luc, being the baby of

the family, took his fair share of shit but was remarkably good at never letting his older brothers get under his skin.

Case in point, Luc merely grinned wider before pivoting around so his back too was to the wall. "I see why you two losers like it over here in the corner. Great view of the womenfolk."

Vincent let himself look in the direction Luc indicated. It was, indeed, an excellent view of the females in the room, and that right there only served to aggravate Vincent's bad mood.

Jill was getting married.

So very absurd was the idea that Vincent had briefly held on to hope that she was just jacking with him.

But no. The ring was real. The nonstop chatter about the dress was real.

The *engagement* was real.

Currently her left hand was the center of a girly circle.

Vincent's sister Elena clasped Jill's wrist firmly as the rest of the women oohed and ahhed over the atrocious rock on her finger.

His sister's enthusiasm, he could see. Jill and Elena had been best friends for years. Maggie and Ava too made sense. The four women had been thick as thieves ever since Luc and Anth had brought Ava and Maggie into the family.

But his *mother* was also making squealy girl-ish noises, fussing with Jill's hair every second, talking about dress shopping and updos and other horrors.

Even Nonna—his feisty, zero-BS grandmother—was getting in on the nonsense, all but hopping around Jill, demanding to be a bridesmaid.

"Who's the guy?" Luc asked quietly.

"Why you asking me?" Vincent asked testily.

"I wasn't," Luc snapped. "I was talking to Anth, who actually knows something about the three months she's been gone."

"Three months," Vin interrupted. "Nobody else thinks it's bullshit that some dude proposed after three months?"

"Didn't you guys talk during that time?" Luc asked.

"Yes, we talked," he ground out.

Barely. Vincent hated talking on the phone, but that's not why he'd tried to keep their phone calls short. He'd tried to limit how much he and Jill talked while she was away because it had reminded him that she wasn't here.

"And she didn't tell you that she was seeing someone?" Anthony asked.

Vincent said nothing, and Luc leaned forward to glare at Anth. "Obviously not."

"I'm just sayin'," Anthony said.

"What?" Vin snapped. "What are you *just sayin'*?"

He felt rather than saw his two brothers exchange a look.

Luc sighed. "I know Jill can be impulsive, but this—"

Yes. *This.* This was . . .

"Whoa, what the hell did I miss?"

All three brothers looked away from the group of women to see their father standing there, looking puzzled.

"Sorry I'm late," he said, pouring himself a glass from the open bottle of champagne. "Did your mother tell you she made me go to the dentist? Tricked me into it, then didn't have the decency to apologize."

"It's a rough life, Dad," Luc said. "Rough life."

Tony Moretti grunted before gesturing with his wineglass toward the women. "So what's going on there? I haven't heard that much squealing since Elena got those new red shoes with the red soles."

"Louboutins," Luc said.

The rest of the men stared at him, and he shrugged. "What? I'm evolved."

"Whatever," Tony muttered. "Why is it so high-pitched in here?"

Again, Luc and Anth did that brotherly look that Vin pretended not to see. Which wasn't hard. He couldn't seem to tear his eyes away from Jill.

She looked...different. Same bright blond hair falling around her face, same wide blue eyes, same ever-present smile.

But tonight, she was...happy. Granted, Jill was always happy. The woman was never without a smile and had more energy than a Chihuahua with a doughnut, but she hadn't been this *glowy* before.

Jill was getting married.

"Jill's getting married," Vincent said to his father. Maybe if he said it out loud, it would start to feel like a comprehendible fact.

He sipped his beer. Waited.

Nope. Still felt totally wrong.

"Bullshit," Tony said.

Vin nearly smiled at that.

His father was, well...exactly what you'd expect a lifelong cop to be who'd once run the entire NYPD without ever having to raise his voice. Tony Moretti was tall, broad, and serious looking, and Vincent sometimes thought his father was the ultimate combination of all his children.

Anth's protectiveness. Marc's smarts. Elena's temper.

Luc's people skills. Vincent's confidence. Or *ego*, if you wanted to speak plainly.

"Jill's not getting married," Tony said, repeating his disbelief.

"She met a guy in Florida when she was staying with her mom," Luc said.

"Who. Who'd she meet?"

"Don't know yet. Haven't really had a chance to ask anything rational over the conversations about the pros and cons of Tiffany blue as an accent color," Anth said.

"How do you feel about this?"

It took Vin several seconds to realize that his father was talking to him. And from the steady looks of his brothers, they seconded their dad's question.

"Why you asking me?" he grumbled.

"Why the hell you think?" Tony shot back. "Maybe because we've been waiting patiently for you to get your head out of your ass about that girl—"

"Patiently? Really?" Luc cut in. "I wouldn't say we've been patient so much as—"

"Pushy, interfering, and completely off base," Vincent said, pushing away from the wall and moving to the table to grab one of the marinated vegetables from his mother's antipasto plate.

He met his father's angry gaze as he chewed, and it was one of those stupid but necessary staring contests.

Vincent wasn't an idiot. He knew his family had long been of the mind-set that he and Jill were just biding their time until their work partnership became a romantic one.

Vin had never paid this any mind.

Neither had Jill. *Obviously*.

"Honey, did you hear the good news?" This from Vin's

mother, who came scurrying over to her husband. "Our Jill's getting married."

Our Jill.

She wasn't going to be the Morettis' Jill much longer. She was going to be some other guy's Jill. She'd never again be . . .

His gut clenched, and Vincent ran a hand down his face. What the hell was wrong with him?

Despite the fact that Jill got under his skin—regularly, and with glee—he cared about her. Cared about her happiness. And she was happy. Any fool could see that.

So why couldn't *he* get happy?

Vincent stepped back again as the men and women melded into one big group. The topic stayed trained on Jill's upcoming nuptials.

No, they hadn't set a date.

Yes, she was excited.

No, she didn't know where the wedding would be.

Yes, she couldn't wait for them to meet Tom when he came out to see her next weekend.

Tom. She was marrying a guy named Tom.

From here on out it would be Tom and Jill. Jill and Tom.

Never again would it be Jill and Vincent.

Vincent went to grab another beer from the fridge. He couldn't do another glass of the celebratory champagne—not knowing what it represented. What they were "celebrating." When he turned around, he almost walked straight into his sister, whose laser-blue eyes were boring into him.

Luc and Elena were the only Moretti offspring to get the dark hair and blue eyes. The rest, Vincent included, had dark hair and dark eyes.

And right now, Elena's blue eyes were seeing way too much.

"How we doing?" she asked.

"*We* are doing just fine."

He started to move past, and she touched his arm. "Vin."

He shook her off. "Don't, El."

Her eyes shifted from wary to hurt. And not hurt for herself. Hurt for *him*, if he was reading it correctly.

Which was stupid. He was fine.

"Okay," she said quietly, giving him a small smile before walking away.

He stared after her in surprise. The fact his stubborn, nosy sister had let it drop was alarming. And not at all a good sign.

Thirty minutes later, food was being put out on the enormous dining table—one of Maggie's new additions to the house—and everyone found their seat.

Vin sat down at the chair within closest reach, and Jill plopped into the seat next to him.

The smell of her familiar citrusy perfume assaulted his nostrils.

She was all smiles as she reached over with a spontaneous grab of his hand as she gave his arm a little shake. "I *love* this. I love being back."

"Good," he grunted, resisting the urge to shake off her touch. She'd always been like that. Touchy. Feely. It didn't usually bother him, but tonight it felt like too much.

She studied him, her wide blue eyes every bit as assessing as Elena's had been earlier.

Damn the prying, observant females.

"You okay?" she asked.

He looked up and looked at her then. Really looked at her. Her blond hair was down around her shoulders, a shorter piece near her forehead falling into her eyes as it so often was.

Her mouth was pink and lipstick free, her pointy upturned nose wrinkled at him in concern.

The face was as familiar to him as his own, and he felt a rough twist in his stomach.

"I'm good," he said.

"So, Jill," Maria said, capturing her attention. "Your man...he lives in Florida?"

Jill's eyes held his for a heartbeat before she released his hand and turned her attention back to his mother.

"Not full-time. He was just there temporarily, doing something with a new condo community. He's in real estate development."

Luc wiggled his eyebrows as the food was being passed around. "So he's loaded."

Ava used a piece of bread to gesture at Jill's left hand. "Look at that ring. Of course he's loaded."

Vincent numbly accepted the salad bowl Anth shoved at him and scooped some onto his plate before handing the bowl to Jill.

But Jill was in the middle of telling her proposal story, both hands flapping around in excitement, so he scooped a pile of salad onto her plate and passed it over her head to his father at the head of the table.

Feeling eyes on him, he glanced across the table to see his mother watching him. She'd clearly seen the gesture and her eyes were...sad.

God.

This misplaced sympathy really had to stop. His

family had to quit acting like he was some victim here. Some little boy left out in the cold because the girl he liked, liked someone else.

Except he didn't like Jill. Not like that.

And even if he did, it wouldn't matter.

Because Jill was getting married.

CHAPTER FIVE

Vincent and Jill both lived in Astoria, a residential neighborhood in Queens that was perfectly lovely.

And not at all close to Manhattan.

Which meant, as usual, Vincent was driving Jill home.

Except *not* like usual, the silence in the car was… deafening.

Jill was used to being silent with Vin. You don't survive a six-year partnership without knowing how to be silent together.

But tonight felt different. Tense.

And it didn't take a genius to identify the elephant in the room. It was sitting on the fourth finger of her left hand.

Vincent Moretti had always been the only person in Jill's life with whom she didn't feel she had to make small talk. Not that she didn't chat his ear off from time to time. She did. Often.

But she'd never felt compelled to fill silence.

Tonight, she did.

But before she could think up a safe, non-wedding-related topic, Vin shocked the hell out of her by beating her to it.

"How's your mom?"

She glanced over at his profile, noting the way the city lights illuminated his harsh, unsmiling features.

"She's good. Really good."

"Glad to hear it. Always liked your mom. Never been able to figure out how a classy woman like that raised a smart-mouthed pain-in-the-ass like you."

"Really?" Jill drawled. "This from someone whose parents are practically saints and yet somehow produced a complete grade-A—"

"And your flight?" he interrupted. "Flight was good?"

Jill stared at him. "Seriously. We're doing this?"

"Doing what?"

Jill reached over and punched him in the shoulder. "I haven't seen you in three months, and you want to talk about my flight?"

He lifted a shoulder. "What do *you* want to talk about?"

Oh, I don't know. How about the fact that you never called. That I barely heard from you. Or hey, here's an idea. How about we talk about the fact that I'm getting married.

And then there was that doughnut.

Sure, it was just a doughnut. A smashed, mutilated doughnut.

But it was her favorite kind. From a bakery not at all near Anth's house, which meant that he'd gone out of his way to get it.

What was *that* about? And why did her stomach fill with happy butterflies every time she thought about it?

"So Maggie's big, huh?" Jill asked, still clamoring for a topic that was safe but not completely generic. "I can't believe we're going to have a baby in the family."

Vincent gave a rare smile. "Yeah. Nonna's already knitted at least a dozen pairs of those little foot cover things."

"Booties," Jill said. "And Nonna knits?"

"Supposedly. Although Mom swears she saw Nonna snipping a Target tag off the last one, so who knows?"

Jill gave a happy sigh as she settled back into her seat. "I missed them."

Missed you too.

"Since when have Anth and Maggie started hosting family dinners?" Jill asked.

"Since Luc moved out."

Ava shook her head at that. "I still can't wrap my head around that. Them not living together anymore?"

"That's what 'move out' means."

"I know," she said somewhat glumly. "But it's like the end of an era."

"Or they just decided to be grown-ups," Vincent muttered.

Although he'd never admit it, Jill was pretty sure that Vin had always been a bit jealous of the fact that his oldest and youngest brothers had roomed together.

Their grandma had an awesome rent-controlled home on the Upper West side. Too good of a deal for someone not to take advantage of, and since it wasn't like Vincent was the "roommate type," Anth and Luc lived together.

Still, despite his insistence that he'd go crazy living there, she sometimes got the feeling that he felt left out.

Especially after their other brother Marco moved to LA awhile back to follow his girlfriend, leaving Vin as the only New York Moretti brother not living on the Upper West Side.

Vincent pulled the car up in front of her apartment, and Jill gave a little happy sigh. *Home.*

Vin was already out of the car, pulling her bags out of the trunk. "Okay, so Luc's moved in with Ava, Maggie's moved in with Anth. What about you?"

He didn't look up as he easily hoisted her bag to the ground. "What about me?"

She rolled her eyes. "How are you?"

Instead of answering, he reached into the trunk, grabbed her second bag. "What the hell's in here, rocks?" he asked, hauling her biggest suitcase out of the trunk.

"Yes. Rocks. I just ran around Mom's backyard this morning finding all the biggest, heaviest rocks I could find and then put them in my suitcase just for you."

He wheeled them up the sidewalk to her front door and Jill followed after him, digging her keys out of her bag.

She brushed past him to unlock the door as she'd done a hundred times before, but tonight she was strangely aware of his closeness. Of his smell, and his warmth, and...

Oh shit. *Shit!*

Tom. She'd forgotten about him.

For one terrible, traitorous moment had she actually forgotten she was engaged?

She glanced at Vincent's irritated profile and swallowed dryly.

Yes. Yes, she had forgotten. *Vin* had made her forget, and that was just all kinds of weird.

Jill shook her head. She needed to call Tom. They'd

texted earlier, the whole "landed safely, love you!" thing, but she needed to talk to him.

Needed to hear his voice.

Needed to stop being so *aware* of Vin.

"Thanks for the ride," she said, turning to face her partner.

He lifted his eyebrows. "You don't want help getting your bags inside?"

She rolled her eyes. "They wheel. I can handle tugging them over the doorstep."

His eyes narrowed slightly as though knowing something else was keeping her from inviting him in, but he said nothing.

They stood still for a long moment, looking at each other.

Jill was oddly relieved to see that he looked exactly as he had when he'd dropped her off at the airport three months ago.

Relieved that despite all the recent changes in her own life, this one thing would stay the same.

His clothes were the same. As homicide detectives, both she and Vin were plainclothed (i.e., no uniform) most of the time, but she liked to joke that Vin had a uniform all his own. Dark jeans. Dark top. Leather jacket.

His always-present aviator glasses were shoved up onto his head, even though the sun had set long ago.

Jill smiled fondly as she reached up to remove them. He always forgot they were there.

"Thanks," he said gruffly, taking the glasses from her without meeting her eyes.

"You got a haircut," Jill said. "It looks nice."

His eyes looked up then, and something flickered. Something she didn't recognize.

Then he shrugged. "I was past due. Mom had been getting on my case."

She nodded, jingling her keys in her palm. This was normally the point where she would have said something. Would have chattered on happily about how she was getting her hair cut later that week, or did his barber still smell like garlic? Or even a teasing *you sure you're not getting gussied up for a girl*?

Tonight, she said none of those things. Tonight, she said what she really wanted to say, even though it betrayed more than she wanted.

"Thanks for the doughnut," she blurted out. "It was... It meant a lot."

He rolled his eyes. "It was just a doughnut, Henley."

Was it though? she wondered.

"Well," she said, looking down at her keys. "Thanks anyway."

"Whatever," he said, shoving his hands in his pockets. "See you tomorrow?"

"Yeah. See you tomorrow."

He turned away without another word and started down the walk to his car.

"Hey, Moretti," she called before she could think better of it.

He turned back.

"I really did miss you," she said.

He said nothing. She didn't expect him to.

But he smiled. A *real* smile.

And that was something.

CHAPTER SIX

Jill's first day back on the job was a big one.

As in...the biggest of her career.

Not because the crime was particularly unique. Being shoved off a staircase wasn't common, but neither was it particularly creative.

No, it wasn't the *crime* that was career breaking.

It was the victim.

Jill hunched down, linking her gloved hands between her knees as she studied the blank, staring eyes of the dead woman.

"Lenora Birch. Who did this to you?"

"I'd forgotten how creepy it is when you talk to the vics," Vincent said.

Jill glanced over to where her partner crouched across from her, his posture mimicking hers on the other side of the victim's body.

He didn't look back at her. His gaze never moved away from the gruesome scene in front of him.

"Well I think it's creepy that you *don't* talk to them," she said. "They're people. Not 'vics.'"

This time he did meet her eyes. "Exactly. They're people. And it's my job to figure out who stole their humanity away from them."

"Right," she said, standing up. "*Your* job. Because I'm just here because you're such great company and I love all the blood."

"Not much blood with this one," he mused, standing with her.

He was right. As far as crime scenes went, it was clean in more ways than one. No footprints, no broken windows, and Jill was willing to bet as soon as the forensics guys finished up...no fingerprints.

But the method of death too was cleaner than most in that there was less blood than a stabbing or a shooting. But somehow the pristine crime scene almost made the death *more* gruesome.

Jill's eyes followed the gorgeous, old-fashioned staircase all the way from the marble floor where they stood up to where it curved up around a magnificent chandelier. Then on to the point where Lenora Birch must have spent her last seconds of life.

"She could have fallen," Jill said.

Vin came to stand beside her, his eyes repeating the exact motion hers had. "She didn't fall."

Jill was inclined to agree; nothing about this scene felt right. But they had to explore all options, as Vincent well knew.

Jill took the stairs two at a time, and Vincent followed

her up. It was an exceptionally beautiful home. Most of
the old walk-ups in this part of town were.

Jill and Vincent didn't get many cases in the Upper
East Side. The crime rate in the uppity part of town was
lower than other parts of New York.

"This is too pretty a place for someone to die," Jill said
quietly. She held her gloved hand over the immaculately
polished wood railing, hovering just an inch above so she
didn't *actually* touch it. "Do you think this is prewar?"

Vincent grunted, his eyes in constant motion as they
ascended the stairs, although she doubted he was marvel-
ing at the decor the way she was.

Still, she couldn't stop herself. The staircase beneath
her feet seemed to be made of the same marble as the
entryway floor. And she didn't know art, but the paintings
on the walls didn't look like prints bought on the Internet
the way all of Jill's were.

This place smelled like money. Old money. And lots of it.

Which made sense, considering one of Hollywood's
most beloved legends lay dead below them.

"I can't believe she's dead," Jill said quietly.

She glanced at Vincent when he said nothing. "You do
know who that is, right?"

Vin rolled his eyes. "Yes, Henley. Even I, an uncul-
tured boor, knows who Lenora Birch is."

"I heard she was once best friends with Audrey Hep-
burn. That she used to hang out with Audrey after takes of
Breakfast at Tiffany's. Did you know that?"

"I said I knew who she was; I didn't say I studied trivia,"
he muttered as they came to stand at the top of the stairs.
He looked down. Pointed. "It would have been here."

Jill nodded and reoriented her thought process. *Right*.

Now was not the time to stroll down memory lane to those carefree days before her dad died, when her little family would curl up on the couch and her parents would introduce her to the classics. Lenora Birch films had made a frequent appearance.

But this wasn't a movie.

It was real life.

They were here to solve Lenora Birch's *death*, not ruminate over her life. That would be for her friends and family to do, and well, most of America. But Vincent and Jill... right now they were homicide detectives first, fans second.

And though neither would say it, they were very much aware that this was a case that could make their career.

Or break it.

Not that they needed much help improving their track record. Jill and Vincent had a lower percentage of unsolved cases than almost anyone in the department.

But still, this was the murder of *Lenora Birch*.

Solving this would put them on the map in a big way. Set them up for promotion well ahead of their time.

But first... to prove it was a murder.

Jill rested her hands on the railing and looked down. "Okay, so she went over here..."

Jill held out her hand, palm to the floor as she measured how high the railing was on her. It hit between belly button and boobs. "How tall do you think Lenora Birch is—was? She's so thin I always picture her being taller..."

"About your height," Vincent said.

Jill nodded. "Okay, so if she's my height and the railing hits me here..." She continued to hold her hand off before taking a couple steps back. "Let's say I stumble..."

She mimed a stumbling motion, and Vincent shook

his head. "Nope. Even if she stumbled against the railing, there wouldn't be enough force."

"You're right," Jill said. "So in order for this to have been a fall..."

She went on her tippy toes and dipped forward.

Vincent swore sharply, and a hand pulled her back from the railing by the waist of her pants.

"What the—" She turned to give him an incredulous look, but his face was stark white, and realization dawned.

"Ohhh," she said knowingly. "I forgot about that little height thing you have."

"Shut up," he said, rubbing a hand over his face.

Jill wisely hid her smile. Vincent may have the reputation as one of the toughest, hardest-to-rattle cops in the NYPD, but he had one teeny-tiny weakness...

He was scared to death of heights.

She wouldn't have thought a second-story railing even qualified, but judging from the slightly nauseous look on his face, it definitely did.

"Sorry," she said, patting his arm. He was wearing his usual work "uniform."

All black.

She didn't judge, as she wore more of the same. Black pants. Black turtleneck. Black shoes.

Jill used to dress up more when she'd first gotten promoted to detective, but now she only busted out the skirts when they were talking to the families of victims or questioning people.

And then, only to soften the fact that Vincent didn't dress up. Ever.

"Okay, so it's reasonably certain that this couldn't have been an accident," Jill said, deliberately steering his attention back to the case.

He shook his head, color returning.

"I know we'll need to look into her mental state," Jill said, because they had to explore all options. "But even if Lenora Birch was depressed and the public didn't know it...I don't think she would have done it like this."

"Why do you say that?"

Jill lifted a shoulder. "A person who was once said to be the most beautiful woman in the world wouldn't want to be found like that."

She gestured toward the floor below.

Vin blew out a breath as he snapped off his gloves and handed them to a passing tech. Jill did the same, although she did it with a smile and said thank you.

"Start with the housekeeper?" he asked.

Jill nodded. "Hopefully she's still waiting in the kitchen like we asked."

The housekeeper had been the one to find the body and call 911. She'd been too distraught to get out more than sobs when they'd first arrived, but Jill was hoping the worst of the shock had worn off and they could at least get some sense of where to start.

Jill felt a little shiver of anticipation roll through her. Not at the death—never the death. But at the thrill of the chase. Of the puzzle. She loved the entire process of putting the pieces together and coming up with the best prize of all: Justice.

"I've missed this," she said, more to herself than to Vincent, who wasn't exactly known for being Mr. Chatty on the job. Or ever.

But to her surprise he studied her. "Yeah?"

"Yeah."

"That why you spent three months on the beach getting

wooed by a millionaire while I got stuck with a Goddamn detective in training?"

"Hey!" she said, stung. "I wasn't sitting on a beach, and you know it. I was making soup for my mother and vacuuming up year-old dust bunnies and going to the pharmacy every other day for her pain meds, and—"

"I know," he cut in gruffly. "Sorry."

She stopped her rampage, mollified only slightly.

He started to head back down the stairs, but she stopped him. "Vin."

He turned around, and she glanced at her shoes, feeling silly for what she was about to say but wanting to say it anyway. Needing to say it so that they could be mavens and focus on work.

"Yeah?" he asked.

"Okay, so I was thinking," she said, licking her lips. "We never talked about . . . you know, me getting married."

He jolted. "You want to talk about it *now*?"

"Well, I mean, we don't have to make a wedding scrapbook together, I just . . . thought it was weird that we haven't really *acknowledged* it."

He said nothing.

"You never even said congratulations," she said quietly.

He stared at her blankly. "What?"

Jill licked her lips, feeling more ridiculous than ever. "I just . . . my engagement. Your entire family was happy for me. But you . . . you didn't say one word."

"Congratulations," he said flatly.

Jill rolled her eyes. "The navigator on my phone's map app has more inflection than you. I don't want you to say it because you're *supposed* to, I want you to say it because you mean it."

"That is such a girly thing to say," he stated gruffly.

She ignored this. She had no problems being girly.

"Everyone, see, is happy for me, but you seem... pissed," she pressed.

It bothered her. She didn't need Vincent's blessing. Didn't need him to sanction her admittedly whirlwind courtship with Tom. Didn't need him to beg to be a brides-maid, but she needed... something.

He held her gaze for several minutes. "Are *you* happy?"

"Of course," she said automatically. *Of course* she was happy. A gorgeous, successful man had approached her in a bar, bought her a drink, and then proceeded to court the hell out of her for the next three months.

No man had ever done that for her. Ever.

Tom Porter was every woman's dream. He was *her* dream. Or at least, a version of it.

"You sure about that?" Vincent asked, coming back toward her.

She frowned in confusion. "Sure about what?"

He moved even closer, his gaze locked on hers. "Are you sure that you're happy?"

He was only a few inches away from her, and for some reason she felt... aware of him. Of his closeness.

She felt the strangest urge to step back from his intensity.

It was just Vincent, she reminded herself.

He was always intense, but this felt different.

"Of course I'm happy," she said.

"Huh." He continued to study her.

"What do you mean, *huh*?" she asked testily.

"Just that twice now you've added an 'of course' to your statement."

"What?" She was thoroughly confused now. "What are you even talking about?"

He rocked back on his heels, then forward again. "I've asked twice if you're happy. You've responded with 'of course.' Twice."

"So?" she asked, throwing up her arms in exasperation.

"So," he said, leaning forward and down so they were face-to-face. "Sounds like you're trying to convince someone."

He turned and walked away then, heading down the stairs, and if Jill had anything to throw at him—anything at all—she would have.

"Who would I be trying to convince?" she called after him, before jumping into motion and all but running down the stairs after him. "You?"

He stopped at the bottom of the stairs, so quickly that she nearly slammed into his back. Vincent's hands found her arms to steady her, even as she glared at him.

He slowly dropped his hands, letting his arms fall to his sides, and something unreadable passed over his expression as he took a step back.

"Who would I be trying to convince?" she asked again.

His expression was both thoughtful and pitying, and once again, Jill longed for something to hurl at him.

"Poor Henley. Your time out of the field has made your deduction skills rusty," he said.

"Meaning?" she asked as he turned on his heel and headed toward the kitchen to question the housekeeper.

"Meaning, I don't think you're trying to convince me of your happiness," he said, not turning around. "I think you're trying to convince *you*."

CHAPTER SEVEN

I think you're trying to convince you.

Jill glared down at her coffee. Vincent was *wrong*.

He was so wrong.

Jill was happy to be marrying Tom. Super happy. She was...

"Yo, Henley, hurry up."

Jill glanced up from where she'd been blindly stirring her white mocha for the past three minutes to find her partner scowling—always with the scowling—down at her.

"Easy, Moretti, I've been waiting for *you*. How long does it take to freaking go to the bathroom?"

"There was a line," he snapped, moving toward the door of Starbucks before she even had a chance to respond.

Jill rolled her eyes and grabbed both her coffee and his, since he apparently expected her to bring it to him.

It would serve the jerk right if she just dropped it in the trash as she walked out the door, but then, if Jill were being *totally* fair, she'd have to admit that he'd carried her coffee plenty of times when she'd zoned out.

He turned around once outside the coffee shop, his eyes immediately going for his cup as she followed him.

"Thanks," he muttered, accepting his boring black coffee. "Totally forgot."

"It's been a long one," she said, taking a sip of her drink.

He looked her over. "How you holding up? First day back on the job and we have a murdered celebrity and nobody even approaching what looks like a viable suspect."

Jill licked away some of the whipped cream from her upper lip, wondering if she imagined the way Vincent's gaze had tracked the motion.

"Not going to lie, my feet hurt, my back hurts, and my head hurts..."

He nodded. "And you love it."

Jill didn't bother to hide the happy grin, her bad mood evaporating, as it usually did.

"I *do* love it. I've really, really missed this," she said as they began walking toward their car.

Vincent surprised her then by glancing down at his coffee, then tossing it in a nearby garbage can.

She skidded to a halt. "Did you just throw away *coffee*? Expensive coffee?"

He lifted a shoulder. "It's six p.m."

"And that's stopped you from guzzling caffeine since... when?"

He stared at her for several long seconds, and she

cradled her coffee to her chest protectively. "Well I'm not throwing out mine."

Vincent didn't seem to hear her. "Do you want to grab a beer?"

It was a casual question.

Nothing special. They'd grabbed drinks a thousand times before after the end of their shift, sometimes without even discussing it. They would just wordlessly find themselves in the same restaurant, sharing a drink or two.

But there was something different tonight. A nervousness, as though he'd been thinking about the question for a while.

It was as though he was afraid she was going to say no. Afraid she was going to choose phone sex with Tom over drinks with him.

Jill glanced down at her coffee. Took one last big sip, then stepped around Vin, dropped the cup in the trash can behind him, and smiled. "Absolutely."

He didn't smile back, but his eyes crinkled in the corners, and that was something.

No, not just something. It was a *big* something.

"Everything okay with you?" Jill asked as she got into the passenger seat. Vincent liked to drive, and she didn't mind one bit. Driving in the city made her crazy.

"Yeah. Why?" he asked.

"I dunno. You've been strange since I've gotten back."

"So, like all of twenty-four hours?"

She studied him.

He gave her a quick glance across the car. "Quit it."

"Quit what?"

"Staring at me."

"I'm not staring."

"You're looking at me without blinking with those big old eyes. It's staring."

She continued to look at him, deliberately trying not to blink now, just to annoy him. "You never told me what you've been up to."

"Huh?"

"While I was gone," she explained with what she thought was admirable patience. "What did you do? Give me the highlights. Any new women or new restaurants discovered? Did you get that weird squeak in your heater fixed? I mean, three months passed. You must have done *something*."

"Three months where you were off getting engaged, you mean."

His statement hung between them for several moments, although she didn't really understand why.

"Yeah. Like that." Her voice was just the tiniest bit touchy, but she really wasn't loving the way he acted pissed about the fact that she was getting married.

It's not like she was expecting him to go dress shopping with her or be the one to give her something borrowed, but Vincent Moretti was . . .

He was her best friend. Not in the traditional sense, of course. He was closed-off and irritable, and most of the time he acted like he didn't even like her. But over the years, they'd become partners in more than just the work-together kind of way.

They were like two halves of . . . something.

Or at least they had been. There seemed to be a rift now, and Jill was oddly desperate to fix it.

"I didn't do much," he muttered finally. "Watched a lot of football. Fixed the heater myself, because my land-lord's useless."

She noticed he didn't answer her question about women, and she should probably just let it go, but...she didn't.

"Did you date?"

He glanced across her again before easily parallel parking into a spot directly across from one of their favorite pubs on the Lower East Side.

"No," he said as he turned off the car. "I didn't date."

Vincent climbed out of the car and slammed the door shut, but Jill sat frozen for several seconds, trying to figure out why his announcement sent such a stab of relief rippling through her.

Relief over *what*, though? That Vin was still single? That shouldn't matter because *Jill* wasn't single.

Not only was she not single, she had a ring on her finger.

Jill closed her eyes and twisted the diamond in an effort to refocus her thoughts on her fiancé. The handsome, kind man she was going to marry. And when she opened her eyes, she'd stop thinking about Vincent. And the fact that he hadn't dated while she was away.

And maybe, just maybe—she'd stop herself from thinking about how much she'd dread the moment when he did find a girlfriend.

CHAPTER EIGHT

Vincent Moretti's adult life had always involved two infallible constants:

(1) his legendary "whodunit" hunch

(2) Jill Henley

It was just his fucking luck that both of those things would give up on him at the exact same time, leaving him feeling a little lost.

And a lot pissed.

When Vin and Jill had gotten the early-morning call about a body at Lenora Birch's house, Vin hadn't even felt a flicker of warning that the case was going to be an elusive one.

In fact, he'd actually been fairly damn confident that it would be an easy one. The more high-profile cases usually were. The more famous the victim, the more people who wanted to be famous by association.

Even if that association was murder.

Vincent had cockily assumed he'd have a solid sense of their guy—or gal—by the time the news hit the media.

They'd bring the suspect in for questioning, and that's when Vincent generally passed the baton to Jill.

If his skill was in figuring out who did it, her skill was coaxing—or tricking—them into confession.

But from the second Vincent had stepped foot in the stunning home of Lenora Birch on Eighty-First and Fifth, he'd known something was wrong.

The scene was clean. Too clean.

He got no immediate vision of what must have happened. No gut sense of how the legendary actress came to be lying dead on her foyer floor.

He hadn't panicked. By the time they talked to all the key players, he'd have something to work with.

But he hadn't.

Nothing from the utterly useless housekeeper.

He hadn't gotten the flicker from Lenora's sister.

Nor Lenora's latest boyfriend.

Nor her ex-boyfriends and ex-husbands.

Hadn't gotten it from her longtime best friend and legendary Broadway actress.

By the time he and Jill had called it a day with some much-needed caffeine, not only did Vincent have *zero* sense of who might have pushed Lenora over her staircase railing, he did not have an idea where to *start*.

Ignorance was not bliss.

Adding to Vin's nagging sense of unease was the woman currently sitting across the table from him.

He didn't know what had compelled him to ask Jill out for drinks.

They did it often enough, but usually it was a natural continuation of their day when they were still knee-deep in work talk.

Today had been different.

Today they'd both been exhausted, frustrated from the lack of leads and lost in their own heads.

He should have left it at coffee. Let them both get enough caffeine to make it through the remaining hours of the day, then dropped Jill off to call her fiancé, while he decompressed with a beer and whatever was on TV from the comfort of his couch.

But then he'd come out of the restroom at Starbucks, seen her lost in thought, smiling to herself, and he'd felt a surge of panic.

Panic that he didn't know what she was thinking.

Panic that he didn't know what was making her smile. (Although he was terrified that he *did* know.)

Panic that he was losing her.

It wasn't supposed to be like this.

She was supposed to have come back from Florida feeling like *he* had that day he impatiently counted the hours until he saw her at the welcome-home party.

She was supposed to feel what he was feeling.

If he only knew what that was.

Jill cradled a beer in her left hand, her phone in her right as she scrolled through. Then she winced and glanced up, holding her phone up to him. "Story broke."

He reached for a handful of the complimentary bar snacks the pub offered to customers. "Took them long enough."

"Right?" Jill said, turning her attention back to her phone. "I'm surprised the media didn't beat us to the scene. How the hell did this stay quiet all day in the age of Twitter?"

"Lenora Birch is old-school. Way old-school. Everyone we interviwed today was in the geriatric set. You really think they're on Twitter spreading the news?"

"Everyone's on Twitter," Jill muttered, never looking up from her phone.

"I'm not."

She snorted. "Please. You can barely maintain a relationship with one person, much less hundreds of followers."

Vin sat back in his chair, and damn if he didn't feel a little...wounded.

It was strange, considering how long they'd been working together, but Vin had never really given conscious consideration to what Jill thought of him. Their relationship had always been both horribly complicated and wonderfully simple.

Those two elements canceled each other out so that when it came right down to it, Jill and Vincent were beyond definition.

They simply *were*.

He'd always thought they'd shared a secret understanding that the fact that what was between them couldn't be named was precisely what made it theirs.

Now, he was realizing that this had been one-sided. That all this time, he'd merely been her colleague while she'd been his...everything.

"Can you put the damn phone away," he heard himself snap.

Jill glanced up in surprise, and he saw guilt flash across her face. She immediately locked her phone and set it facedown on the table.

"Of course. I'm sorry."

Her apology was simple. Sincere.

And yet it did nothing to mollify him. He didn't want Jill to pay attention to him just because he begged her to. He didn't want to have to compete for Jill's attention at all. He wanted—

Fuck. He didn't have a clue.

He reached for his beer, then instead changed course and grabbed one of the laminated menus at the back of the table.

"You hungry?"

"Always," she said. "Nachos? Wings? Ooh, we could split a burger!"

Vin lowered the menu and gave her a look. "One does not *split* a burger."

"One can and one *should* when the burger is as big as it is here," she said.

In the end, they ordered nachos for her and a burger for him.

"I'm not sharing," he said, pointing his newly refilled beer at her.

"Of course not," she said soothingly, picking through all of the nuts to get at the almonds and leaving the peanuts for him.

Vin grunted. He knew that voice. He was definitely going to end up sharing that burger.

"I must be out of practice," Jill said with a tired sigh. "Because for the life of me, I don't know where we start tomorrow with this case."

"Me either," he admitted.

She lifted an eyebrow. "I *wondered* why I wasn't getting your smug, I-know-it-was-you vibe all day. I thought I was rusty on my Vincent-reading skills too."

You are, he wanted to say.

But that wasn't fair. Not really.

He couldn't expect her to read him, when he didn't have a read on himself.

He didn't know what he wanted her to look at him and scc. He only knew that something was very, very wrong. Starting with the fact that she was going to marry another man in...

"When's the wedding?" he asked.

Jill's beer glass froze halfway to her mouth, and she lowered it without taking a sip. "So I guess we're not talking about the case then."

He popped a handful of nuts in his mouth. "We're off the clock."

"That hasn't stopped us from talking about work before."

He narrowed his eyes. "Are you avoiding the question?"

Jill puffed out her cheeks and then slowly blew out a breath the way she always did when she was annoyed. He took a sip of his own beer and studied her.

Interesting.

Interesting that she should be annoyed about a topic that should send her over the moon.

And she'd been *plenty* happy to talk about wedding stuff with the women of his family last night, so it was obviously just with him that she didn't want to discuss it.

He leaned forward. "Come on. If you can't give me a date, at least promise me I'll get to be a bridesmaid."

She smiled, and he was relieved to see that it reached her eyes. "You're going to look so pretty in pink."

He winced. "Don't tell Nonna that. She'll make it her

life's mission to get me into a pink bow tie. Seriously though, when's the big day?"

"We don't know yet." She fiddled with her glass. "It's all been happening so fast."

"You think?"

She glanced up. "If you don't approve, you can just say so."

"Who said I didn't approve?"

She gave him a look. "Your scowls. Your grunts. Your silences."

He shrugged. "I'm always like that. Even when I'm happy."

This time it was Jill who leaned forward. "So you *are* happy?"

"You are so damn annoying," he muttered.

She sat back in her seat and studied him, then leaned forward again, her face all kinds of animated. "Okay, two things. First, that is *such* a pathetic non-answer. I'm disappointed in you. Second, it doesn't even make *sense* considering earlier today you accused me of not being happy."

He leaned even closer. "Speaking of non-answers, you didn't exactly rush to reassure me that you're over the moon about your fiancé."

He drew out the last word, and it came out just slightly mocking.

She didn't look away, but he had the sense that she wanted to. "I answered."

"So you *are* happy?" he asked, turning her own game around on her.

Someone who didn't know her as well might not have noticed the half-second pause. But he noticed.

"I'm happy," she said.

"Uh-huh. So just to be clear, you're one hundred percent happy to be marrying this Tom guy, whom you've known for all of three months?"

"Absolutely. Very happy."

He studied her face for several seconds, then shrugged. "Then it's like I said. I'm happy if you're happy."

That was mostly true.

"You don't mean it."

"Well, you'll have to excuse me if the news of you marrying some tassel-shoed millionaire isn't the impetus I need to turn into Mr. Smiley."

"What *is* the impetus you'd need then?" Jill snapped back. "Because I've known you for years, and I've yet to see a damn thing that makes you feel anything other than irritable."

Vincent took a sip of his beer, annoyed to realize that this was the second time in one evening that he'd felt an uncomfortable sting at her words. Vin had no illusions about the type of man that he was. He knew he was prickly and guarded and too intense.

But for some reason, he'd always thought that Jill saw past all that—beyond it. He'd always thought that Jill *got* him. Liked him for who he was.

But now—now he wasn't so sure. Maybe she didn't know him.

Because he sure as hell wasn't sure that he knew her anymore.

"Why are you looking at me like that?" she asked quietly.

"Like what?"

"With so much...dislike."

"I'm not."

Jill threw her hands up in frustration. "I'm so glad you asked me to drinks so that you could alternate between telling me how unhappy I am about my engagement and then not talking to me at all."

"I've never been particularly talkative," he said slowly. "Never seemed to bother you before."

"Well, it bothers me now," she said, mostly to herself.

They were saved from a full-blown argument by the arrival of their food, and before he realized what he was doing, Vin was cutting off part of his burger—not quite half, but at least a third—and was putting it on a side plate and sliding it across the table.

He watched her face, feeling almost shy . . . wondering if she would accept the shared burger for what it was. A peace offering.

And from the sunny smile she gave him, he warmed just a little. She understood.

But the warmth vanished as quickly as it arrived with her next words.

"You asked about a wedding date. We're thinking June."

June. That was in four months.

The fry and ketchup in his mouth suddenly didn't taste as good.

"That's fast," he said eventually, because he had to say something. "You got a hankering to be a June bride or something?"

"Not really." She fiddled with a burned corn chip on the edge of the nacho platter and didn't look at him. "Tom thinks we should get married before we move."

Vincent's burger paused in midair, halfway to his face. He slowly put it back down again.

"Move?" His voice sounded rusty. He cleared his throat and tried again. "Move where?"

She was slow to meet his eyes. "Tom's opening up a new property. It'll take up all his time, and we want to spend our first months as newlyweds together, so—"

"Jill," he interrupted. "Move. Where?"

She licked her lips. "Chicago. We're moving to Chicago in the summer."

It was the second time in twenty-four hours that Jill Henley had dropped a bomb on his head, but this time, his subconscious must have been prepared.

Because no sooner were the words out of her mouth, then Vincent *knew*.

Knew that there was no way he was letting Jill Henley walk away from him. Walk away from them, and what they had.

Whatever that was.

He only knew that the thought of her moving away...

... It felt like he couldn't breathe.

CHAPTER NINE

Even before Vincent and Jill had become partners—before they'd even known of the other person's existence—they'd both lived in Astoria, Queens.

Manhattan rent was outside of a comfortable cop's salary (unless you were like Vin's brothers and had a grandmother hooked up with rent control).

Brooklyn was *slightly* more affordable—or at least it had been, back when Jill was looking for her first New York apartment a few years ago—but then she'd toured the cozy one-bedroom in Astoria and she'd felt...

Home.

Sure, it was a longer-than-desirable commute into the city, and yeah, there was nothing trendy or particularly sexy about it. It wasn't the New York City one saw on TVs or the movies, or even the gritty NYC one saw in the *other* types of movies.

Astoria was one of those New York neighborhoods that inspired loyalty in its residents for reasons they could never quite explain to nonresidents. You either lived there and *got it*...or you didn't.

But Vincent? He got it.

Jill knew this because he, like her, had never voiced interest in moving anywhere else, even when their most recent raise might have allowed for it.

And living just a few minutes away from her partner had other perks, like easy carpooling.

The morning after her and Vincent's gorge on nachos and burgers and beer, Jill dropped into the passenger seat of the car with a grumpy huff.

"Caffeine," she said. "I need *all* the caffeine."

She jumped a little in surprise when a travel mug appeared in front of her face. She started to push his wrist aside. "No, not *your* coffee. You know I don't like it all thick and tarlike."

It was one of their many differences. Vin preferred his coffee blacker than his wardrobe. Jill preferred cream. And sugar. Preferably mass amounts of both.

"You know, all this time together, and I never realized how you drink your coffee," Vincent said in a sarcastic voice.

Jill turned to look at him.

He looked...the same.

Same aviator glasses, same simply styled black hair. Same dark shirt, same leather jacket, same dark pants.

But something was different today.

She narrowed her eyes as he extended the mug to her once more with his right hand. And this time she registered that he had a second mug in his left hand.

One for him...

And one for her?

"Don't worry," he said, giving it a little shake. "I dumped in all sorts of cavity-causing goodness for you."

"Thanks?" Jill said. She accepted the mug, taking a tentative sip. It was good. Really good. Not just a packet of sugar and a splash of milk good, but like...

"Is this vanilla flavored?" she asked, staring down at the mug.

Vincent still hadn't pulled away from the curb outside of her apartment. "French vanilla if you want to get fancy."

She shifted in her seat to stare at him. "This is your backup travel cup, which tells me you brought this from home, not a coffee shop. Which begs the question... why does a man who thinks anything other than black coffee is a sin have French vanilla coffee creamer at his apartment?"

He looked at her over the rim of his own mug. Took a sip without a response.

She sat up straighter. "Did you meet a woman while I was gone? A sweet-flavored-coffee-loving woman?"

Vincent merely held her gaze, and Jill kept her smile in place, but she also wanted to shake him. To demand that he answer.

"I already told you I'm not seeing anyone," he said.

Jill felt her shoulders relax a little; told herself that it wasn't because she didn't want Vincent to have met someone. Of *course* she wanted her partner to meet a nice woman. To settle down and—

She pushed the thought aside. Lifted her mug. "Explain."

He shrugged before putting his mug in the cup holder and turning the ignition. "I stopped at the store last night for eggs and paper towels. Then I saw the foofy coffee creamer stuff, knew that you rarely get your ass out of bed in time to make your own coffee..."

Vincent broke off with a shrug as he began to drive, and Jill could only stare at him in puzzlement.

"Six years we've been doing this," she said, "and you've never made me coffee. *Brought* me coffee, yes. Picked up a cup for both of us while we're working OT, sure. But this..."

She held up her mug and stared at it.

Vincent made an irritable sound like he wanted to rip the mug away from her, but then he surprised her— again—by changing the conversation once more.

"How'd you sleep?"

Jill sighed and took a sip of coffee—a big one. "Didn't. Not much anyway."

"Me either."

She tapped her nails against the cup, stared out the window. "I'd forgotten about this part. Forgot that it's always like this on the first night of a new case. Especially one that doesn't have so much as a hint of a clue."

"Same."

Jill pivoted her head to look at him. "I think we should start with the scene. There's got to be something we missed. Maybe run through a couple scenarios..."

"I was thinking we start with questioning the sister," he said. "Her prints are all over the place."

"Yeah, because it's her *sister*," Jill said. "The house-keeper said Dorothy was at Lenora's all the time."

"Still want to question her," he said.

If Vincent bringing her coffee had shocked the hell out of Jill, it was nothing compared to the jolt his next sentence had on her:

"If you're okay with that," he said slowly, flicking his eyes to her.

Her mouth dropped open. "Okay, who are you and what have you done with my partner?"

He said nothing, and she punched his arm. "No, seriously. I don't even recognize this thoughtful guy who brings me caffeine and asks my permission before interviewing someone."

"We're partners," he said roughly. "Of course I need your permission."

Jill laughed. "Since when? Since when have you done anything other than bark out directives and expect me to go along?"

He sighed as he rubbed a hand over his hair. "That makes it sound like I don't respect you."

"Yeah it does, doesn't it?" she teased.

But then her smile slipped, because he looked troubled.

She hadn't meant it that way. It was true that Vin could be an ass, but he was never chauvinistic. Had never made her feel like less than an equal despite his penchant for taking charge when he had a hunch.

"For the record," she said, "whenever you do utter your grumpy directives...I trust you."

That too was true.

Sure, his bossiness had grated in their first months together when they were trying to figure out their rhythm, but over the years she realized that he'd never boss her around for the sake of being bossy.

When he insisted they do something, it was always with good reason. The man was very nearly always right, which was why...

"Okay then," Jill said with a shrug. "The sister it is."

"Good. She already knows we're coming."

Jill smiled, and they fell silent for the rest of the drive to Lenora's sister's place.

To a non–New Yorker, Dorothy Birch and her now deceased sister were practically neighbors. Dorothy lived on Eighty-Ninth and First, Lenora had lived on Eighty-First and Fifth.

On a map, they were close.

But in New York reality? They were worlds apart.

Not that Dorothy Birch lived in a hovel, by any means. Her Yorkville apartment building was a lovely pre-war mid-rise with a doorman and carefully laid flowers outside.

It just lacked the splendor and prestige of Lenora's Upper East Side brownstone.

As Jill stepped out of the car and looked up at the building, she wondered how much that distinction bothered Dorothy.

Yesterday when they'd come to deliver the sad news of her sister's passing, Dorothy had been as distraught as one might expect.

Disbelieving at first. Followed quickly by shock.

Jill wondered if Dorothy had moved into grief yet. That was always the worst part...seeing the moment a family member moved beyond the shock and into the heart-wrenching reality that their loved one was really, truly gone.

It was easily one of the worst parts of Jill and Vincent's job.

Vincent came to stand beside her. "What're you thinking?"

Jill tilted her head back to look at him. "Why her? Why start with the sister?"

He shrugged. "Only surviving relative, save for the ex-husbands."

Jill blew out a breath. "So no magical Spidey sense? Not one of your legendary hunches?"

Vincent shook his head. "Nope. Just good old-fashioned by-the-book investigating."

"That's the worst kind," Jill muttered as she followed him into the building.

Dorothy Birch had indeed moved into the grief stage, if her puffy eyes and red nose were any indication, but she was remarkably poised as she carried a tray over to the coffee table.

Jill sat on the love seat and watched the older woman carefully.

Like her more famous sister, Dorothy Birch was tall, slim, although not frail, despite the fact that Jill knew her to be sixty-six.

Two years younger than Lenora had been when someone had shoved her to her death.

"You two are certainly up and at 'em early," Dorothy said with a faint smile as she set down an antique gold tray on the table.

Dorothy had told them she was making tea for herself, and although she'd offered to make a pot of coffee as well, Jill hadn't wanted to burden the grieving woman so she'd accepted tea on behalf of herself and Vincent as well.

A fact Vin was clearly not pleased about, judging from the glare he gave Jill when, with a sweet smile, she handed him his dainty teacup.

His big hand dwarfed the feminine-patterned china as he accepted it.

"Ms. Birch—"

"Dorothy, please," the woman said as she settled onto the love seat opposite Jill. Vincent retained his standing place against the window. He'd never been good at sitting.

"Dorothy," Jill said sincerely, "let us just say again how sorry we are for your loss."

"Thank you." The woman's lips pressed together firmly, a trick that Jill knew could be quite effective in staving off a crying bout. "I don't—Lenora is all I have. Had."

"You never married?" Vincent asked rudely from behind Jill.

It was all Jill could do not to roll her eyes at his lack of sensitivity.

But Dorothy merely gave him a mild look. "No, Detective. Never married."

"But Lenora was," Vincent pressed. "Several times."

Dorothy's smile was genuine. "Yes, four times. Engaged two more than that, although those never came to pass. She always kept our last name though. Never took her husband's on account of her being so famous."

"Did you resent her for that?"

Oh, for God's sake. Jill could shake the man.

"Well, resentment would have been pointless, now, wouldn't it?" Dorothy said, leaning back, lost in thought. "Some say my sister was rivaled only by Marilyn Monroe in terms of her legendary appeal for men."

"That must have been—"

Jill cut Vincent off before he could further insult a grieving woman who'd been nothing but cooperative and kind thus far.

"Did Lenora keep in contact with any of her exes?" Jill asked.

They'd spoken with Lenora's latest beau yesterday. A wealthy widower who'd only recently moved to the city from Dallas.

Of everyone they'd spoken with, he'd been the most visibly upset by the news. Really, truly upset. And as they weren't married, he had no financial motivation to kill her. Even if the man weren't loaded himself—and he was definitely loaded—he had to have known that he wouldn't earn a penny from her death.

But money could be a powerful motivator for her *exes*. If she was on good terms with any of them, there was always a chance they could end up in her will.

"Oh, goodness no," Dorothy said with a dismissive wave. "As skilled as Lenora was at drawing men to her, she was equally adept at driving them away when she tired of them."

"Tired of them?" Vincent asked. "They're not shoes."

Jill silently echoed the question.

It was an odd way of describing a failed relationship. It spoke of a woman who entered relationships to stave off boredom, or a woman prone to fits and starts of passion as little more than a whim.

"No, of course men aren't shoes, Detective." Dorothy took a sip of her tea. "But for Lenora, they may as well have been."

"She was...fickle?" Jill asked, searching for the right word.

Dorothy's lips pursed. "More like...Hmm, how do I say this? Lenora was always very aware of how removed she could be from other people. Men in particular. She tended to throw herself into one relationship after another in hopes of connecting with someone."

"Did she ever? Connect, I mean?" Jill asked, taking a sip of her own tea to be polite. She didn't have to turn around to know that Vincent probably hadn't touched his.

"Oh, for a time she would. A few months. A couple years, with some of them. But they always wanted more than she had to give. They'd get jealous. Demanding. Needy. And that's when Lenora would move on."

"So it was always her that ended the relationship?" Jill asked.

"Generally, yes."

Jill silently cursed.

It wasn't ideal for crime solving. She'd hoped for one ex in particular that had been discarded. It would be a starting point. But from the way it was looking, they had four ex-husbands, two ex-fiancés, and an unknown number of unnamed lovers that could have been wooed and discarded by the famous Hollywood siren.

"Well except for Clayton Wallace," Dorothy said as she pulled a delicate macaroon off a china plate and took a tiny nibble.

"Clayton Wallace?" Vin asked.

"Her third husband," Jill said.

She'd done her homework last night when she couldn't sleep.

"And he was different from the others?" Vincent prompted, the impatience in his voice seeping through as it always did.

Dorothy carefully wiped her fingers on a cloth napkin. "Only in that he was the only man who ever dumped Lenora."

Jill leaned forward. "Why?"

Perhaps Lenora had cheated, or there'd been some sort of scandal. Perhaps one that Clayton Wallace hadn't let go of, even after fifteen years...

Dorothy lifted one slim shoulder. "He was gay, of course. He and Lenora remained the best of friends, though. I believe he's living in California now."

Jill had to stop herself from slumping. A gay ex-husband with whom the victim was "the best of friends" was not exactly a prime suspect.

Vincent came around to the two women then and sat down beside Jill.

They weren't touching...not quite. But suddenly Jill was distracted, because he smelled...like soap.

Not fancy cologne, no expensive aftershave.

Vincent Moretti smelled like soap, and it was...nice.

Had he always smelled like this? Maybe he'd gotten new soap. Maybe...

"Detective?"

Vincent was staring at her in confusion, and too late Jill realized that she was all but leaning into him. And judging from the expectant look on both of their faces, a question had been directed at her and Jill had missed it because she'd been too busy—

"Sorry, what?" she asked.

Vincent's gaze dropped to her mouth for a single moment before his dark eyes lifted back to hers. "Ms. Birch asked if you'd care for more tea?"

"Oh. Oh! Yes. I'd love some."

He lifted an eyebrow and flicked his eyes to her cup. It was nearly full.

She ignored this—and him—as she extended her cup and saucer to Dorothy, who politely didn't comment on

Jill's full cup as she added just the tiniest splash from the pot.

"Yesterday you said that my sister had fallen—was likely pushed," Dorothy was saying, her voice remarkably steady.

"Yes, ma'am," Vincent said.

"And there was no chance it could have been an accident?"

"We don't think so," Jill said quietly. "The height of the railing...it would have taken some force—"

She broke off, not wanting to go into more details than she had to about this woman's sister's death.

Vin leaned forward. "Of course, we can't officially rule it a homicide until we rule out suicide—"

Dorothy gave a delicate, feminine snort. "Don't be ridiculous. Lenora was far too fond of herself to take her own life. And even if she had, she wouldn't have done so in such a messy manner."

Dorothy Birch's words echoed Jill's from yesterday. She resisted the urge to kick Vincent and mutter, *I told you so.*

The older woman sighed and set her cup aside. "I suppose you're here because you want to know if I have any ideas on who might have done it."

"Yes," Jill said quickly before Vincent could inform Dorothy that they were actually here to see if *she* might have done it.

"Well, I have no idea," Dorothy said.

Jill didn't even bother to sigh. It was about what she'd expected.

"But if I were to hazard a guess..." Dorothy continued.

Jill and Vincent sat up straighter.

"...I'd start with Malcolm Torres."

"Her second husband," Jill said, mostly for Vin's sake.

"Yes," Dorothy said, taking a sip of her tea.

"Why him?" Vincent asked.

"Because of the death threats, of course."

Vin and Jill turned to stare at each other. Of course.

CHAPTER TEN

Vincent spotted his two brothers the moment he walked into the completely generic sports bar.

Both Luc and Anthony were already halfway through their beers, so they'd obviously been here awhile, despite the fact that Vin had arrived five minutes *earlier* than when Anthony had told him to show up.

The fact that they were deep in conversation confirmed Vin's fears: they were talking about him.

This was confirmed when they ended their conversation the moment they saw him approach.

"Having a nice gossip session, girls?" he asked, dropping onto the stool across from them.

Neither had the decency to look the least bit apologetic.

Anthony glanced over at the bartender, signaled another round.

Vincent shrugged off his leather jacket as they moved

to a table, and set it on an empty seat. "Tell me again why we're grabbing beers at this crap hole when we're supposed to be at Elena's in"—he glanced at his watch—"twenty-five minutes?"

Anth jerked his head in Luc's direction. "Ava tipped Luc off that Elena has been experimenting with a signature cocktail."

"Ah," Vin said. "Say no more."

Their sister was a decent cook; hard not to be with the way their mother had determined to raise her only daughter to learn every Italian cooking tip she had flowing through her veins.

But for reasons that nobody understood, Elena could never be satisfied with just serving wine and beer when she hosted the family.

For that matter, she wasn't satisfied with just basic cocktail ingredients either. Martinis. Manhattans. Gin and tonic. All fine.

No, Elena had a penchant for trying things like Elder-flower Spritzes, and Parsley Lemongrass Margaritas.

In other words, his little sister had a serious skill for messing up good booze.

"Thanks," he muttered to the bored-looking bartender who delivered three beers to their table.

He took a long sip. Then another. It wasn't that he had to be plied with alcohol before family gatherings, but for this one . . .

He took another drink.

"Thanks," he said to his brothers. Not *thanks* for the beer, so much as thanks for, well . . . understanding.

Understanding that he needed this for what was to come.

Jill's boyfriend—no, *fiancé*—was in town.

Tom *Whatshisface* had arrived last night, and Elena had been planning his "welcome to the family" party all week.

Vin knew that he'd have to meet the guy eventually. Hell, he wanted to meet him, so he knew what he was up against. It was just…

He wasn't looking forward to it.

"So you ready to talk about it?" Luc asked.

Vincent glanced up to find both brothers watching him, their expressions more serenely patient than usual.

"Talk about what?" Vin asked.

Anthony linked his fingers, set them on the table, and leaned forward. "Honestly, Vin? Cut the bullshit. We did this the other night, the whole dance around the topic. You're our brother. We know you."

Vincent opened his mouth to argue, but Luc picked up where Anth stopped. "If you don't want to talk about it, we'll respect that, but don't pretend it's nothing. Don't pretend that you're thrown off by the fact that your woman is getting married to someone else."

Your woman.

He'd known, of course, that his brothers thought of Jill as his.

Knew that his whole family thought that. The Morettis, as a group, were not inclined toward subtlety.

But had *Vincent* ever known it?

He wasn't sure.

He only knew that when faced with the prospect of her walking down the aisle toward another man…

His stomach clenched.

He took a deep breath. "Jill's moving to Chicago."

"No," Anthony replied immediately, and the same second Luc let loose with, "The hell she is."

"Yup. Fancy Pants Fiancé is opening up a hotel there or some shit."

"And she's going to what, just pack it up and follow him?" Anth said. "Become the little woman? Because that's not—"

"She's apparently got connections at Chicago PD. Or Tom does," Vincent said, staring at the table. "She's not done being a cop, she's just done being a New York cop."

Done being his partner.

Luc shook his head. "This has gone too far. What's your plan?"

It took Vincent a moment to register that Luc was directing the question to him. "What makes you think I have a plan?"

What makes you think I have a say?

Anthony again leaned forward, his sanctimonious Big Brother face still firmly in place.

"Luc's right. Enough with the playing-dumb bullshit. Are you in love with Jill Henley, or are you not?"

Vincent choked on his beer.

Cleared his throat, tried to talk, and started coughing again.

"I thought we agreed we weren't going to freak him out," Luc said under his breath to Anth.

"He can handle it," Anthony said with a shrug.

"Look at him!" Luc pointed at Vincent. "He looks ready to pass out."

Vincent *felt* ready to pass out.

How the hell had his brothers got it in their heads that he was in love with Jill? Or with anyone?

Vincent wasn't even sure he knew what love was.

Family love, sure. He loved his parents. His sister. Loved his brothers, when they weren't being delusional morons. He was crazy about his grandmother, and even Ava and Maggie, who were new to his life, but might as well be sisters...

But *in love* was a different animal altogether.

One that Vincent had never encountered.

He'd dated, sure. Not so much recently. Okay, so it had been a couple years since he'd done more than hook up with random women.

He didn't do *dating*, not in the traditional sense. Not in the out-to-dinner, bring-her-home-to-Mom kind of way.

And he'd certainly never felt anything more than passing lust for the women whom he'd brought to his bed.

It wasn't that Vin didn't believe in love, the all-consuming, turn-you-into-a-sappy-moron thing. He wasn't that cynical. He'd seen it every day growing up between his parents.

Hell, it had taken him seconds to understand what happened to Luc the second he met Ava, only to watch it all over again when Anthony met Maggie.

He believed in love. He did.

He just didn't believe in it *for him*.

Not because he had any gory emotional wounds, not because he had some brokenhearted past.

He was just... he didn't *feel* like other people did.

He wasn't some sort of sociopathic weirdo, he just had never really absorbed things to his very soul the way his sister, and to a lesser extent his brothers, had.

So, no.

Vincent certainly wasn't in love with Jill Henley.

"Do you need smelling salts, honey?" Luc asked politely.

Vincent finally recovered from his shock and shot his brother the finger. Then his other brother too just for good measure.

"Where the hell did you two idiots get that idea?" he asked.

Luc sighed and slumped back. "Still in denial, I see."

Vincent ran a hand over the back of his neck, feeling strangely itchy. "Look, I'll admit that I'm having a hard time with these changes with Jill. But only because I don't want her to make a mistake. Because she's a *friend*."

He may have emphasized this last word a bit too desperately, and he could have sworn he saw Anth hide a smirk.

"So you're just going to let her go off to Chicago?" Luc asked.

"Hell no," Vincent grumbled.

"So, let me get this straight," Anth said slowly. "You're not in love with her...but you're also not going to let her go be in love with someone else?"

Vincent drained the last of his bottle, set it on the table with a clink. "She's not in love with this Tom guy."

"Really? Because the big-ass rock on her hand says otherwise."

Vin pulled his wallet out of his back pocket and fished out a couple of bills. "Jill's in love with the idea of love. Always has been."

"Can I be there when you tell her that? Please?" Luc begged.

Vincent stood. "Better idea. How about you two stay out of mine and Jill's relationship."

"Ah, so it *is* a relationship."

Vincent ignored this.

What he and Jill had was...undefinable. It didn't need names, or labels. All he knew was that he was suddenly itching to get to Elena's party. Itching to meet this guy who'd somehow managed to wrap Jill around his finger.

To his brothers' credit, they finally backed off, and the walk over to their sister's was blissfully free of talk about women.

Instead, Vin filled them in on the details of the Lenora case, which after a week was still at a complete standstill.

Dorothy Birch's tip about the ex-husband hadn't panned out. The man was a hothead for sure, and Vincent had no trouble picturing the son of a bitch uttering death threats.

But his alibi was solid.

He'd been on a Caribbean cruise at the time of Lenora's death, and only recently returned to town. There were literally hundreds of witnesses, right down to the captain of the cruise ship with whom Malcolm had gotten his picture taken, dated the night of Lenora's death.

As far as alibis went, being on a crowded ship in the middle of the Caribbean was ironclad.

Anthony had picked a bar close to Elena's midtown apartment, so in under five minutes, the three Moretti brothers were waiting impatiently for her snotty doorman to find them on her list of approved guests.

Vincent loved his sister but absolutely *hated* her apartment. It was one of those brand-new, sixty-plus-floor monstrosities that completely ruined the character of the city. The outside was all generic shiny glass, the inside all bizarre modern art.

For the life of him, he couldn't figure out why she spent

an exorbitant amount of money on something so soulless, but then . . . he supposed it was because she *could*.

Elena was the only Moretti sibling not in law enforcement, which would have been fine had her chosen career not been a slap in the face to the NYPD.

It wasn't just that Elena was a lawyer.

That was fine. No, Elena had to go and be a *defense* attorney. She fought to defend the very jackasses her brothers and father fought to put away.

Still, much as Vin hated her profession, he had to admit that his sister had done quite well for herself. He might not share her penchant for all things new and swanky, but he could respect that Elena knew what she wanted, went for it, and got it.

Once they made it up to her floor, Anth paused before knocking. "Remember, if whatever drink she's serving has floating flowers in it, we all take turns distracting her while the others dump it. Agreed?"

"Agreed."

But then they were inside Elena's apartment, and Vin realized rather abruptly that he'd drink whatever his sister put in his hand as long as it had alcohol.

Because there was Jill.

And there was her new man.

And holy hell, *he wasn't sure that he could do this*.

Luc clamped him once on the shoulder before seeking out Ava, and Vin stood in the foyer for several long moments wondering if maybe he could sneak away, plead a stomachache . . .

Jill spotted him, and the happy smile on her face drew him forward.

He blew out a breath. *He could do this*. He had to.

"You came!" Jill said, all but bounding over to him.

"Of course I came," he muttered.

Jill's hair was in its usual ponytail, but that's where *his* Jill ended, because he barely recognized her from the neck down.

She was wearing a dress. A short, white strapless thing that made her look young, and well...bridal.

Jill linked her arm in Vin's, oblivious to his turmoil.

He wanted to jerk his arm away. Wanted to bark at her to, for once, give him some Goddamn distance.

Except he wasn't sure he wanted distance. He wanted...

"How's the new guy fitting in?" he asked.

"Hmm," she said, seeming to consider the question.

She took a sip of her drink, which true to Anth's prediction, had some sort of floating flower in it.

"He's doing great. Everyone loves him," she said, taking another sip of drink.

A quick scan of the situation verified this. The entire Moretti clan looked ready to fall at Tom's feet.

"And this is a problem, because...?"

"It's not!" she said brightly. "It's great."

He gave her a look. "Jill."

She bit her lip. "Okay, fine, but if you repeat what I'm about to say, I will kill you."

"Spit it out."

"Do you think there's such a thing as too nice?" she asked. "*Too* friendly?"

"Yes," he deadpanned. "I know there is. I've dealt with it every day for the past six years."

She pinched his arm. "I'm serious."

"So am I. Henley, you're like the human equivalent of a rainbow."

There was a burst of laughter, and she and Vin shifted to see the crowd around Tom laughing as he told a story.

Jill took another sip of her drink, and everything clicked into place.

"Are you *jealous*, Detective?"

She glared at him. "Jealous of what?"

He nudged her shoulder. "That your boy over there is the center of attention. That for once, you're not the funniest, brightest person in the room?"

Her face fell a little, and he instantly regretted his teasing. He itched to tell her that she was always the brightest person in the room. That she was *his* light.

"I just don't want Tom to feel like he has to try so hard to make people like him," she said.

Tom. Just hearing another man's name on her lips made him irritable.

"What do *you* think of him?" she asked, gesturing with her glass.

Oh God. Don't ask me that.

"Haven't talked to him. Don't want to make snap decisions," he said.

Jill snorted. "You make snap decisions all the time. Come on, use your Spidey sense."

Vincent forced himself to look at her fiancé again. He looked like Tom Fucking Brady. Even the first name was the same.

And yet... good-looking as the man was, something was off. Not off in that there was something wrong with the guy, but the man hadn't once looked at Jill.

He was too busy working the room. Not even in a smarmy way, just the way of someone who made it his business to be liked.

Much like Jill.

He wouldn't admit it to her when her mood was fluttering on the edge of cranky, but she might be onto something with the two of them being too much alike.

Almost as though their matching, ready smiles would cancel each other out.

"Does he play polo?" Vin asked. "He totally looks like the type of dude that would play polo."

She gave him a look. "Stop. Just because he doesn't wear a leather jacket doesn't mean he's preppy."

"How much white does he have in his closet? Tell me honestly," Vin said, glancing down at her.

She started to giggle, then slapped a hand over her mouth, as though catching herself. "Stop. Come on. I'll introduce you."

Please don't.

But of course, he followed her. It had to happen sometime. Might as well get it over with.

And as it turned out, Tom had all sorts of pretty manners to go with the pretty face.

Vincent hated him. Mainly because there was nothing to hate.

"It's nice to finally meet you," Tom said sincerely, reaching out to shake Vincent's hand.

Ignoring the hand was tempting—very—but even he had his limits of rudeness, and endured a firm handshake.

"Jill's said plenty about you," Tom said, taking a drink of the flowery cocktail and not wincing in the least.

"Nothing good," Jill chimed in cheerfully.

"I knew within minutes of talking to Jill about her job that you were her other half," Tom said.

Vincent glanced at Jill then, curious how she would respond to that assessment, and found her watching him.

She looked away the second their eyes met, something fleeting and unidentifiable flashing across her face.

Vincent was saved from having to rummage up some requisite response when Elena appeared.

"You're late." She shoved a glass of something sugary and pink into his hand as she lifted to her toes and kissed his cheek.

Elena was dressed to kill as always in a form-fitting gray dress and high heels that, despite being light gray suede, were inexplicably clean.

The dirt was probably scared of her.

He glanced at his beverage. "Got any beer?"

His sister tapped a manicured fingernail against his hand. "You didn't even try it."

"Because there's a flower floating in it."

"It's an edible flower. Did you know that some of the fancy grocery stores carry those in their herb section? It's just this cute little box called edible flowers."

Vincent stared at her. "Do I look like I would know that?"

Elena rolled her eyes and turned her attention to Tom and Jill. "Vincent here thinks that if he doesn't grunt and scowl eighty times a day, we'll all forget he's a man."

He lifted the glass to his face. Sniffed. It smelled like booze. That was promising. Vincent studied it more carefully, curious if there was a way to avoid the sugar rim. Nope.

He took a tentative sip.

"Well?" Elena asked, finally ripping her glare away from Tom. "What do you think?"

"It's terrible," he said.

Although, it wasn't really. A little sweeter than he would have liked, and he'd have preferred a beer or a glass of red wine, but it was alcohol.

Tom's hand found Jill's back, and Vincent took another sip. Bigger this time.

"You *do* like the drink!" Elena said.

"Something like that," he muttered.

The smell of familiar flowery perfume drew Vin's attention to his grandmother, who materialized at his side with surprising speed considering her advanced years.

"Your mother got the wrong kind of prosciutto."

"Nonna, there is no wrong kind of prosciutto," Elena explained gently.

Vincent nodded, inclined for once to agree with his sister.

Nonna shook her head stubbornly. "No, she got it from that dodgy butcher on Staten Island when I specifically told her—"

Elena held up her hand. "Wait, why are either of you bringing prosciutto? I told you I was getting this catered."

Nonna gave a furtive look over her shoulder. "Yes, I've seen your caterer. Wouldn't know al dente pasta if it bit her in the ass."

"Which is fine," Elena explained through gritted teeth. "Because we're not having Italian food."

Nonna puffed up. "But we're Italian."

"Yes, but they're not," Elena said, gesturing at Jill and Tom. "And it's their night, so I wanted to do something more traditionally American."

"I'm sure we'll love whatever you serve, Italian or not,"

Tom said, earning beaming smiles from both Nonna and Elena.

"Vin, you got a sec?" Jill interrupted, dragging Vincent toward the kitchen. "I had a thought on the case."

"What's up?" he asked. "Tell me you've figured out who the hell killed Lenora Birch, because the higher-ups are starting to get—"

"No, I don't have a freaking clue," she said. "I just need a drink. I need a minute."

"Need a minute from…the man you're going to marry?"

"Mmm," she murmured distractedly as she glanced over her shoulder and then dumped her drink down the drain.

Jill reached for his drink and followed suit.

"I thought you liked sweet stuff," he said.

"I do, but that drink was just wrong," she muttered as she rummaged through Elena's fridge.

She pulled out a bottle of white wine, which wasn't Vincent's preferred beverage, but at least it was flower-free.

"Come here often?" he said dryly, watching as she located Elena's corkscrew and wineglasses without having to search.

"She hosts a lot of our girls' nights," she said, defiantly opening the bottle and pouring them two generous portions.

"Where you talk about boys and lipstick?" he asked, accepting the glass she handed him.

"God no," she replied. "Mostly we talk about the kind of sex we're not getting."

Vincent choked on his wine. *Don't ask. Don't ask.*

"What kind of sex is that?"

He'd asked.

Jill merely looked at him over the rim of her wineglass before giving a little shrug. "You know. Hot. Raunchy. Often."

He opened his mouth to respond, only to realize there was no response to that.

None.

Jill was already skipping out of the kitchen to rejoin the party.

Vin almost followed her, then stopped, jerked open the freezer door, and put his head in.

A few moments later, the frigid air of the freezer had helped cool his body.

But not his mind.

Raunchy sex. Jill Henley wanted hot, raunchy sex.

There wasn't enough cold air on the planet to cool his mind from *that* visual.

CHAPTER ELEVEN

As far as leads went, a retired actress who lived three hours away from the scene of the crime wasn't much to go on.

But Jill and Vincent were officially out of suspects.

Every last one of Lenora Birch's current and former lovers either had alibis or lacked motivation.

Jealous family members? None.

Bitter friends? None.

Disgruntled employees? None.

The latest lead—and it was a weak one—was Holly Adams, an actress whose career had revved to life about the same time as Lenora's fifty years earlier.

But whereas Lenora's career and reputation continued to grow over the years, Holly's fizzled almost as quickly as it had taken off. Not because she'd lacked talent.

But the combination of a couple bad movie choices plus more than a few cheating scandals, and Holly had been toppled—no, *thrown*—off the America's Sweetheart pedestal.

Leaving Lenora with the spotlight all to herself.

It wasn't exactly a unique story, but according to Lenora's sister, Holly Adams had blamed Lenora for her fall from grace.

In addition, the two women had run into each other at a Broadway premiere just weeks before Lenora's death, and the run-in had been icy.

Which was why Jill and Vincent were driving out to Connecticut to figure out if Holly's anger had shifted from icy to white hot and murderous.

"I can't believe we're driving to the middle of nowhere on the ridiculous possibility that a seventy-two-year-old washed-up starlet made a three-hour trek into the city to push another starlet over a banister, then managed to get away without leaving a single clue," Vincent grumbled.

Jill ignored his griping, all of her attention focused on the map on her phone. "Turn right here. Right! Here!"

He turned quickly with a curse.

"Oh wait," she muttered when the phone gave her a rerouting message.

"Henley, I swear to God..."

"It's not my fault," she shot back. "I get almost no signal out here. The GPS keeps losing track of where we are."

"It's Connecticut, not Wyoming, how can it—"

"There," she said, her arm whipping out, bumping against his chest. "There's a sign for the Holly Haven. That's it."

Vincent pulled into the driveway and then slowed as they approached an enormous metal gate.

"I thought you said she was a washed-up actress," he

said as he rolled down the window to dial the call box. "She's apparently loaded."

"She's had a couple of wealthy marriages," Jill said, leaning forward to peer onto the property while Vincent announced them.

The gate opened and Vincent drove forward on what seemed to be a private country club. The grass was perfectly manicured. The trees lining the driveway were evenly spaced.

"How big is this property?" he asked. "I don't even see a house—"

And then they saw it.

"That's because it's not a house," Jill said, her voice just a little bit awed. "It's like a French chateau."

"Yeah? You've been to a lot of those?" he asked as they both climbed out of the car, staring up at the enormous structure.

She felt a little pang at his casual question. She hated reminders that she'd never left the country. Never left the continent.

Never had anyone to travel with.

She pushed the maudlin thought aside. She had Tom now. Maybe for their honeymoon...

Vincent glanced up at the sky. "Henley, you did check the weather report before we left?"

"Yeah, that's the first thing I do when we go off to interview a murder suspect," she said sarcastically. "Check the weather."

Then she too looked up at the sky and understood immediately what he meant. She may have grown up in Florida, but she'd lived in New York long enough to know what snow looked like.

They exchanged a glance. "Let's make this fast," Vincent said.

An hour later, it was clear that Holly Adams had other ideas.

"You just can't know how lonely it gets around here," she said with a bright smile. "I love to entertain, so you can imagine how excited I was to hear I was having guests!"

Jill hid a smile.

She was pretty sure that this was the first time that homicide detectives at the NYPD had been described as guests.

And Jill was definitely certain that it was the first time they'd been treated to a three-course meal.

The food had been amazing, although not quite as amazing as watching Vincent carefully eat butternut squash bisque with an itty-bitty spoon.

"So, Ms. Adams," he said as the housekeeper set chocolate mousse in front of them. "About Lenora Birch..."

Holly sighed from where she sat proudly at the head of the table. The woman had refused to discuss the death of a "dear friend" while eating, but Vincent was apparently out of patience. Jill was surprised he'd made it all the way to dessert.

"Ms. Adams, can you tell us about the last time you saw Lenora?" Jill asked, leaning forward.

"Please. Call me Holly." She fiddled with her spoon.

Jill studied the older woman, trying to get a read on her and failing.

She was beautiful, even in her mid-seventies. She was short and curvy, and even with her advanced age, Jill could definitely see the outline of what must have been a rather phenomenal figure back in her day.

She and Lenora must have made quite a pair, one tall, thin, and regal, the other short, curvy, and coquettish.

"We used to be friends, you know," Holly said on a sigh. "Best friends."

Her voice was just slightly petulant, although Jill wasn't sure if it was from old wounds or annoyance that she was being questioned in the death of a former friend.

But the former part was why they were here.

"What happened? To the friendship, I mean," Jill asked.

Holly spooned up a tiny bit of chocolate mousse and slipped it between coral-colored lips. "Isn't it obvious? She shoved me out of the way so that she'd be the only Hollywood darling. Took all the prime roles, stole all the men—"

"All the men?" Vincent asked.

Holly waved her hand. "You know what I mean, Detective. All the good ones."

"You've been married three times," Vincent said dryly. "Were they the good ones?"

Holly huffed and gazed at him with sharp eyes.

Then she shifted her attention to Jill. "Your partner's a cynic."

Jill smiled. "A bit, yes."

Holly's hand glanced to Jill's left hand. "I see you're not. Married?"

"Engaged," Jill responded.

Holly's face lit up. "Oh, I do love a good engagement! They're so much fun. I miss them."

"More fun than the marriages themselves?" Vincent cut in again.

Jill's lips twitched, but Vin brought up a good point.

All signs were definitely pointing to Holly Adams being spoiled and shallow.

But murderous? She just wasn't sure. At all.

"So your and Lenora's friendship ended. What caused the final break?" Jill asked, bringing their attention back to the case.

"Well." Holly plucked at the skirt of her Chanel suit. "It was over a man."

"Naturally," Vincent muttered into his water glass.

Jill tried to kick him under the table, but the massive dining table was too large for her to reach.

"He was my beau first," Holly said. "We met at Bemelman's. You've been?"

Jill shook her head, and Holly clapped her hands together. "Oh, you simply must. It's this lovely—"

"So how did Lenora steal him?" Vincent asked, his patience officially frayed.

Holly slumped again. "I invited her out to drinks with the two of us. I wanted her to meet him."

Or wanted to show him off, Jill thought, taking a bite of rather excellent chocolate mousse.

"Anyway, the two of them fought like crazy," Holly said. "I'd never seen anything like it. Hate at first sight. Or so I thought."

Jill saw Vincent sit up straighter and wondered if he was getting one of his premonitions. Although over what, she had no idea. Holly Adams might be a vain snot, but Jill doubted she'd have killed a former friend over a decades-old grudge over a man whom neither had gone on to marry.

"Anyway," Holly said moodily, "turns out all that 'fighting' was really something else."

"They had an affair?" Jill asked, keeping her voice kind.

"They said they didn't," Holly said. "But Henry—that was his name—ended things with me. When I asked him why, he said he had feelings for someone else. Two weeks later, they showed up together at the premiere of Lenora's latest film."

"That upset you," Vincent said.

Holly gave him a vaguely incredulous look. "Clearly you've never had another man steal someone of yours, Detective. Of course I was upset."

Jill should have been watching Holly then. Should have been assessing the older woman to determine whether or not by *upset* she actually meant homicidal.

But instead she found herself watching her partner.

Something on his face just then. When Holly had said he'd never had another man steal someone of his . . .

Suddenly, Jill wanted to press. Wanted to know what Vincent was thinking right that very second, because it felt important—vital. As well as she knew Vincent (and she supposed she knew him as well as anyone), she had a sense that she was missing something.

"Ms. Adams, where were you the night Lenora Birch was murdered?"

Jill jumped to attention at that, her attention swerving back to Holly at Vincent's direct question.

She had to admit, it was well played. Vin had a habit of being a bit too hasty with the accusations, and he could sometimes put suspects on edge too soon, but he was right to try to throw Holly Adams off her game.

And he'd succeeded given that the woman clutched at her necklace with white knuckles.

"Why, I—how dare you—"

"Oh, come now, Holly," Jill said kindly. "You had a very public argument with Ms. Birch just days before she was murdered. Surely you knew two homicide detectives didn't drive all the way out from New York just to share a meal."

Holly glared at her, and for the first time, Jill found herself on the receiving end of a suspect's irritation. Usually she played the good cop, but Holly was starting to rub her the wrong way.

The woman was lonely, true, but she was also petulant and manipulative—two flaws Jill had always found particularly irritating.

"I was here," Holly Adams said finally, picking up her spoon and determinedly scraping at the last of her chocolate mousse. "I was here like I always am, alone like I always am."

"So nobody can verify your whereabouts?"

She lifted a shoulder. "My housekeeper, of course. And Martin. He manages security and the occasional odd job around the house."

Both were employees who could be easily bought, Jill thought.

Still, it was far-fetched. Possible, yes. Possible that Holly Adams could have found her way to the city, visited an old frenemy, and then, in arguing about old times, pushed her in a fit of rage.

But there was no proof. Not even circumstantial evidence.

Holly was sharper than Jill originally gave her credit for, because the older woman seemed to sense Jill's lack of conviction and played on it.

She reached out a hand, although the table was so enormous it stopped several feet short of Jill before dropping delicately. "I didn't kill Lenora," she said. "I don't even have the energy to dislike her anymore. When you'll get to my age...you'll see. You'll understand. It takes a grievance far worse than a straying lover to carry on that kind of hatred for decades. We had a spat a few weeks ago, true, but it was more for old times' sake than anything else. There was no real heat to it. I'm sure Lenora would say the same."

"Except she can't. Because she's dead." Vincent put his napkin down after this sharp deceleration and stood, indicating that the meal was over.

The interview was over as well. Jill knew there was nothing more to get out of Holly at the moment. She had that clammed-up look of a woman who was gearing up for a good sulk.

"May we speak with your housekeeper and this Martin?" Jill asked, standing as well.

Holly sniffed. "Of course. I have nothing to hide."

As expected, the housekeeper and security guy backed up their employer's claims that she rarely left the home. Apparently Holly hadn't been away from the house except to see the show in the city on the night she argued with Lenora, as well as to a friend's house for cocktails a couple nights earlier.

Jill didn't see any of the classic warning signs that they were lying, but neither did she get that gut-level instinct that they were completely honest.

Though, that sort of people-reading hunch was more Vincent's thing. Maybe he'd picked something up.

Vincent and Jill said a chilly good-bye to a thoroughly

pissed-off Holly Adams, who had left the dining room and now sat watching reruns of *I Love Lucy* in a fully decked-out media room.

"You can see yourself out, I trust?" Holly said, not looking away from the screen.

"We'll manage," Vin said with a roll of his eyes at Jill.

They barely managed. It took two wrong turns in the massive house before they found their way back to the formal foyer.

"That chandelier is bigger than my entire apartment," Vin muttered.

"Probably costs as much too," Jill said, pausing to take one last look at the opulent home. "It's a little sad, isn't it? All of this grandness and nobody to share it with?"

"Doesn't have to be sad. Some people like being alone."

She glanced at him knowingly. "You're talking about you, huh?"

Her voice was teasing, but he merely looked away. Didn't answer as he opened the door and started to head outside.

Vincent skidded to a halt and when Jill glanced around him, she knew why.

The sky had made good on its threat of snow.

Lots of it.

CHAPTER TWELVE

Jill and Vincent made a solid go of it, but ten minutes after leaving Holly Adams's house, they realized that trying to make it back to Manhattan in a near blizzard was stupid and dangerous.

"There," Jill said, squinting through the white blur of their windshield. "I think that's a motel up on the right."

" 'Motel' is a strong word," Vincent said as they inched closer, pulling into the near-deserted parking lot.

Jill reached for the door handle, but Vincent gave her a skeptical look. "You do know that deserted motels like this are where people come to die, right?"

She leaned over and patted his thigh. "You've got a gun, big guy."

The woman behind the reception desk had both the whitest skin and the blackest hair Jill had ever seen. Add to that a complete inability to smile, an obvious disdain for her job, and a disarming habit of maintaining eye contact for three beats too long, and Vincent had a pretty solid point about the whole death-in-motel theory.

The place was seriously creepy.

"Good thing Holly served us a big old meal so we won't have to worry about dinner," Jill said as they made their way to their side-by-side rooms.

"Or not," she muttered, watching as Vincent stopped in front of a vending machine, pulled out some cash, and began punching buttons for everything from mixed nuts to M&M's.

Their rooms were on the first floor. "This is me," Jill said, pointing at 104. The "0" was missing, but as long as the bed was clean and the bathroom spider-free, she'd make do.

Vincent nodded at 105. "I'm next door if you need anything."

"I'll be good," she said. "I have every intention of taking a hot shower and then watching some truly appalling old movie on TV."

"And calling Tom," Vin said.

She'd started to put her key in the lock but glanced over her shoulder in surprise at that.

"Sure," she said, a little confused by the sudden and unprompted mention of her fiancé. "And calling Tom."

She hadn't thought much about it actually. But they talked most nights, so yeah . . . she'd check in.

Vin nodded once before taking a couple steps toward his own room. He passed before entering, glancing at her once. "If you hear me scream . . . save me?"

Jill grinned. "You got it, partner. Be brave in there."

Then, to her utter surprise, Vincent Moretti smiled at

her. Not a big toothy grin...the man didn't have any of those...that she knew of.

But it was a definite smile. As rare as it was beautiful.

She stood there for several seconds even after he'd shut his door, still feeling a little off balance.

Jill shook it off and went into her motel room. It was about what one would expect from a roadside motel in a town whose borders took all of five minutes to drive through.

The carpet was less than pristine. The bedspread was standard, ugly floral print. The pillows looked flat, the lighting horrible.

But it was clean—ish. No hairballs in the bathroom, no dead bugs on the nightstand. Jill abandoned the shower idea after remembering that she'd have no clean underwear to put on after.

Instead, she set her gun in the drawer of the nightstand, pulled off her boots and bulky sweater, and settled back on the bed in her white camisole and pants. She made herself as comfortable as possible against the two pathetic pillows and pulled out her cell phone.

And got Tom's voice mail.

She settled for a text. Call me when you get a chance. Interesting day.

Jill started to set the phone aside, then paused, and wrote another message.

Love you.

She stared down at her screen for several moments, wondering if maybe he'd respond right away with a "love you too" as he usually did.

Nothing.

Jill shrugged. Tom was still in Florida, in the last phases of that deal before he'd shift his attention to

Chicago. No doubt he was out schmoozing some businessmen and -women.

He wanted her to fly down next weekend. She hadn't seen him since last week when he'd come up to meet the Morettis, and she tried not to let herself get freaked out by the fact that since he'd slipped a ring on her finger, they'd been apart more than they'd been together.

She *should* go down to Florida. There was no reason not to make the short trip. She wouldn't have to miss work if she kept it short, and she could totally go for a dose of sunshine.

And it was important—vital—somehow, that she keep Tom fresh in her memory.

And her in his.

"You're being ridiculous," she muttered to herself, tapping her fingers against her mouth. "You're marrying the man. It's not like he's going to forget you."

Jill dropped her hand to her lap and stood staring at the wall, wondering if this is what people meant by pre-wedding jitters.

Granted their wedding was still several months away, and she didn't have jitters so much as...

She didn't know what. But it was *something*.

Not in the mood to deal with it, and blaming it on the fact that she was in a small, gross motel without any clean clothes in the middle of a snowstorm, she reached for the TV remote.

"Are you freaking kidding me?" she said ten seconds later.

Every single channel was doing the staticky thing.

She pushed all the standard "fix it" buttons on the remote. Nothing. Got up and fiddled with a few things on the TV set itself.

Still nothing.

A call to the front desk confirmed her worst nightmare.

"Our fix-it guy could normally be here in a half hour, but in this snow..."

"I can take another room," Jill said. It's not like she had any heavy luggage that had to be moved.

"Well...I think 219 is clean, and 201 is supposed to be..."

Jill pulled at her ponytail in irritation. "Never mind," she muttered. "Do you guys have any books? You know, a shelf of books left behind?"

Maybe she could read. A nice mystery or romance would do just the trick...

"Books?" the receptionist said.

Jill closed her eyes. "Forget it. Thanks anyway."

She hung up the phone and gently banged her head against the wall behind her. She could probably just go to bed early...get caught up on some sleep.

Jill glanced at the clock on the nightstand. It wasn't even seven o'clock.

Standing, Jill pulled her sweater and boots back on, grabbed her gun and purse.

Ten seconds later she was knocking on Vincent's door.

"I came to save you—" she started to say the second the door opened.

And then she broke off.

And stared.

And stared some more.

Vincent Moretti was shirtless.

Jill didn't trust herself to speak.

Because the only word her dazed mind seemed to be able to come up with was *mouthwatering*.

CHAPTER THIRTEEN

He hadn't meant to open the door without a shirt.

But taking in Jill's stunned expression, he was glad that he had.

Call it payback for her *raunchy sex* comment at Elena's party that had kept him up for more nights than he cared to admit.

Jill still hadn't lifted her eyes from his torso, and he put his hand on the doorjamb, leaning just slightly.

When her eyes finally met his, he was wearing an all-out grin.

"Why are you... panting?" she asked.

Why are you? he wanted to ask back.

Instead he shrugged. "Doing some push-ups."

"You do those every night?" she asked.

"And every morning."

Actually, his twice-daily workouts were usually a good

deal more than push-ups, but he was in a tiny-ass motel room. He did what he could.

"Huh." Her eyes drifted lower again.

He smirked. "Can I help you with something, Henley?"

"Um..."

There was a very satisfying pause, and Vincent felt his grin grow wider.

She pointed to her room. "My TV's not working."

Damn. Not what he was hoping she'd say.

"Ah. What room are they moving you to?" he asked, assuming she was stopping by to tell him of her relocation.

"They're not."

And then she ducked, slipping under the barricade his arm had made across the doorway and entering his hotel room.

"Um, okay." He shut the door and turned to face her.

She'd already found the remote on the nightstand and wiggled it at him. "You mind?"

"You're watching TV *here*?"

"Why not? If you need to finish your push-ups, I'll promise not to watch."

"*Really*," he said dryly.

"Nope." She grinned. "Not really. Seriously, Moretti, that's an impressive upper body you've been hiding from me all this time."

"I'd be happy to implement shirtless Saturdays if you are."

"Eh, you're getting the bad end of the bargain there, my friend. The only exercise I do on a daily basis is lifting beverages to my face. Coffee in the morning, wine in the evenings—"

Vin tuned out her rambling. He was too busy picturing shirtless Jill, and somehow he didn't think he'd be disappointed.

Jill was slim, yes, and her small breasts were not exactly the type to land the *Sports Illustrated* swimsuit cover, but Vincent had never been a boobs guy.

He liked his women on the smaller end of the spectrum, liked when he could lift them, hold their tight, perfect ass in his hands as he...

The TV turned on and his dirty thoughts scattered.

"I guess you're staying then," he muttered.

"It wasn't really ever up for negotiation," she said, her mouth full of M&M's as she flipped through the stations.

"Thought you 'couldn't possibly eat'?" he said.

She shot him a patient look before patting the mattress next to her. "Come watch this stupid movie with me. It'll help ease your bad mood."

He glanced at the TV. "Isn't this *Transformers*, or something equally awful?"

She wiggled her eyebrows at him. "You know you want to."

And in spite of himself, he did.

Not the movie so much, but the idea of relaxing beside someone else, even if it was in a shitty little motel room with no clean clothes and a fucking blizzard outside, held a strange appeal.

Vincent walked around the bed and sat beside her, both of them propped against the headboard. And he realized he was wrong. It wasn't relaxing beside someone that appealed.

It was relaxing beside Jill.

She glanced over at him, then did a double take before bouncing off the bed and grabbing his undershirt from the chair in the corner where he'd set it.

Jill flung it at him, and he caught it just before it whacked him in the face.

"Put that on," she ordered.

"I usually go to bed shirtless," he said, flexing just to mess with her.

"And I usually watch TV pantless," she shot back.

Vin lifted an eyebrow. "I'm game if you're game."

She pointed at him. "Get dressed, Moretti."

He complied, but only because an annoying thought cropped up. "Did you talk to Tom?"

Jill was in the process of flinging herself on the bed, but she faltered a little at that. "You sure are concerned with the state of my relationship."

"Just making conversation," he muttered, turning his attention back to the TV. It was commercials.

"Since when?" she asked, pressing the issue. "Since when have you 'just made conversation' with *anyone*?"

There was a sharper-than-usual edge to her voice, and Vincent scooted down so he was lying on his side of the bed, head propped on his hand, facing her. "What's going on, Henley? You're testy."

She fished out an M&M, started to lift it to her mouth, and then frowned at it.

"Everything okay?" he asked, tongue in his cheek. This disgruntled version of Jill was kind of . . . cute.

"I don't like the brown ones," she said, as though this were completely reasonable.

She held it out to him between two fingers, and Vincent surprised them both by leaning forward and nipping it out of her fingers with his mouth.

The lips-to-fingers contact was brief. A second at most, but he felt it in his gut. Heard it in her intake of breath.

Vin lifted his eyes to hers, but the second he did, she

looked back at the M&M's bag, shaking it violently until she found a blue one.

She rattled the bag again, going at it like a raccoon with a take-out bag, and he reached out, touched her hand. "Jill?"

Abruptly she dropped the bag of candy and scooted down until she was flat on her back on the bed. She flung both arms over her face, the crook of her crossed elbows hiding her eyes.

He didn't ask her what was up. Didn't push. Just sat and waited. She was still for several minutes, and then she rolled over onto her side to face him, propping her head on her hand, mimicking his position.

"Do you think I'm making a mistake?"

His chest clenched. *Don't ask me that.*

But her gaze was level, her voice steady. She really wanted to know. Wanted his opinion.

He fished an M&M out of the bag—a brown one—to stall. "I assume that we're talking about your shotgun wedding?"

She nodded.

"What's going on? Trouble in paradise?"

"Not really," she said, glancing down at the bed. "We're not fighting. It's just . . . we never see each other."

"Which sucks," he said slowly. "But plenty of couples make long-distance work, at least in the short term."

"Yeah, because you know so much about couples," she said crankily.

"It'll get better," he forced himself to say. "Just throw yourself into the wedding planning. Remind yourself all the reasons that these tough months are worth it."

Jill smiled. "I think you might be the first guy in history to tell a woman to throw herself into wedding planning."

"Yeah well ... I'm not the one you're marrying, now am I? I won't have to deal with the worst of it."

He intentionally kept his voice light, but her smile dimmed, just a little, before she seemed to force herself to recover. "Very true. And yet you *will* have to see me every day, so you just remember this little chat while I'm talking to you about chair covers and canapés and white lingerie."

"That last one, I'm down with," he said.

She smiled, and he smiled back. "You sure you're okay?" he asked.

"Sure. Just been getting a lot of the jitters lately," she said, rolling herself into a seated position and crossing her legs on the bed.

"Movie's back," she said, reaching for the remote and turning it up.

Okay then.

The conversation was apparently over. Usually it was him finding ways to stop talking, but tonight, he wanted to keep the conversation going. He wanted to know more about what was going on with her and Tom.

Wanted to hear more about these second thoughts she was having.

Instead, he reached for a candy bar and tore it open with his teeth as he turned his attention toward the noisy, brainless, yet fully entertaining movie.

Forty minutes later the credits started rolling and Vin waited for Jill to turn the channel.

And waited ... and waited ...

"Yo, Henley—"

He broke off when he glanced over and saw her. She was sound asleep.

Vincent gently pulled the remote out from under her

hand and turned down the volume, thoroughly amused when he heard gentle snores coming out of his partner.

Jill Henley snored. How . . .

Cute.

It was cute.

He grinned to himself, reaching for his phone so he could capture it on video and use it for some good-natured blackmail in the future, only to find that his thumb didn't hit Record like he meant it to.

Instead he found himself putting the phone away.

And then he looked at her. It was probably creepy, a man staring at a sleeping woman who was not his wife or girlfriend, but he couldn't look away.

Jill looked younger than her age, even when awake. She had a girlish face and figure that gave her a perpetual twenty-three look, something he knew she loathed and loved in waves.

But sleeping, she looked . . . womanly.

Not old, not haggard, but as though she held all of the secrets of the world in her dreams; secrets only she knew.

Secrets that he wanted to beg her to share.

She made a smacking sound with her mouth and then rolled onto her side, one hand sliding up under her cheek, the other . . .

The other reached out toward him.

He froze, staring down at her small hand where it lay between them on the bed.

She hadn't been reaching for *him*, obviously. She was asleep. Didn't know that he was there.

And yet, he suddenly found it hard to swallow. Found it hard to look away from her pointy little nose, and the way a few strands of straight blond hair escaped her ponytail to lay against her cheek.

Before he realized what he was doing, he slid his hand along the bed until his fingertips were millimeters from hers.

And then he touched her hand. Just softly. His fingertip against her knuckle, the rough pad of his finger against her smooth skin.

He allowed himself to linger, just for a moment, his finger tracing each of hers. Drawing circles on the back of her hand.

Vincent wanted to flip her hand over. Wanted to touch his fingers to the nerve endings of her palm. Wanted to press his lips there. Wanted to lever himself over her, and—

Vincent pulled his hand back. Slowly.

He squeezed his eyes shut.

The touch had been almost nothing—it was less than chaste.

And yet he thought of it, long, long into the night.

CHAPTER FOURTEEN

Hey, babe."

"What's up?" Jill asked, not looking up from where she was carefully chopping an onion. Maria Moretti had always made this look easy, but Jill had nearly taken off the tip of her middle finger.

"Are you aware that you have eight different types of pasta in here?"

"Um, you try being practically adopted by the Morettis and not come to think of it as a food group."

Tom kissed the side of her head as he passed her from the pantry on his way to the fridge. "They're lucky to have you."

Jill smiled and rolled her eyes. "Biased much?"

Tom was too busy peering into her fridge, debating white wine options. "Annnnnd, every last white is Italian. Another Moretti influence?"

She gave him a quick glance, searching for any sign of irritation, but saw only amusement.

"They're all good, I promise. Even the ones you've never heard of."

He glanced at her and lifted an eyebrow. "Oh, I've heard of all of them."

Jill snorted and set the knife aside. The onion was close enough to chopped. "You're such a snob."

"Didn't hear you whining about my wine prowess while I was verbally dueling every sommelier in Florida," Tom said, pulling out a bottle as he wiggled his eyebrows.

"What, do you guys draw corkscrews at dawn on your yacht?"

"Don't be ridiculous," he said as he searched her cupboards for wineglasses. "We never drink before noon on my yacht."

Jill accepted the glass he handed her, and he clinked their glasses together. "To my second time in your apartment," he said warmly.

She smiled and tried to ignore the implication behind his teasing words.

She was going to marry a man who'd been in her apartment twice. A man who hadn't known what cupboard she kept her wineglasses in, a man who hadn't even been the slightest bit irritable despite the fact that his plane had sat on the tarmac for two hours, a man who...

Jill paused as she was sipping her wine. "Tom, you don't really have a yacht, do you?"

He smiled, his blue eyes crinkling at the corners. "Do you really want me to answer that?"

Oh God. He had a yacht. She was marrying a man with a yacht.

Tom glanced down at the massacre on her cutting board before flicking at a too-big piece of onion. He gave the barely minced garlic a skeptical look.

"Darling."

"Mmm?" The wine was delicious as she wanted it to be.

"How deft are your cooking skills?"

"You really want me to answer that?" she asked, repeating his earlier question.

He bent his knees slightly and captured her mouth for a kiss. "Want me to take over?"

She pulled back from the kiss. "You own a yacht and you cook?"

Tom winked. "Did I mention I can best most sommeliers at wine trivia?"

Jill shook her head. "What are you doing with me? I had Captain Crunch for breakfast. Out of the box. Later I found a piece between my boobs where it had fallen into my bra."

He hooked a finger into her shirt and pretended to take a look. "Still there?"

She batted his hand away. "My point is, you're *so* far out of my league."

"Then I guess it's a good thing I'm crazy about you," he said, ushering her aside. "Now step aside, drink your wine, and let me make you something fabulous."

Jill did as she was told, hoisting herself onto her kitchen counter as she watched Tom chop the onion into more manageable pieces.

This was her life. This, right here, was going to be the rest of her life. Sipping wine with Tom at the end of the day while he cooked for her.

The thought was . . . nice.

And if somewhere in the back of her mind, she wondered if it shouldn't be nicer, she ignored it.

"So how's the case coming along?" he asked as he made easy work of the onion and moved on to the garlic.

"Ugh. Stagnant," she said.

There was a vibrating news alert sounding from her purse, and she leaned across the counter, fishing her phone out as she took another sip of wine.

She bit her lip when she saw that the text was from Vin.

Ordered Chinese. You want?

For one horrible, terrible moment, Jill wanted nothing more than to respond and say yes.

What was *with* that?

She was sitting here in her cozy kitchen with delicious wine, as a gorgeous man cooked for her.

And she wanted to leave all that to go have mediocre takeout with a man who'd probably either want to review crime scene photos or watch a game while they ate?

No. No, she didn't want that.

This was where she belonged. With a man who was good at conversation, and good at kissing, and good at being nice...

Still, she regretted not telling Vin that Tom was coming into town for the weekend. She'd meant to. It was just... she didn't like talking to Vincent about Tom, any more than she liked talking to Tom about Vin.

It was like they were two parts of her life that she wanted to keep as separate as possible, and had no idea why.

Or maybe she had every idea why, which is why she couldn't let herself think about it.

"So, my sister's cousin is a real estate broker in

Chicago," Tom said, oblivious to Jill's turmoil. "She said we're looking at the perfect time to move. There are a bunch of brand-new buildings going up near the lake. Which will be brutal in winter, of course, but that's why we'll have a place in Florida as a getaway."

"I'll still have to work in winter," she said with a bit more bite than she intended.

He looked up. "Yeah. I know."

Did he?

"The option to get away to a nicer climate sounds nice," she said, softening her tone. "Maybe I can save up vacation time."

"And if not, we'll hunker down in Chicago and drink red wine in front of the fire," he said. "Maybe binge on whatever show's the next Netflix rage."

Jill's mind happily entered the cozy picture he described. It was everything she'd ever wanted. Someone to cuddle with on the couch, watching crappy TV with excellent wine…maybe even a foot rub. Maybe Vin would suggest ordering extra cheese on the pizza, and she'd pretend to protest because it was too fattening, and—

Jill sat up a little straighter. Wait. Whoa.

Vin?

How had her partner entered that picture?

He'd be back here in New York when she and Tom were in Chicago. Not like he'd be stopping by any longer, and there certainly wouldn't be any cuddling since she'd be married.

Jill glanced down at her phone, where Vincent's text sat unresponded to.

That sad text combined with her strange, out-of-place vision made her chest ache.

She took a deep breath and forced herself to reply to his message. If they had any chance of preserving their friendship after her marriage, she had to keep being open with him the way she had before Tom.

Can't. She wrote back. Tom's in town. Have an extra egg roll for me.

Jill set her phone aside and asked Tom about the most recent deal he was working on.

Her phone buzzed beside her as Tom talked, and Jill ordered herself not to look at it. Reminded herself that looking at your phone when anyone was talking was rude. And when it was your fiancé, it was downright unforgivable.

And yet, the second Tom stopped talking to peruse her spice rack, Jill tugged the phone closer to read Vin's response.

Please don't be mad, please don't be mad...

K. Also, opened your fortune cookie. Says right here that you'll die young unless you buy your partner Starbucks for the rest of the week.

She smiled as she wrote back. What does yours say?

That I'm brilliant. Also, well-endowed.

Jill nearly choked on her sip of of wine. Isn't that what it said last time?

I know, weird, right. Think I should laminate this and hand it out in bars?

"Something funny?" Tom asked as he turned back with a polite smile.

"Nah, it's nothing," she said, putting her phone away with a little pang.

But it didn't feel like nothing.

It felt like...something.

CHAPTER FIFTEEN

Oh, *that* one," Maggie exclaimed. "That's the one!"

Elena gave her sister-in-law an indulgent look over her glass of champagne. "You've said that about the last five."

Maggie sighed and leaned back on the pink sofa of the bridal shop, and rubbed her ever-growing belly. "Don't judge me. *You* have champagne while I only get this stupid sparkling cider. Also, it's the hormones. They're killing me. Yesterday I cried when I saw a pigeon eating a French fry."

Jill was barely listening as she pivoted in slow circles in front of the enormous mirrors. "I don't know—I don't think I'm liking that big bow in back."

"It dwarfs you," Ava said in her bossiest voice. "You need something that enhances your small frame, not overwhelms it."

"But I kind of like the poofy princess dress," Jill said, her voice just shy of petulant.

Elena tilted her head and gave Jill a look. "Really? Because two dresses ago you insisted on no poof."

Jill scowled at Elena in the reflection of the mirror. "I changed my mind."

She saw the look Ava and Elena exchanged. Not that they were trying very hard to hide it.

Jill whipped around, her finger pointing at them. "What was that? What was that look?"

Elena didn't miss a beat as she smoothly stood up and swooped Jill's champagne flute from the side table and came to stand beside her. "You're edgy, darling. Talk to us."

Jill accepted the flute and stared at her best friend.

Elena looked perfectly together and gorgeous as always. She was wearing one of those pencil skirts that she seemed to own a million of, in every color, and a simple white blouse. Her black hair was pulled back in a neat chignon, her makeup flawless, her manicure un-chipped.

She made Jill feel small and frumpy.

Which wasn't fair. At all.

It wasn't Elena's fault that she was gorgeous.

Nor was it Elena's fault that Jill had been in the mother-of-all funks for the past week.

It wasn't Elena's fault that Tom had been busy and hardly remembered to call. Or that when he *did* call, Jill was always working on the time-consuming Lenora Birch case.

Or that said case had yet to turn up so much as a potential clue, much less an actual suspect.

Jill pressed a thumb between her eyebrows. "Ladies, what say you we abandon the dress shopping for the day?"

"Done," Ava said, not bothering to hide her relief.

"We can go back to my place," Elena said. "Eat junk food and bash boys?"

Jill gave her friend a look. "You're having guy trouble?"

"It's not for me, honey," Elena said soothingly, petting Jill's head. "Is everything okay with you and Tom?"

"Yes," she said automatically. "Everything's great."

Elena narrowed her eyes.

"Really," Jill said. "He's such a good guy. You all liked him."

"Well yeah, but it doesn't matter that we liked him," Ava said.

"I like him too. Obviously. I love him," Jill said.

And she did. It was just...

Every time they'd talked on the phone lately, it had felt... well, almost sibling-like.

He asked about her day, she about his. They laughed, and there were no awkward silences. She cared about what he had to say.

But something wasn't right. She smiled whenever she saw his name on the caller ID, but there were no tummy flips. No slightly dry-of-mouth excitement to talk to him.

And there *should* be. Their relationship was young. They should absolutely still be in the tummy-flip stage.

And yet...

Had Jill and Tom ever really been in the tummy-flip stage?

Jill threw back the rest of her champagne.

The four women strolled out of the bridal shop empty-handed and headed toward Fifth where they'd have better luck hailing a cab.

Elena and Ava walked ahead, but Jill held back with Maggie, who was entering the *waddling* stage of her pregnancy and moving a bit slower.

Maggie linked her arm with Jill as they walked side-by-side in companionable silence.

All four women were good friends—Jill had known Elena the longest, of course. And then Ava had started dating Luc, and fit in marvelously.

And then came Maggie, who was welcomed to the group enthusiastically when she'd captured Anth's heart.

But of all of them, Maggie was perhaps the kindest.

A kindness that Jill was occasionally jealous of.

Maggie was so damn sure of who she was, and who she was was just *good*. Maggie had once been the waitress at the diner the Morettis treated like their second home, but she'd recently made a career shift over to publishing.

A pretty perfect fit considering Mags was an author in her own right; she'd recently landed a book deal for a teen love story.

Add in the fact that she was married to the love of her life and pregnant with the first Moretti grandchild...

The bitter truth was, Maggie had everything Jill wanted.

Her footsteps faltered slightly as an alarming thought hit her upside the head.

What if *that* was the reason Jill had said yes to Tom's spontaneous proposal?

Not because she wanted to marry *Tom*, but because she wanted everything that came with it.

Maggie stopped with her, turning her warm brown eyes on Jill in concern.

"You okay?"

"Yeah," Jill said, tugging her ponytail. "Maybe not. I don't know."

Maggie glanced up ahead at the other two women. "You want to go somewhere? Talk?"

Jill smiled. "You mean without Elena interrupting every five seconds?"

Maggie smiled back. "My sister-in-law can be... opinionated."

Jill sucked in a breath at Maggie's statement.

There. *That* was what was bothering her. When Maggie had said *sister-in-law*, Jill felt it all the way to her bones.

The truth of what was bugging Jill hit her like a bucket of ice water. Her three best friends were all part of the Moretti clan. Officially.

Elena *was* a Moretti. Maggie was a Moretti by marriage. And Jill had no doubt that Luc and Ava had a wedding in their future.

Which meant...

It meant that Jill was the only one of the group who *wasn't* a Moretti. Would *never* be a Moretti.

And sure, they treated her like family now, but what about when she married Tom? What about if—*when*—she moved to Chicago...?

Jill sucked in a gasping breath.

Maggie put her hand on Jill's back in alarm. "What's going on, honey?"

"I don't want to move to Chicago," Jill said. The declaration came out a little breathy.

She bent over and rested both hands on her knees. Her breathing got even shorter—the air harder to come by as though it refused to enter her lungs.

Elena and Ava had apparently realized that they'd lost two of their group and turned back, and then they were there, each of them every bit as concerned as Maggie.

"What's going on?" Ava asked.

"No big deal," Jill said weakly. "Just having a breakdown here on the sidewalk for all to see."

"Talk to us, Jilly," Elena said, her voice gentler than usual.

Jill opened her mouth, but no words came out.

"She doesn't want to move to Chicago," Maggie explained quietly.

"Well, of course she doesn't," Elena cooed, cupping Jill's face and searching her features as though looking for open wounds. "*We're* not in Chicago."

Jill smiled. Weakly, but still a smile.

"Have you told Tom this?" Ava asked.

Jill shook her head.

"You have to," Ava said firmly. Kindly. "You're one half of the relationship. You get a say."

"I know," Jill said, biting her lip. "I know that. And it's not like he made a unilateral decision. We talked about it, and I agreed, thinking that maybe a change would..."

She broke off and the other three women waited patiently for whatever breakthrough Jill wasn't sure she had the courage to reach for.

Maggie's hand stroked her back. "A change would what—what do you need to change?"

Jill glanced at the ground, and Elena made a knowing, understanding sound. "Vincent."

Jill's head snapped up. "Vin and I are fine."

Nobody said anything for several long seconds.

Ava broke the silence. "Maybe that's the problem, hun. Maybe you want more than fine."

Jill would have backed away from them had they not been surrounding her so completely. Instead, she settled for shaking her head. "I'm not following."

It was a cop-out. She knew exactly what they were getting at. But denial was the easier path. And right now, Jill *needed* easy.

Elena's fingers gently wrapped around Jill's arm as she tugged her forward. "Let's finish this conversation at my place."

"There's nothing to discuss," Jill said stubbornly. "Vincent's my partner, and he's happy for me. We work great together, sure, but he's the best detective in the city. He'll get another partner, and—"

"And what?" Ava prompted as she lifted her slim arm to hail a cab.

Vincent will find another partner.

She'd be replaced.

Granted, it'd be of her own doing. She'd be leaving *him*. But the thought of him showing up to a crime scene with someone else by his side, talking over beers about a case with someone else...

Jill's mouth tasted distinctly bitter.

"It's just work," she said quietly, to nobody in particular. "We're just partners."

None of the other women responded as they piled into the cab, and the long silence held an uncomfortable truth:

What if *just partners* was no longer enough?

CHAPTER SIXTEEN

You're grumpy today," Vincent said, handing Jill a mocha.

She took a sip of her sugary coffee. "That's supposed to be my line."

He studied her through the dark lenses of his sunglasses. "You good?"

"Yeah, *real* good," she snapped.

She wasn't good. At all.

Tom was flying in from Florida tonight, and she should be over the moon, but instead she felt...nervous.

She had butterflies, but not the kind she'd been wishing for just days earlier. Instead she had a terrible sense of foreboding.

"Really? Because you look kind of—"

"Can we just focus on the case?" Jill snapped, interrupting whatever insult Vincent likely had at the ready.

He was silent, and for a moment Jill had the strangest sense that maybe her rejection had hurt him. That maybe he wanted her to talk—to confide in him.

And then he shrugged. "Works for me. Got any new thoughts?"

No.

No, she did *not* have any new thoughts on who freaking killed Lenora Birch, and it was starting to get ridiculous.

Worst of all, their lack of progress had led to other investigators being assigned to the case. Something that had never happened in Jill's career. Or Vincent's.

"Why aren't you more upset?" she asked as they headed toward their car.

"'Bout what?"

"About the fact that they had to bring in extra resources for the case because we can't do our job."

He shrugged. "Whatever catches the killer."

She jumped in front of him, holding up a hand so he had to stop. "Okay, my turn to ask. What's going on with you?"

"Don't know what you mean."

"You're *seriously* okay with the fact that this case is destroying our perfect record? That there's a very real chance someone else will solve this before we will?"

Vincent shrugged. "They can throw as many resources at this as they want, but it's still going to be us that finds the guy. Or the woman."

She narrowed her eyes. "How can you be so sure?"

He grinned, completely confident. "Because we're the best, baby."

Baby? Jill watched in puzzlement as he moved around her and continued down the sidewalk.

Something was weird with him. Definitely.

Jill darted after him. "Okay, well then, what's our next move because I can only talk to the same people so many times. Should we go back to question Holly Adams? She's the only one who—"

Vin shook his head. "I don't want to make that trek again until we have something else to go off of."

"So then what?"

He rocked back on his heels. "We start over."

"Sorry, come again?"

"We start the case all over. Repeat from the very beginning when we arrived at Lenora's house."

"Sort of hard to do a do-over in a homicide investigation case," she said. "The whole lack of body, and whatnot."

"So we'll pretend."

"And the point of this exercise?" she asked as she jerked open the car door.

He glanced at her over the hood, tapping his fingers against his cup thoughtfully, looking very serene, and very un-Vincent-like.

"We missed something, Henley. It's the only explanation. Think about it: we've never had this much trouble on a case. It's never taken us more than a couple days to have a solid list of suspects, and most of the time we're leaning toward one suspect—the right one. But this case... we did something wrong. So let's go fix it."

He lowered himself into the car, and Jill rolled her eyes, following suit.

"Why do you think we missed something?" she asked as he turned the ignition.

"We were off our game. Unused to each other after your three months away."

"Ah," she said, understanding why he was so Zen about all of this. "*That's* why you're okay with this. Because you've transferred the blame to me. *I* was the one who left. *I* was the one who was gone for three months. *I'm* the one who messed up our routine..."

He said nothing as he headed toward the Upper East Side—to Lenora Birch's house, which was still lined in yellow tape.

"Please, stop with all fervent denials," she muttered.

He glanced over at her. "I don't blame you for going to Florida to take care of your mom, if that's what you're getting at."

"Just the getting engaged to another man part?"

Jill hadn't meant to let that last part out. She heard the way that it had come out and cringed. Why had she thrown in the "another man" part. It made it sound like she and Vincent had some history—

He said nothing for several moments. Not until he'd pulled up to the curb a couple blocks down from the Birch home.

He pivoted in his seat, one hand going around to the back of her headrest as he studied her.

Still, he was silent, and Jill's temper snapped. She leaned forward and plucked the damn glasses off his face, tossing them none-too-gently up on the dash.

But seeing his eyes did nothing to diffuse the strange tension in the car. If anything, their eye-to-eye contact made it worse.

What the hell was going on here?

Also, why was it so damn hot in this car? It was winter, for God's sake.

He jerked his eyes away then, and without a word climbed out of the car, slamming the door.

Jill's temper was good and truly bubbling now, and she was out of the car in record time, just as he was coming around the front of the car.

"Listen, Moretti. You don't get to just walk away when I'm talking to you, you—"

Vincent never stopped moving. Not until he was in her face, crowding her until her back was all the way against the car, mere inches separating their tense bodies.

Jill was appalled to realize that she was breathing hard. So was he, both of them all but vibrating with anger, and...and something else.

His dark gaze was furious as it burned down into hers.

"You're spoiling for a fight, Henley."

"I'm not—"

"You are," he interrupted. "You keep poking at me, baiting me. You want me to say something, but damned if I know what you're looking for."

Jill swallowed nervously then and had to look away, because damn it...he was right. He was totally, totally right, on all counts.

"I—"

He moved imperceptibly closer. She felt his breath on her face, coffee mingled with the mint, and suddenly she couldn't look away from his mouth.

"Let's get one thing straight," he said in a gravelly voice. "You were right before. You were the one who left. You were the one who met a man. You were the one who got a ring on your fourth finger in record time. You left me, yes. But I don't resent you for it, and I never have. You got that?"

"Yeah," she said softly. "I got that."

"I may not be the effusive type, but I care about you,

Henley. I want you to be happy, even if that means you and I part ways. You got that too?"

Jill's heart should have flown at that moment. He cared about her. *He cared about her.* He'd never come even remotely close to admitting it, and just a few months ago, the admission would have sent Jill flying over the moon.

Vincent Moretti cared about her. He wanted her to be happy . . .

And yet . . . she wasn't happy. Not at the moment.

Because as quickly as the euphoria had come on, it fled. For some utterly unidentifiable reason, his admission left her more melancholy than if he hadn't spoken at all.

Almost as though it wasn't enough.

He pulled back slowly, and she felt the loss of his body warmth acutely. She lifted her hands to pull him back, only to realize the utter insanity of that. Instead she shoved them in her pockets and squeezed her eyes shut.

Tom. Think of Tom. You'll see him in just a few hours, and everything will be fine . . .

"Henley, let's get a move on it. We've got a case to solve," Vincent called, already several feet down the sidewalk.

Right. She took a deep breath, opened her eyes.

They had a case to solve.

Likely the last they'd have together.

Might as well make it a good one.

CHAPTER SEVENTEEN

Vincent's apartment was the one place where the Moretti family never gathered. Ever.

He didn't blame them.

His place was quintessential bachelor pad.

Beat-up hardwood floors. A Spartan black leather sectional that had probably seen better days even back in the Reagan administration. A dented coffee table. Nary a throw pillow in sight. A big-ass TV that had cost far more than the couch, coffee table, and nonexistent throw pillows combined.

He kept the kitchen clean, but it was small; just big enough for him to keep himself fed, and certainly not large enough to host his big, chronically hungry Italian family.

Vincent was also the only family member to live in Queens. His parents were on Staten Island, Elena in

Midtown, and his grandmother and brothers in Upper West Side. His place wasn't exactly "on the way" to anything.

But none of that was why his family avoided his house like the plague—especially come feeding time.

No, the reason that his house was Absolute Last Choice of Moretti family gathering spaces had to do with the fact that while the rest of his place was rather Spartan, his walls were colorfully and frequently adorned.

With crime scene photos.

Corkboards competed for space only with the dry erase whiteboards, and every last surface was generally covered with pictures, notes, charts, and even the occasional good, old-fashioned, *I-thought-they-only-did-that-in-the-movies* string running among various pieces of evidence.

Technically speaking—he wasn't supposed to have any of this out of the office.

But Vincent had never been a stickler for the rules.

This was how he solved crimes. This was *where* he solved crimes. Sure, he had a desk at the precinct, and he put in the bare minimum of face time in order to not get his ass fired.

But the office was bullpen style. A bunch of desks pushed together, his one of dozens in the middle of a crowded, ever-buzzing room.

He couldn't think there. Couldn't get inside the mind of the victims, and certainly not inside the head of the suspects.

Vin needed space, and visuals, and above all else, *quiet*.

It was that last one that was turning out to be really fucking hard to come by on a Sunday evening.

The phone would not stop ringing.

"What," he snapped into the phone without glancing at the caller ID.

He'd already heard from:

His mother (how come you never come to dinner anymore?).

His father (did you catch the guy yet?).

His grandmother (will you pick me up from my colonoscopy on Tuesday?).

Luc (Jill's not seriously marrying that guy, right?).

And Elena (do you want to buy my old smoothie machine? I'm getting an upgrade? No? What if I give it to you? Still no?).

Vin figured it was Anthony's turn. His big brother wasn't the chatty type, but he'd been known to take his hobby of lecturing to the cell phone once or twice.

But it wasn't Anth.

"There's that sweet voice I know and love," the low voice on the other end said in a cooing, mocking voice.

Vincent grinned. "Well, son of a bitch. If it isn't the prodigal son."

"Prodigal brother to you," Marco said.

"What's that? You seem to be breaking up—must be because you're in *Goddamn California*."

"Easy, Grandpa. This isn't a World War One radio. Cell towers work just as well here as they do there. Probably better."

Vin sat down on his couch, well aware that he was still wearing an atypical, broad smile.

Of all his brothers, Marc had always been the one to piss him off the least. Younger than Vin by two years, he'd been easier to relate to than Anth, who'd always pissed everyone off with his interfering tendencies.

And Marc had been the *cool* brother. The one who was always just a couple inches taller than you, just a little bit better than you in sports, and in the case of Marco and Vincent, was about ten times *nicer* than you.

It wasn't that Marc was soft. Not in the least. The man was six feet two inches of sheer muscle, and his intolerance for the "bad guys" ran blood-deep. He could also be stubborn, impatient, and intense.

But people *liked* Marc. Liked his quick smile, his sense of humor, his good-old-boy charm.

So yeah, Vincent had idolized his brother as a kid, even though the other was younger.

As adults, they'd been close too. Closer than he was with Luc or Anth. And then Marc had up and left for California with barely a month of warning, all for a woman.

"How's Hollywood?" Vin asked just to needle his brother. "You busy working on your tan?"

Marc didn't live anywhere close to Hollywood, but the thoroughly East Coast Morettis clung to California clichés whenever they talked to Marc.

Partially out of ignorance, but more so out of persistent dismay that one of their own had up and left them for the other coast.

"Absolutely," Marc said. "Just got done pruning my poolside palm trees."

Vin smiled. Marc was just about the only brother who'd mastered the skill of not letting his siblings get under his skin.

"And Mandy?" Vin asked, not that he much cared.

Marc's girlfriend was...well, suffice it to say, none of the Morettis had ever been able to figure out what Marc saw in Mandy Breslin.

She was pretty, yes. Stunning, even, in a Barbie-esque kind of way. She was also manipulative, selfish, and completely allergic to anything resembling work.

It galled Vin that they'd moved to California for her "acting" career, and yet they were living off of Marc's salary while Mandy waited for her big break.

"She's good," Marc said.

Vincent's eyes narrowed, noticing the delay in Marc's response. "Gone on any auditions lately?"

Another pause. "No. Her agent's called with a few possible commercial slots, but she wants to hold out for something bigger."

Of course she did.

"How's Jill?" Marc asked before Vincent could press the issue. "Rumor has it she's getting married."

Well played, Big Brother. Well played.

"Yup." Vincent's voice was curt.

Marc didn't take the hint. "And how do we feel about that?"

"We, being the Moretti collective, or . . . ?"

"Good point," Marc said. "I already know how the rest of the Morettis feel about it. How are *you* handling the news?"

Vincent slouched back on the couch. "Not much to handle. My colleague is getting married. Not exactly earth-shattering."

Marc snorted. "Really? That's where you're going with this? Jill's a colleague now?"

"She's my partner."

"I know who and what she is," Marc said quietly. "I also know who and what she is to *you*."

Do you? Because I sure as fuck don't know.

"Can we not talk about this?" Vincent grumbled.

"Sure," Marc said easily. "How about you tell me about this case you and your *colleague* are working on."

That, Vincent could do.

Hell, he needed to do it. He'd been staring at his boards for hours now and couldn't shake the sense that something was just out of reach...

He filled Marc in on the Lenora Birch case.

Told him of finding the body but without a single sense of what might have gone down. Told him that they'd interviewed all of the usual suspects—ex-lovers, ex-husbands, jealous ex-lovers of Lenora's ex-lovers...

And nothing.

He and Jill had been following Vincent's suggestion of "starting over." They'd interviewed everyone again with fresh eyes and ears, and they weren't any further along than they were before.

Vincent stood to stare at his board, his eyes locking on the wide-eyed stare of a deceased Lenora Birch, silently begging her to tell him her secrets.

He rubbed the back of his neck. "I don't know, man," he told his brother with a shake of his head. "The method—shoving someone over a railing—screams crime of passion. But the complete lack of evidence, the lack of fingerprints, or so much as a hair could mean premeditation..."

"Or someone who's remarkably cool under pressure," Marc said. "A crime of passion followed immediately by levelheaded damage control."

"Could be," Vin mused. "But that's the part that's tripping me up. Crimes of passion generally stem from, well, passion. And Lenora Birch's love life, while not uncomplicated, hasn't turned up anything worth killing over. Best as we can tell, she held herself apart from other people. She was...removed."

"Huh. Someone scared to connect, to get too close to another person," Marc said. "Sounds...familiar."

"I don't think she was scared," Vincent mused, ignoring Marc's not-so-subtle jab about Vincent's lack of relationships. "It's like she focused her energy somewhere else."

"Well, we can get that right?" Marc said. "Sure, we Morettis are all husbands or boyfriends or brothers or sons, but aren't there times when we're a cop first? When that takes up all of us. Those days when we're married to the job, you know?"

Vincent froze in the middle of his pacing, a familiar prickle of knowing rippling along his spine.

"Say that last part again," he commanded his brother.

"Um," Marc said. "I said we were cops first...that some of us were boyfriends, although of course not you, because you just have a *colleague*—"

"That's it," Vincent said, interrupting yet another jab.

"What's what?"

"What if it was a crime of passion," Vincent said excitedly. "But not passion in the sense that we usually think of it. Love and sex and all that."

"Um—"

Vincent tucked the phone under his ear, moved toward the board, and began plucking down pictures of ex-lovers.

"You said we were married to our job," Vincent said hurriedly. "What if Lenora Birch was the same. What if the reason she held herself apart from people all those years was because her focus—her *heart*—was her career."

"Not following. Remember, of the two of us, you're the

detective who solves crimes. I'm the sergeant who chases bank robbers. Spell it out for me."

Vincent didn't respond. His brain was humming with the hunch that had been eluding him this entire case.

"Marc, you're a fucking genius," he muttered.

"Thanks?"

"I gotta go," Vincent said, hanging up before even giving his brother a chance to say good-bye.

Two seconds later, he was making another phone call, this time to his partner.

"Henley," he said the second she picked up the phone. "Get your butt over here. Now."

CHAPTER EIGHTEEN

Jill's place was a ten-minute walk from Vincent's apartment, which was handy when he had what she thought of as his "fits." Those abrupt, semifrantic phone calls that meant he was onto something.

Hadn't happened in a while though.

Both because she'd been in Florida for three months, and because in the month she'd been back, they'd both been thoroughly stumped by the Lenora Birch case.

Funny how she'd almost missed his barked commands to drop whatever she was doing and come over.

This interruption in particular had been welcome. Jill had been sitting on the center of her bed, surrounded by bridal magazines and trying to get excited about...something. Anything.

What did it say about her that the latest trend in bridal bouquets (yellow roses were apparently "in") didn't even cause a blip on her radar, but a lead in a homicide case revved her motors?

Right now, Jill didn't care.

Because she and Vin were *back*. She could feel it.

She knocked at his door, but he didn't answer, so she let herself in.

"You know, you should really lock your front door," she called, shrugging out of her coat. "Being a cop and all."

Still no answer. She walked toward his living room and found him precisely where she expected to. Where she'd found him a thousand times before.

Scribbling frantically at his whiteboard.

She watched him for a moment. He was wearing jeans and a white T-shirt, a surprising change from his usual black. The muscles of his back rippled beneath the thin fabric as his arm moved furiously across the board, scribbling whatever was going through his head at warp speed.

His black marker was starting to run out, and Jill wordlessly went to the small, utilitarian desk in the corner and pulled out a fresh pen.

She moved to his side, uncapping it and then fluidly swapping the dying pen in his hand with the fresh one in hers.

He barely paused. Didn't grunt so much as a thank-you, and Jill smiled.

She'd missed this.

She tossed the dead pen in the trash and then settled down on his couch to wait.

And wait, and wait.

She tried to read his notes as he wrote them but his handwriting was atrocious, and he kept moving back and forth from one end of the board to the other.

Finally, finally he stopped, although likely it was more a function of him running out of space than his brain slowing down.

He capped the pen.

Stepped back, and stared at the board.

He held up the marker without turning around. "Thanks for this."

Jill lifted an eyebrow. Acknowledgment of her usefulness. That was... new.

She pushed off the couch and moved beside him so they stood shoulder-to-shoulder. Actually, more like shoulder to waist, since he was several inches taller.

"What am I looking at?" she asked.

He tossed the marker on the coffee table, then linked his fingers behind his head, turning in a circle.

"I had a breakthrough."

She smiled. "Yeah, I figured."

He glanced at her then, seeming to see her for the first time since she'd arrived, and he dropped his hands, looking her up and down.

"You're in your pajamas."

She glanced down at her pink-and-white-striped flannel pants and white tank. "Well, you called me at nine o'clock on a Sunday night. Not quite my bedtime, but let's just say I'd put my ball gown away for the evening."

He'd already turned back to his boards. His main one—the one he called *the* board—was more barren than last time she'd seen it, and the stack of papers on the table told her that he'd recently decided he was on the wrong track.

"Talk to me," she said patiently.

"We've decided that pushing someone over a railing

smells more like impulse than premeditation, right? If you're going to show up at someone's house with the intent to kill, you take a gun, maybe a knife—"

"Right," Jill said. "You don't think, 'gosh, I want to off someone; I'm going to wait until they're in a prime position on the second-floor landing and then push them.'"

"Exactly. So we've been operating under the assumption that this is a crime of passion."

"Right..." she said, waiting.

"It *is* a crime of passion, but we got the passion wrong," he said, turning to face her, eyes excited.

Jill shook her head. "Explain?"

"Something's been bothering me about the way she died," he continued hurriedly. "We know that someone pushed her, likely in a fit of rage."

"Sure, but that's not all that unusual—"

Vincent held up a finger. "No, what's been bothering me is that everything we've learned about Lenora Birch says that she's not the type to provoke someone. Almost everyone we've talked to, from the housekeeper to her boyfriend, said she's hard to rattle. Cool to the point of being cold."

Jill nodded, still having no idea where he was going with all this.

"Everyone except one person said that," he said.

Jill chewed her lip as she mentally ran through every conversation they'd had, every person they'd interviewed.

"Her agent," Jill said. "The Lenora that her agent described was a different person. Fiery, temperamental, passionate."

"Exactly." He took a step nearer, his eyes blazing. "Passionate. This was a crime of passion, but not of the romantic, sexual nature. If Lenora could be provoked into saying something that would piss off another person to the point of murder, it means they would *both* have to be fired up."

"Okay?"

He breathed out a sigh of irritation. "We've been looking at her lovers, and lovers of her lovers. But the Lenora we keep hearing about would have been indifferent if she were talking about a husband or a boyfriend, and nobody pushes an indifferent person to their death."

"Not entirely true," Jill said, holding up a finger. "For some people there might be no more trigger quite as hot as being ignored by someone you love."

He shook his head. "Lenora was nearly seventy. The people in her life would have learned not to love her that deeply. They would have been used to it."

"So what are you saying?"

"I'm saying that we've been trying to figure out the murder's trigger, when what we really should have been looking for is Lenora's. What would have set her off enough to say something that would drive another person to murder her. She's not a woman that inspires great passion because she doesn't *feel* great passion. Except when talking about—"

"Her career," Jill said, finally understanding what he was getting out. "Lenora Birch cared about her career—her legacy—more than anything."

He nodded. "Someone that threatened that—challenged that—it would have pissed her off. She would have been—"

"Cruel," Jill finished for him. "Her agent said that Lenora could be cruel when she felt her legacy as an actress was threatened."

"We've been looking at people that Lenora's wronged on the personal front, but it's the professional one we need to pay attention to. It didn't dawn on me before, because she's retired, but then I thought of my dad. He's retired, but so much of his self-worth still stems from his identity as a cop."

Jill wandered closer to his board, feeling both elated and overwhelmed. "The woman's been in acting since she was fifteen. There are literally decades of old rivalries. Holly Adams was just the tip of the iceberg…"

"So we start with her," Vincent said. "Something tells me the woman will be all too happy to provide a list of all her and Lenora's old acting buddies that might be holding a grudge."

"Yes, she will," Jill said slowly, as everything began to settle around her. She felt both the most calm she'd been in weeks—months—and the most invigorated.

She turned back toward Vincent and saw that he was feeling the same things as her. Elation. Relief.

"We did it," he said, sounding slightly awestruck. "We fucking did it."

Vincent lifted his hands to his sides as a wide grin spread over his face, and then he looked at his hands in surprise, as though not sure what to do with them—not sure what to do with the unfamiliar sensation of happiness.

And then he apparently figured it out. Vincent's hands found their way to either side of her face, and he bent his head to hers.

And kissed her.

The kiss was over before Jill even realized it had begun.

Nothing but a firm meeting of lips.

A victory kiss, if you will. The type of kiss a friend gives another friend in an impulsive moment of triumph.

There was nothing romantic.

Nothing sexual.

Vincent had already moved away from her, his attention shifted back to his precious board.

Jill lifted her fingers to her lips.

It was nothing. It meant nothing.

But if it was nothing...why was her hand shaking? Why were her lips tingling?

If it was nothing...

Why did she want him to do it again?

CHAPTER NINETEEN

Vin helped himself to yet another piece of pizza and tried not to stare at Jill's profile as she chewed absently on the end of a pencil.

She looked completely unperturbed. As though an hour earlier their lips hadn't collided in a careless, casual victory kiss.

He took a sip of beer. *Casual my ass.*

That kiss had been...

There were at least half a dozen reasons he shouldn't have done it. The fact that she belonged to another man being number one.

But reason number two was a very close second.

He shouldn't have done it, because now he couldn't stop thinking about it.

Couldn't stop wanting to do it again.

Except longer this time—he would linger. Let his hands

explore her curves as his tongue slipped into her mouth, learning what she liked...

"Fuck," he muttered.

She glanced up from her notebook. "What's up?"

"Nothing."

Jill reached out and grabbed the neck of her own beer bottle, twisting it between her fingers before taking a sip and staring at him all the while.

"What?" he asked, irritated.

"Nothing," she said sweetly.

He glared. "Are you mocking me right now?"

"Only because you're so cute when you're riled."

"You're a nightmare," he muttered.

"Oh, come on," she said. "I think I've been pretty good lately. I haven't played the 'what's your favorite color' game, or tried to set you up with that cute barista at the Times Square Starbucks. I haven't forced any Abba sing-along, or..."

"What, you, like, want a medal for not driving me nuts?"

She sat back and smiled, happy with herself. "So I'm not driving you nuts?"

Damn. He'd walked right into that one. "You are."

She sighed. "I can't win with you these days. You gripe if I talk about the wedding too much. If I don't talk about the wedding at all, you make snide 'trouble in paradise' comments. It's like—"

"Don't move to Chicago."

Jill broke off and stared at him in shock. "What?"

Vincent wiped his mouth with the paper towel doubling as a napkin as he finished chewing his pizza. "You heard me."

She let out a little laugh. "Yeah, I was sort of hoping I heard you wrong."

He forced himself to meet her gaze steadily. "Don't leave, Jill. You belong in New York."

You belong with me.

She set her beer carefully on the table. "It's not that I want to leave New York, Vin—"

"Then don't."

"It's not that simple," she said, her voice rising a notch.

"Well, make it that simple."

She snapped her notebook on the table. "You're impossible. Just because you've got this whole lone wolf thing going on doesn't mean that the rest of us want to be alone forever."

Now it was his turn to toss his notebook aside. "Who said shit about being alone forever? That's why you're moving to Chicago? You think you're *alone*?"

"No, I just—" She reached up and tightened her ponytail the way she did when she was stressed. "Come on, Vin. You knew things were going to change when one of us met someone. We can't just keep doing this forever, being each other's everything."

He knew she didn't mean her words to hurt, but they cut like a knife all the same. "I'm not asking you to be my everything," he said quietly. "I just hate that this guy swoops into your life for all of a couple months, and you're ready to throw it all away."

Vin didn't look at her as he said it. It was the closest he'd come to admitting…something, and he couldn't bear to see what might be laughter on her face.

He heard the sound of her chair scooting backward before she moved closer, dropping into the chair right next to his.

Her hand found his knee. "Is that what you think? That I'm throwing you away?"

He said nothing.

Her fingers squeezed and she leaned down, trying to catch his eye. "I'm always here for you. Even if I'm in a different time zone, you can call me anytime and I'll come running. You know that."

He swallowed. He did know that. Knew that he'd do the same for her.

He also knew that if he kept on with this push-pull thing, he'd risk losing her. He'd put a rift between them that couldn't be fixed with a doughnut.

Vin forced himself to meet her eyes. "I'm sorry about the kiss."

Her head snapped back a little. "Oh. Don't apologize. It was...nothing."

Burn. "Right. I know. But I was out of line. I mean, if Tom found out."

She gave a small smile. "Relax. It's not like you slipped me tongue and copped a feel."

Good God. Even her joking, off-the-cuff comment made him horny.

"Yeah, right," he said, forcing a smile.

There was a moment of silence before she gave his leg a little squeeze. "We're okay, right?"

"Sure."

She pulled back, looking frustrated. "Would you talk to me? Please. I feel like there's so much going on inside your head, but the second we get anywhere, you pull back. It's almost like—"

"Almost like what?"

Their eyes clashed for several long tense moments, until she finally shook her head. "Nothing. Almost like nothing."

Vincent felt a brief stab of disappointment until he reminded himself that it was for the best. That this was a conversation they could never have.

He pushed back from the table, grabbing at their empty plates so he had an excuse to walk away.

Vin heard her sigh of frustration and ignored it. He didn't know what the hell she wanted from him. Sure, she thought she wanted honesty. She thought she wanted him to spill his guts.

But if she had a clue—even the tiniest clue—as to what had been going through his head for the past few weeks, she'd probably find a way to escape to Chicago early.

He dropped the plates noisily into the sink to be dealt with later and then braced his hands on the counter, letting his chin drop, just for a second, willing himself to get it together.

Vin was so lost in his dark thoughts that he didn't realize Jill had approached until her arms wrapped around him from behind.

She squeezed his waist hard, and he felt her cheek nuzzle against the center of his back. Vin wasn't particularly tall, but Jill was downright short. Perfect.

She'd always been perfect.

"We're gonna be okay, right?" she asked, her voice muffled against his shirt.

Vin closed his eyes as his hand closed over clasped arms, his head tilting back so that the back of his head rested lightly on the top of hers.

And because he cared about her—cared about her so damn much—he did the only thing that he could.

He lied. "Yeah. Yeah, we're gonna be all right."

CHAPTER TWENTY

Two weeks after her and Vincent's awkward non-kiss and the even more awkward conversation that had followed, Jill was feeling the best she had in months.

She and Vincent were *back*. Really, truly, dynamic-duo kind of back.

And if maybe some distant part of her brain was buzzing with warning that they were merely in the calm before the storm, she ignored it.

She'd given him an opening. Given him a chance to say something . . . and he hadn't.

Which was fine. Great. Maybe all his bad moods lately really were just what they seemed: typical Moretti Moods.

She had bigger things to worry about.

Like the fact that she had a wedding to plan.

Like the fact that they still hadn't caught Lenora Birch's killer, and it was getting, well, embarrassing.

But neither had the other homicide investigators assigned to the case, which lessened the embarrassment. Slightly.

Everyone had a theory. But nobody had even a lick of proof.

The only *good* news about the whole thing was that the media had backed off. After nearly constant Who Killed Lenora Birch coverage, everyone had tired of the lack of updates.

Nobody more so than Vin and Jill.

They were, however, getting closer. She could feel it down to the tip of her ponytail, and Vincent had been increasingly doing that edgy, snippy thing that meant his brain was working in overdrive.

"I can't believe she invited us to stay the night," he griped for about the thirtieth time since they'd left Queens early that morning.

"You have to admit, it would have been convenient," she said, not looking up from her phone, where she read the latest e-mail from the wedding caterer.

"It's inappropriate. She's a suspect."

"Which is why I politely declined," Jill said patiently. "Hey, do you think meatballs are too pedestrian? It says here they can stick rosemary in them as little skewers, which sounds kind of nice..."

"It sounds ridiculous," he muttered.

She sighed and put her phone down. "If you don't want me to talk about the wedding, you can just say so."

"I don't want you to talk about the wedding."

She narrowed her eyes at him. "*Fine.*"

Jill felt irrationally annoyed, which wasn't fair. Of course Vin didn't want to talk about the wedding. Not many dudes gave a shit about appetizers and party favors.

Well, Tom did. But that's because it was Tom's wedding. And because he was, well... perfect.

Perfection was tiresome.

Jill shoved the thought away before it had a chance to fully form.

What was *wrong* with her?

She was *marrying* Tom.

And yet she couldn't seem to stop needling *this* man. This man who'd always been there for her, in his crusty, monotone kind of way.

Jill put her phone and her notebook away. No more wedding talk. It always put her in a bad mood.

And if the fact that planning her wedding put her in a bad mood was really alarming, she pushed that thought aside too.

"Hey, has your Spidey sense given you any more tingles about Holly Adams?" she said. "Since we discovered that she wasn't as forthcoming about her and Lenora's history as she could have been?"

That was a major understatement.

In Jill's research to unearth Lenora Birch's complicated career in Hollywood, there was one name that came up over and over:

Holly Adams.

Despite early rumors that Holly Adams would be cast as the lead, it was just announced that the much coveted role went to Lenora Birch...

Once again, Holly Adams and Lenora Birch are fighting for a plum role. Casting insiders say their money's on Lenora...

Holly Adams has made no secret of her excitement about the project, but early rumors indicate

*that it was Lenora Adams's audition that wowed
the producer...*

"I need to spend some time with her," Vincent
grumbled. "I can't pluck theories out of the air."

"Really?" Jill asked dryly. "Since when?"

"She wasn't straight with us last time," Vincent said.
"Which wouldn't bother me if she hadn't made such an
effort to convince us she was telling all."

"You're mad because she played us," Jill concluded.

He was silent for several moments. "Yes."

She smiled, surprised at the admission. "Well, she's an
actress. It's her job to fool people. Don't beat yourself up."

"That's the problem with our growing list of suspects.
They're *all* actors. Speaking of which, how's the list
coming?"

Ah yes. A list. Jill *loved* her lists.

Jill and Vincent's partnership was a solid one for two
reasons:

The first was the most obvious—he was bad cop, she
was good cop. They practically defined the cliché.

The second was subtler.

Vin was the feelings guy; the one who paced and
observed and pondered until a breakthrough occurred.

Jill was more about the data; she trusted his hunch—
always. But then it fell to *her* to figure out how to act on it.
Where to look for the proof. How to maneuver the suspect
into a confession.

Or in complicated cases like this one, how to nar-
row down their suspects from all of Hollywood to a viable list.

Jill had spent the last ten days glued to her computer,

most of those with Vincent hovering over her shoulder, which hadn't been annoying *at all*.

"The list is almost done," she said, stalling.

He glanced over. "You're not telling me something."

Jill turned to look out the window, wondering if now was a good time to give him the news, since he was preoccupied with driving, or if it would make him swerve off the road in irritation.

"You know, I don't think you realize how lucky we are that Holly Adams lives so close to New York," she said, deciding to ease into it.

"Close? We've been in the car for two hours, and we're not even halfway there. Fucking rush hour."

Here we go.

"She's a lot closer than the rest of the suspects."

He was silent. "Explain."

"Lenora Birch was an actress, Vin. A *Hollywood* actress."

More silence. "Tell me you're not suggesting what I think you're suggesting," he said. "Tell me we're not—"

"Going to California?"

He groaned. "No. No fucking way. I don't care how many enemies she has in Beverly Hills, she didn't die there. The crime was committed in New York."

"I'm aware of that, thanks. But based on what I've learned, if you're a big name in Hollywood, you're either in LA, or you're in New York. There's a lot of crossover. And four of the names I keep coming across on the Lenora Birch enemy list?"

"Don't tell me. Do not tell me what I think you're going to tell me."

"They were in Manhattan at the time of her murder. But they *live* in California."

Vincent swore softly. "What the hell is wrong with these old folks, all jetting around across the country all willy-nilly?"

"Wait, and you think *they're* the old folks? Are you kidding me with the *willy-nilly*?"

"Nonna says it," he grumbled. "And California? Really?"

Jill smiled. "You're going to look so great with a tan."

She reached out to playfully poke his cheek and he batted her hand away. "Why don't we just fly *them* out *here*?"

"Yeah, the department's really gonna go for that. Flying out four suspects from LAX to JFK, then paying for their transportation, then hotels…"

"Well, they're not going to go for flying us out there either."

"Maybe not. But if we chipped in on flights, I'm guessing they'd spot the hotel room."

"Why the hell would we do that?" he asked.

She stared at him. "Waiting for it…"

"Fuck," he muttered the second it clicked. "You're thinking we can see Marco."

"Come on. You know you miss him."

Jill knew she was right. She could see it in his stillness.

Jill didn't know Vin's other brother as well as she did Luc and Anthony. By the time she and Vin had gotten really close, and she'd been all but welcomed into the family, he'd already moved.

But she remembered him being a good sort—just like the rest of the Morettis.

Handsome as sin, too. Again, just like the rest of the Morettis.

"When?" he grunted.

"I was thinking next week. Enough time for us to get a plan together, but I don't think we can wait much longer. The captain swore at me for at least an hour yesterday about how our asses were on the line if we didn't give him an update he could, and I quote, "fucking do something fucking with.""

"I hate California."

"Of course you do. All that sunshine," she said sweetly.

Vin flexed his fingers on the steering wheel and then tilted his neck from side to side as though trying to work out a kink, although whether it was in his neck or his attitude, she wasn't sure.

"We really have to go?" he asked.

"No. But I think we should."

"Damn," he breathed softly.

Relieved to have dropped the bomb with relatively little fallout, Jill turned her attention to the world that was whizzing by at oh, twenty miles an hour. Vin hadn't been joking about traffic being a total bitch.

And it would be even worse in LA. Weren't they supposed to have the worst traffic, like, ever? And crappy air quality, and...

Oh, who was she kidding?

Jill couldn't *wait* to go to California, even if it was for work.

With her mother living in Florida, most of her "sunny getaways" involved the Atlantic Ocean over the Pacific. She'd been to California... once. Her parents had taken her to Yellowstone as a kid.

But she barely remembered it, and Yosemite, while lovely, wasn't exactly the quintessential California described by the Beach Boys, or Katy Perry.

But more than the destination itself was the chance to get away. A chance to get out of her routine, to get some distance from wedding planning and the looming changes in her future.

A chance to...think.

She didn't know what she needed to think about. Just knew that she needed to.

An hour later, California was the last thing on her mind, because she was too busy trying to stifle her laughter.

Holly Adams was every bit as over-the-top welcoming as she'd been last time they questioned her.

But she'd tweaked her approach, to play up her, um, assets.

In all their years together, Jill didn't think she'd seen Vincent Moretti quite so uncomfortable. Hell, until today, she hadn't realized that he *could* be uncomfortable.

But then, he'd probably never had an elderly femme fatale dressed in a red gown—yes, gown—draped all over him before.

"Um, Ms. Adams," Vincent said, making yet another futile attempt to shift away from the older woman. "You were telling us about the time that Lenora won the *Moonlight Damsel* role?"

"Stole," Holly said with a smile, setting her hand on Vin's arm. "She *stole* my role. And my my, do you work out?"

Yes. Yes, he does, Jill thought, remembering all too vividly that moment when Vincent had opened the motel door sans shirt.

Holly's arm ran up Vincent's bicep. Squeezed. Vin gave Jill a panicked look, and she took pity on him.

"Ms. Adams, when you say that Lenora stole your role, what do you mean by that? Did she bribe someone? Sabotage your audition?"

Holly's attention snapped to Jill and her eyes narrowed. "Why are you two so interested in forty-year-old films?"

"You know why," Jill said steadily. "It's the same reason we're here. Again. You have a murky past with Lenora Birch, and now she's dead."

Holly leaned forward, her still-impressive bosom all but heaving out of her dress. Vincent's eyes lifted toward the ceiling.

"And your best bet is looking at aging film stars?" Holly asked. "I have arthritis. Lenora probably did too. Even if we wanted to try and push each other over the staircase, or however she died, it would take agility and coordination that we don't have."

Jill kept her face impassive, but damned if she didn't agree just a little bit with Holly's assessment. This whole case was starting to feel like a farce.

A geriatric version of Clue.

"Who do you think did it then?" Jill asked.

Holly sat back with a wave of her hand. "The help? Maybe the driver felt underpaid, or the housekeeper got sick of having to pick up Lenora's dentures from the coffee table. Someone young and angry, not someone old and tired."

"I don't think you're quite so indifferent to old grudges as you'd have us believe," Vincent said.

Holly's hand froze in the process of sliding up his thigh. "Oh?"

Vin flicked his gaze to Jill, who picked up on the cue and reached into her bag. Pulled out a Ziploc bag.

She held it out to Holly, who hesitated briefly. "What's this?"

"A letter you sent to Caroline Jones four months ago. One in which you said if any of the old crew deserved an early death, it was Lenora."

Holly touched the bag only for a moment before letting it flutter to the table. The corner dipped into the tea and Vincent plucked it back out again, wiping the moisture away before holding it up to the older woman's face.

"This is your handwriting, yes? Your signature?"

"That bitch," Holly breathed.

"Careful now," Vin said easily. "If Caroline Jones ends up dead, you're going to wish you hadn't said that in front of two homicide detectives."

She gave a dismissive wave of her hand. "All I'm trying to say is maybe you should look a little harder at the woman who gave you that letter."

"She's not the one that wished an early death on Lenora Birch."

"How do you know?" Holly shot back. "Do you have her side of the correspondence?"

Vin and Jill exchanged a glance. She had a good point.

"Do you have it?" Holly pressed. "Well, of course not," she huffed. "*Her* letters are rambling and boring. I throw them out after I skim them. But I can assure you there's plenty of ranting about Lenora on her end as well."

Jill subtly blew out a breath without showing Holly how frustrated she was. Not that she'd put a lot of stock in the letter. Caroline Jones had called their office about a half dozen times with "crucial information to the case," and had been just a tad too eager to send over Holly's letter.

It smelled more of aging, petty rivalry than it did

useful evidence, but in a case that seemed to be nothing *but* aging, petty rivalries, they couldn't afford not to act on it.

Holly slapped her palms slightly against her thighs. "Oh, I almost forgot...I have something for you."

Holly brushed needlessly against Vincent as she stood, and he shot Jill another exasperated look. She grinned widely at him as Holly went to a small writing desk in the corner.

Vin was just starting to stand—no doubt to move to safety—when Holly returned waving an envelope. "Here we go!"

Jill watched Vincent's face as he accepted the already-open envelope, his eyes scanning the return address with a slight frown before pulling out the paper inside.

His jaw tensed as he read it, and when he lifted his eyes to Jill, she knew then...knew that whatever was in that letter meant that any hope they had of Holly Adams breaking down and admitting guilt had just gone out the window.

He handed it across the coffee table to Jill.

"You didn't think to mention this last time?" he asked Holly.

Holly sat down beside him once more, crossing her legs and blinking innocently up at him. "Well, you'll pardon me if I'm unaccustomed to being questioned in a murder investigation. I wasn't exactly thinking clearly."

Jill scanned the contents of the letter, taking in the seemingly official logo, the cookie-cutter phrasing of the letter that indicated it was a form letter, which in this case, made it all the more believable.

The pages that followed sealed the deal.

Jill looked up. "You called the cable company the night Lenora Birch was murdered."

"The Wi-Fi wasn't working," Holly said, almost proudly. She pronounced "Wi-Fi" just a bit too precisely, the way someone unfamiliar with the technology would be.

Vincent pinched the bridge of his nose. "And all calls are recorded."

"Yup," Holly said, sounding quite pleased with herself. "I wrote them a letter asking if they could provide a transcript of the conversation, and that's what you see there."

Jill glanced down again at the transcript. A quick scan showed that it was exactly what one would expect from a tech-savvy customer service rep and a seventy-something woman who "couldn't get to The Google." Lots of, "I understand your frustration, ma'am," countered with, "back in my day..."

And Holly couldn't know it, as time of death wasn't common knowledge, but the time stamp meant that Holly Adams was listening to an explanation of the difference between *modem* and *router* at the precise moment Lenora Birch had been pushed over that balcony.

"You two don't seem happy," Holly said, looking between Vincent and Jill.

"Of course we are," Jill said with an automatic, not-entirely-genuine smile. "Just because we like to solve crimes doesn't mean we enjoy finding people guilty."

Vincent's expression said otherwise.

"No, that's not what I meant," Holly said, fiddling with the oversized ruby around her neck—just a tad overdressed for entertaining homicide detectives on a random Wednesday. "I meant that you aren't happy. Soul happy."

Vincent glanced at Jill and mouthed *soul happy?* with a lift of his eyebrow.

Jill kept her smile firmly in place. "I assure you, everything is just fine with us. Just the usual exhaustion from trying to solve a case."

Holly pursed her lips. "No. That's not it."

"Excuse me?" Jill said, her smile slipping. She knew better to engage with a woman who'd proven she loved nothing more than to play games, but without knowing it, Holly Adams had hit on a nerve.

Or hell. Knowing Holly, she probably *had* known it.

"How's the wedding planning coming along, Detective Henley?" Holly's voice was sweet as sugar.

Jill kept hers just as sweet, even as her body went on high alert. "So great, thanks for asking."

"Mm. Your young man, he's handsome?"

"Very."

"More handsome than *this* young man?" Holly asked with a speculative look at Vincent.

Jill nearly laughed at the obviousness of Holly's ploy. She leaned forward. "Ms. Adams, the time to be matchmaker is *before* one of the people has a ring on her finger."

Holly mimicked Jill's posture, leaning forward with dancing, mischievous eyes. "You didn't answer the question, Detective."

Jill's eyes flicked to Vin, even as she told herself not to humor the interfering older woman.

He was watching her with barely concealed amusement. Not exactly helping her out, but then, she supposed that was fair for the way she'd smirked at him earlier when Holly employed her best flirting techniques.

Then he lifted an eyebrow.

Oh, so that's how it's going to be.

She shifted her attention back to Holly, her voice even more sugary than before. "I'm sure plenty of women would find Detective Moretti perfectly handsome." Jill let her shoulders lift in a little shrug. "But he's more like a brother to me. I really can't see him like that."

"Mmm-hmm," Holly said, sounding skeptical as she shifted her attention to Vin. "And you, Detective. Do you think of your partner like a sister?"

Jill looked at Vin, a little smile on her lips as she waited for whatever his one-up would be on her jab.

He stared at her for what seemed like an uncomfortably long time.

"No," he said finally. "No, I've never thought of Detective Henley as a sister."

Jill's smile dropped. Not so much because of the words. But the look on his face. The heat in his eyes.

And irrationally, she felt angry. At him.

"Oh really?" Holly said, her eyes wide, her hand laying against her heart in a forced, oh-my-goodness-me manner.

Jill stuffed the printed transcript back into the envelope not as gently as she should have, and held it up. "Can we take this?" she asked.

"Of course," Holly murmured, her attention still locked on Vincent's steely profile. "Detective Moretti, how did you feel upon learning your partner was getting married?"

"Oh, for Pete's sake," Jill muttered as she stood. "Vin, let's head out."

He didn't stand with her, although he didn't stop looking at her as he answered Holly's question. "I don't love it. I don't love the fact that she's getting married."

Her jaw dropped. "Seriously? We are not doing this here."

And then she completely contradicted herself by sitting down once more. "What do you mean you don't love it? It's not for you to love. Or decide. You get no say."

He shrugged. "I didn't say I did. Just said I didn't like it."

"Well that's just...that's just..." *Unfair.*

She had nothing to say to Vincent, so she shifted her attention to Holly. "What are you doing?"

"Oh, I'm sorry, dear, am I stirring the pot?"

"You know perfectly well that you are," she said quietly. "Vin. Let's head out."

"If you don't mind me asking," Holly said, holding out her hand.

"I do," Jill snapped, knowing that she wouldn't like what was going to come out of Holly Adams's mouth next.

Seriously, why the hell was Vin just sitting there?

He didn't let his own mother ask questions about his personal life, and here he was letting a meddling stranger just have at it.

And then it hit her...that sense she'd been having all week that a storm was coming. This was it. *This* was the storm she'd been fearing.

Holly had shifted all of her attention to Vincent now, who had a placid, you-can-ask-me-anything look on his face, and abruptly Jill realized that they'd somehow just switched roles.

She'd become the snippy bad cop, and he was the cooperative one.

"Have you and Detective Henley ever dated?" Holly asked Vincent.

Vin didn't look at her as he responded with a clipped "No."

"Hmm, that surprises me," Holly said, leaning forward and pouring both herself and Vincent more tea from a porcelain pot. She didn't offer Jill any.

"How's that?" Vincent asked.

"The way you look at her."

It was a good thing Jill wasn't offered any more tea. She would have dropped the cup just then.

Vincent, on the other hand, went perfectly still. Nothing except his eyes moved.

Eyes that found Jill's.

"How do I look at her?" His voice was low. Gravelly.

This was, without a doubt, the most bizarre, the most insane, the most *painful* interrogation she'd ever been on.

"You're letting her take control of the conversation," Jill said. "This is beyond inappropriate."

"I don't give a shit about appropriateness," he said.

"Well, I do!"

"You do not," Vincent said, leaning forward and setting his teacup on the table. "This isn't about what's *appropriate*. This is about you not wanting to have this conversation."

"I didn't even know there was a conversation to be had!" she said.

"That's bullshit," he shot back. "You've been goading me every chance you get. The other day I told you I was happy for you. And yet still, you keep poking at me with your talk of meatballs and honeymoon locations and black tie versus cocktail attire."

"I wasn't *goading*, I was asking you because you're my friend."

"Am I? Really? Because a *friend* doesn't disappear for three months, come back engaged with not so much as a word of warning."

"Well, pardon me for assuming that my gruff, non-talkative partner would care about my love life."

"I cared!" he roared. "I've always fucking cared!"

Jill stared at him, speechless, both of them breathing too hard.

Holly continued to sip her tea, looking pleased as punch with herself. No doubt this was the best entertainment she'd had in years.

"We shouldn't be having this conversation in front of a suspect."

"I'm still a suspect then?" Holly asked petulantly.

"Yes," Jill snapped at the same time Vincent muttered, "No."

There was a long, pained silence, before Jill took a deep breath and looked at Holly. "We just need to verify the authenticity of the letter is all."

"Well then!" Holly said, all chipper-like. "You'd best get on that! I'd like my name cleared as quickly as possible."

Should have thought of that before you decided to stir the pot.

This time when Jill stood, Vincent did as well. But he didn't look at her.

Not when they walked to the door and bid a terse farewell to a far-too-chipper Holly. Not when they got into the car.

Not on the entire drive back to New York.

They rode in ice-cold silence.

Protocol demanded that they stop by the station. File some paperwork, put Holly's letter into evidence . . .

But Vincent was apparently far beyond protocol, because he drove them straight home to Queens. Which Jill was just fine with. She didn't think she could be civil to him right now if someone paid her.

It will be better in the morning, she told herself. *We'll cool off. He'll realize he was just trying to piss me off.*

He pulled up in front of her apartment, and Jill knew it was rude, but she didn't say a word to him as she grabbed her purse.

She slammed the door as she got out because it felt good.

It wasn't until she reached the front door that she realized Vin was right behind her.

"What are you—"

She spun around, only to find herself backed against the door by one very livid, very close cop.

Wordlessly, he pulled her keys from her hand and without moving away from her, slowly reached around and unlocked her door.

He unlocked it, pushing it open just barely.

"What the hell, Moretti? In case it wasn't evident by the last three hours of silence, I have no interest in talking—"

"Oh, we're talking," he said, his voice gravelly.

His hand slowly, deliberately rested low on her throat as he pushed her backward into her house.

Followed her inside.

His brown eyes were black with anger. "We're having this talk, and we're having it now."

CHAPTER TWENTY-ONE

Vincent could feel Jill's heartbeat against his palm as he roughly pushed her back into her apartment.

He told himself the feel of it didn't excite him—that *her* excitement didn't excite him—but he'd be lying.

And it was excitement Jill was feeling, at least for a moment. He saw it in the flash of her eyes, the catch of her breath.

But then her pointy little chin jutted out in defiance as the anger overtook her once more.

Her anger was justified.

She had every right to be downright pissed, because damned if he hadn't been widely out of line by allowing Holly Adams to manipulate them.

But damn. The old biddy had known all the buttons to push. Buttons that had been blinking red in Vincent's peripheral vision since Jill'd returned from Florida with that fucking rock on her finger.

And he'd just... lost it.

"You don't get to decide when we talk," Jill was saying. "You don't get to just stew for months—no, *years*— and then snap your fingers and decide to become an open book. In front of a suspect, no less."

"Holly Adams didn't kill Lenora Birch, and you know it," he growled.

"Doesn't mean we should be talking about our personal life in front of her!"

He leaned down so their faces were inches apart. "So you admit we have a personal life."

"Of course we do. We're friends. Although we won't be if you keep this up."

Vin yanked his palm back from where it had been resting against her collarbone.

It was as though she burned him. Not by the warmth of her skin, but by the white-chill fire of her words.

Friends.

Jill thought of him as a friend.

Vincent swallowed.

When had friends stopped feeling like enough?

When had that one simple word ripped down to his very gut?

She lifted her hands as she opened her mouth, then let them fall, and the defeated slump of her shoulders was a little jab to his heart.

"What's going on, Vin?"

What's going on is that I can't stand the thought that in a couple short months, you'll be some other man's.

What's going on is that I only have a few weeks left to convince you that…

Fuck.

Fuck!

What did he want to convince Jill of?

That he was the man for her?

Because he wasn't.

Jill's favorite holiday was Valentine's Day, for Chrissake.

Vincent didn't do hearts and flowers. Or love.

But companionship and sex? He wanted those things.

With Jill?

He closed his eyes and rubbed a hand over his face. "I don't know."

"Well, you seemed to know when you were gossiping with Holly Adams," she said, starting to put her hands on her hips, confrontation-style, only ending up wrapping her arms around her middle. Defensive-like.

She was *literally* withdrawing from him, and it made Vin want to punch something.

He moved past her toward the kitchen.

Vincent was no stranger to Jill's home. They'd had dozens—*hundreds*—of working dinners at her kitchen table, arguing over Chinese food.

There'd been birthday parties, and dinner parties, and random Saturday night movie marathons when neither of them had any plans.

But as he opened her fridge, it hit him that this was the first time he'd been here since she'd gotten back from Florida.

Yet another testament to how much had changed between them, and yet one more thing that had Vin wanting to hit something.

Jill followed him in, not saying a word as he rummaged around in her fridge looking for a much-needed beer.

Not finding anything, he moved to the small cabinet where she sometimes kept wine and pulled out a bottle of Chianti and wordlessly held it up to her in question.

She shrugged out of her jacket, dropped it on the back of a kitchen chair, and hesitated only briefly before nodding.

He found her corkscrew in its usual spot in the drawer to the right of the sink. Watched out of the corner of his eye as she opened the freezer and pulled out a frozen pizza.

Jill put the pizza in the oven while he poured them both hefty glasses of the under-ten-dollar Chianti.

He held out a glass to her and she reached for it, although he noticed that she seemed strangely careful not to let their fingers brush.

They hadn't said a word since their heated exchange in the foyer, and Vincent held up a glass. "Truce?"

Jill rolled her eyes as she clinked her glass to his. "I don't even know what we're trucing over."

He took a sip of wine and watched her. *Get out of this, man. Take it back to safe territory. Fix it!*

"How are you?" he asked.

Her glass paused halfway to her mouth, and her nose wrinkled. "How *am* I?"

Vincent shrugged, not really sure why he asked, and yet instinctively knowing that someone needed to ask her.

And that someone should be him.

"You spend four to five days a week with me," Jill said with a little laugh. "You know how I am."

"Do I?" he asked.

Do you? Vincent said the words to himself. *Do you know how you are?*

She blew out a breath, then took her wine to the kitchen table, where she folded one leg up beneath her and sat down, both hands cupped around her glass.

"I don't know how I am," she said.

He leaned back against the counter and nodded once, hoping she'd continue.

"I feel…" She glanced up. "I feel lost. I don't know if it's the case, or the wedding planning, or the fact that Tom and I are apart more often than we're together."

He withheld his flinch, barely.

Then she shook her head. "Actually, that's not it. None of that is the problem."

"No?" he asked.

Her eyes locked on his. "No. The problem is you."

"Me."

"Look, Vin, we've always been open with each other, so I'm going to lay it out for you. Since I've been back, you and me… we've been off. Horribly so."

"I know," he replied quietly.

"What the hell happened today?" Jill asked. "One minute we were interrogating a suspect, and the next we were interrogating each other, although I'm not even sure what about."

He sipped his wine, then wordlessly turned his back, pulling two plates out of her cupboard, then two paper towels, before checking the pizza in the oven.

Vin was buying time—stalling—so that he could think, and Jill probably knew it, but she didn't pester him.

The pizza wasn't done for another five minutes, and he didn't speak that entire time.

Only once he'd cut them each a hefty slice and sat across from her at the table did he finally speak.

"It's the same thing I told you the other night. I don't want you to go to Chicago," he said.

Jill had just started to bite and choked, a stringy piece of cheese clinging to her chin.

She chewed as she wiped the cheese away with her paper towel. "I have to."

"Do you?" he countered, taking his own bite of pizza. It wasn't great. Typical frozen-quality with the crust only a shade better than cardboard, but it had everything but the kitchen sink piled on top, which helped a little.

She reached for her wineglass. "Tom's job is there."

"And your job is *here*."

Jill's eyes glanced to her plate, and he knew he'd struck a nerve. Or if not a nerve, at least he was voicing something out loud that she'd put plenty of thought toward.

"Okay, I'm having déjà vu," she said. "Didn't we just do this two weeks ago? And we ended up hugging in your kitchen, agreeing everything was okay?"

"Well, it's not okay, Henley. It's all fucked up."

She blinked a little, probably surprised at his forthrightness considering he'd been anything but direct with her all day. All month.

Vincent pushed his plate away, pizza barely touched, and he'd grabbed her hand before he realized what the hell he was doing.

The shock of her fingers in his rippled through him; the same surprise echoed on Jill's face as she stared down at where his right hand rested on her left.

She didn't pull away, but her features went immediately wary.

He didn't know what he was going to say, only knew that he had to say something, had to convince her that she belonged here. In New York. With him.

That he couldn't imagine what his days would look like without her.

That he didn't know how to be without her.

"Jill, I—" The words got lodged in his throat.

And then they became permanently lodged there, because...

Jill's phone rang.

They stared at each other for several long moments as the unmistakable sound of a vibrating cell phone buzzed from her purse.

For one wonderful, hopeful moment, he thought she might let it go to voice mail. That she needed to hear what he had to say as urgently as he needed to speak it.

Then her hand pulled away from his.

Jill licked her lips nervously, glancing in the direction of her purse. "I should get that. It could be—"

She broke off, but not before Vincent dropped his head in defeat as he silently finished her sentence for her.

Tom. It could be Tom.

Jill touched his shoulder as she passed, just briefly, and he all but batted her hand away. Her touch was the touch of someone who felt sorry for the other person.

Objectively, he knew it was meant to appease him. To ease his ache. Instead it made it worse.

And then she picked up her phone with a quiet "hey."

She didn't say Tom's name. She was kind enough for that. But she slipped into her bedroom and quietly closed the door.

He took both their plates to the sink. Rinsed his

wineglass and put it away. He could still hear Jill's voice coming from the bedroom. Muffled as though she were intentionally keeping her voice down.

For his sake?

Maybe.

Vincent braced both hands on Jill's kitchen counter as he stared blindly at her coffeepot for several long, torturous moments.

He breathed in, breathed out.

He waited for a minute. Two minutes. Five.

Waited for Jill to remember he was out here. Remember that they had a conversation that needed to happen.

He waited ten minutes.

Waited for Jill to choose him.

Her door stayed shut.

And then he realized...Jill wasn't going to choose him. Not now.

Not ever.

CHAPTER TWENTY-TWO

Jill knew she should be happy that the Morettis and Tom were getting to know each other. Knew that in theory, it was a good thing that the two most important areas of her life were blending.

But right now?

Right now she felt just about anything but happy.

It had seemed like a good idea at the time—having a spontaneous dinner party at her place. She'd wanted Tom to get to know her friends in a casual, "let's all hang out and eat pasta and drink wine" kind of way.

The way they did it on her favorite TV shows.

She'd set it up two weeks ago. Back before she and Vincent had had the mother of all fights. Back when they were still talking.

It had been two days since their tense talk over pizza at her kitchen table. Two days since she'd come out of her bedroom after her conversations with Tom, and found him gone—as though he'd never been there in the first place.

They'd barely exchanged a word since.

No easy task, since they were partners and all, but they'd managed.

Jill had never been so miserable.

Worst of all, people had noticed. Tom had noticed. He'd practically given her an inquisition when he'd flown in last night. Elena had noticed when she'd shown up early to help Jill set up.

And now, of all people, it was Anthony who'd cornered her in her own home.

"Talk," he said curtly. Like Vincent, nearly everything Anthony said came out like a near-bark. His marriage to the sweet Maggie had softened Vincent's older brother slightly, but there was nothing soft about him right now as he stood glaring down at Jill.

She glared up at him with, "Were you just standing here waiting for me to come out of the bathroom?"

Anthony crossed his arms and said nothing. Waited.

She huffed and started to move around him, but he moved with her, blocking her from walking back into the kitchen.

"Look, Anth, I respect the big brother thing you have going on, but let's remember that you're not *my* brother, hmm?" she said, trying to dodge him again.

He moved once more, blocking her way as he spoke. "Just because we're not related by blood doesn't mean I don't love you like a sister."

Jill froze. None of the Moretti siblings were overly demonstrative, but it was particularly unnerving to hear the word "love" from the mouth of the taciturn eldest.

But Jill couldn't deny the effect it had on her. Suddenly she found herself wanting to lean into Anth's tallness and beg for a hug. Because the sibling love went both ways.

Still, it wasn't the time. Or the place.

Instead she crossed her arms over her middle and cupped her elbows as she glanced to the right of Anthony toward her living room. "It's nothing."

"Jill."

She gave a little sigh. Then she shifted so she could look around Anthony's other side, since the man was entirely too tall for her to see *over* his shoulder. "Fine. I'll play annoying little sister to your overbearing big brother. You want to know what's crawled up my ass? It has to do with the fact that I have a certain bad-tempered homicide detective in my living room who can't be bothered to look up from his cell phone for—"

"He's looked up," Anthony interupped.

Jill gave him a look. "Not that I've seen."

"That's because he only looks up when you're looking away."

Jill glanced again at Vincent where he sat perched on her bar stool in a long-sleeve black shirt, jeans, and a scowl. "I don't think—"

"He's been looking at *you*," Anthony cut in.

Jill's eyes flew back to Anth's gaze, which was surprisingly patient.

"He's always looking at you," Anth said, his voice quieter this time.

"I—"

"What are you doing, Jill?" His voice was tired.

"Excuse me?" she asked with an incredulous little laugh.

"You know what I'm asking," he said, keeping his voice low. "I'm not saying that Tom's not a great guy. I'm not saying that you're not allowed to marry whomever you want—"

"Damn straight I'm allowed to marry whom I want!" Jill said, temper spiking.

She'd seen Anthony get high-and-mighty with his younger siblings before, but this was the first time she'd been on the receiving end. And she could totally see why the younger Morettis were always itching to strike at Anth, in all his control-freakish—

"Calm down," he said, irritating her even further. "Don't cause a scene."

"*I'm* not the one who cornered someone else coming out of the bathroom." Jill lowered her voice, but it came out as a hiss.

"Look, all I'm saying is that any idiot can see that something is going on with you and Vincent. Something's been going on for years. If you care for him, at all, address it. And then let him go, Jill."

Her mouth dropped open. "Me, let *him* go? Your fraternal observations are a bit shortsighted, Anth. I've been right in front of Vincent for years, and he waits until I decide to get married to start acting weird. If anyone needs to do the letting go, it's him."

"He's trying," Anthony said through gritted teeth. "What do you want from him? Any fool can see that he just wants you to be happy."

Jill's shoulders slumped. "Yeah, he keeps saying that. But then he turns around and bites my head off about getting married."

"It's because you're giving mixed signals," Anth said, his voice quiet.

Her head snapped up. "I'm not."

His look was sympathetic, and that made it all the worse. "You are. You know how I said that he looks at you every time you're not paying attention? You do the same. And may I just say, you've been looking at Vin a hell of a lot more than you've been looking at Tom tonight."

Jill felt her cheeks go hot. With anger. *How dare he!* With embarrassment. *Oh God, was he right?*

And then shame. *Yes. Yes, he was absolutely right.*

She closed her eyes and swayed just a little. "I don't know what to do."

Anth lifted his shoulders slightly in a shrug. "You've got to choose."

Jill licked her lips and gave a nervous laugh. "I don't know that it's that simple. I mean it's not like Vin even wants—"

She broke off, and her eyes found the quiet man sitting at her kitchen stool, looking so utterly alone.

"Take it from a brother that knows Vincent better than he realizes. He *wants*."

Jill shook her head. She didn't want to hear this. Didn't want to deal with any of it.

"I'm getting *married*, Anth," she said.

"Fine," he said with a lift of his shoulders. "Just make sure that's what you want."

"Of course it's what I want."

He merely looked down at her, and Jill resisted the urge to shove him. "What is it with you Morettis waiting until now to have this conversation with me? You couldn't have told me earlier that Vin might have wanted—something?"

"Would that have changed anything?" Anth asked.

Jill's eyes went once more to her partner. Her best friend. Her everything.

She didn't answer Anthony.

But her heart responded loud and clear.

Yes. Yes, it would have changed *everything*.

"Oh my God," she whispered, her hand lifting to her mouth at the realization of what she had to do.

Anthony's hand rested kindly on her shoulder. "It's going to be okay."

Easy for him to say. He's not the one that had to tell a perfectly nice man that *she wasn't going to marry him*.

CHAPTER TWENTY-THREE

When Tom texted to ask if they could cancel dinner reservations, and do room service in his hotel room instead, Jill had been torn between relief and alarm.

Relief, because it had been a crappy day. She and Vincent had endured yet another of those icy, bare-minimum-of-words exchanges. The high heels that had seemed like a great idea this morning were pinching like crazy. The thought of going to a fancy dinner, sitting across from Tom, and pretending that she was excited to talk about seating arrangements felt...

Unbearable.

But on the other hand, being alone in Tom's hotel, just the two of them?

Also unbearable.

Jill told herself she didn't take her sweet time paying the cab driver, but the truth was, she was dreading the evening that lay ahead.

It was definitely time to face the fact that something was seriously very, very wrong with the direction her life was headed.

Anthony had been right. She couldn't marry one man while her head was all wrapped up in another.

It was time to put on her big girl panties and deal with it.

Tomorrow.

She'd deal with it tomorrow.

Right now all she wanted was a dinner—preferably something caloric and filled with carbs, and maybe a beer to take the edge off. And comfortable shoes. She could really, *really* go for comfortable shoes right about now.

The elevator ride up to the thirty-eighth floor was faster than Jill was ready for, and too soon, she found herself pasting on what she'd come to think of as her happy face.

At least tonight, she only had to do the happy face for Tom, and not an entire restaurant.

But in some ways that was worse. More chance of exposure.

More opportunity for him to finally open his eyes and see her and ask the dreaded question:

Is everything okay?

And no. No, everything was not okay.

Tom opened the door with his usual wide smile, but she noted that there were tired lines around his eyes. She'd always loved his smile lines, but today there was a hardness about them.

As though the smile had been forced into place for far too long.

She knew that feeling all too well. Knew what it was like to smile when you didn't want to, to talk when you wanted to be silent. To sparkle when you just wanted a freaking nap.

Too late, Jill wondered how long had that been going on. How long had she and Tom been failing to *see* each other?

She wasn't sure she wanted the answer to that question.

"I already ordered some food," he said as Jill came inside and shrugged out of her jacket. "Hope that's okay. Skipped lunch today, so I'm starving."

"No problem," she said distractedly, heading toward the window where the Brooklyn Bridge looked like something out of a picture.

"The view's gorgeous," she said.

He didn't respond, and Jill turned around to find him watching her with a pensive look on his face.

Maybe he could read her after all.

She smiled. He smiled back.

Both smiles were—not *fake*, exactly—but weary.

Warning bells rang faintly in the back of Jill's mind, but she seemed to lack the energy to get really, truly worried.

The arrival of room service stalled what was happening—or not happening—between her and Tom.

"Roast beef sandwich, or roast chicken?" Tom asked, pulling the silver lids off both plates.

She shrugged, pulling a fry off the plate with the sandwich and halfheartedly chewing it.

Objectively she knew she was hungry, but the faintest flicker of butterflies in her stomach made both food options look unappealing.

"You pick," she said.

He nodded, but despite his earlier claims of hunger, didn't seem in a rush for either plate.

The mood wasn't awkward so much as...expectant. Like the calm before a storm you've always known was coming.

Jill sat on the bed, looking across the room at Tom as he leaned against the small hotel desk. His long legs were stretched out in front of him, crossed at the ankle. He was still in his suit—always in a suit—although he'd ditched the tie.

But there were tension lines around his eyes and mouth. His knuckles were white where they gripped the desk.

Jill opened her mouth, wondering what she could say to make this all go away.

In the end, she didn't have to. He spoke first.

"Whatever it is, you can just say it."

Jill was suddenly really glad she hadn't eaten more than the single French fry.

The gentle butterflies in her stomach turned into bats. Big ones.

"Tom—"

He blew out a long breath. "You don't want to marry me, do you?"

She could only stare at him.

He smiled gently. "I'm not asking if you care about me. I'm not asking if you think I'm a great guy. I'm not even asking whether or not you think I'd be a great husband. I'm asking whether you want to *marry* me."

She pushed her plate aside. "I *do* care about you. And I think we'd have a pretty damn content marriage. But I want more than that. Don't you?"

He blew out a long breath and dipped his head.

"Yes. Yes, I do want more," he replied softly.

Tom blew out a laugh and then dipped his head forward, staring at his hands clasped between his legs.

She scooted to sit beside him. "Are you mad?"

"Mad." He stared at his hands for a while. "You know, I'm not? Embarrassed, maybe. But not mad. Not even hurt. And I guess that says it all right there, huh?"

She smiled sadly. "Maybe."

"I think maybe I always knew it wasn't right, but I kept trying…"

"Me too," she said.

They were both silent for several seconds, and then Jill let out a little laugh at the absurdity of it all and flopped back on the bed.

"Do you get the sense we're getting off way too easy here?" she asked. "We're calling off a *wedding*."

He leaned back so he was lying beside her, both of them on their backs, shoulders nearly touching, feet dangling off the end of a random hotel bed.

"True. Although, not gonna lie, right now my imagination is playing over scenarios in which you tell me you changed your mind."

"Oh yeah?" She turned her head to look at him. "What do I sound like in your head?"

His voice pitched up several octaves. "Tom, *noo*, I was so wrong, Tom, my dearest beloved…"

Jill cracked up. "That's terrible."

He grinned. "Am I close?"

She rolled toward him, tucking her arm beneath her head. "Can I ask you something?"

"Only if I get to ask you something after."

"Deal." She took a deep breath. "Why did you propose? We barely knew each other—"

Tom stared up at the ceiling for several seconds. "It's going to sound awful."

"Try me."

Tom blew out a long breath. "You have ... you have this light. No, more like you *are* light. And when I saw you sitting across the bar that first day ... well let's just say it was very moth-to-flame."

"Romantic," she said teasingly. "But that explains why you approached me, not why you asked me out again, and again, and then proposed."

He turned his head to look at her, seeming to search her face. There was fondness on his face, but no passion—had there ever been passion?

Did she care?

"It took me all of a week to realize that that light I saw in you? It was love. You have so much damn love to give, and I ... I wanted some of it."

Jill's mouth parted in surprise. "Everyone has love to give."

"Sure. But you have it in spades," he said, his finger running along her nose. "And I think that's why you said yes. Because that love was ready to burst out of you, and you needed to give it away."

Jill stared at him. Was he right?

It felt ... right. Sometimes she did feel like she was going to explode with ... something.

"I guess you just answered *your* question," she said lightly. "Why I said yes."

Tom shook his head. "That's not what I was going to ask."

"No?"

He rolled onto his back, linking his hands behind his head. "I was going to ask what's going on with you and Vincent Moretti. I mean, really."

Jill's heart stopped. "Nothing! Tom, you have to believe—"

"I know you didn't cheat on me, Jill," he said, his voice quiet. "But you can't tell me that there's not something there."

She swallowed. "But...I don't—we don't—"

She flung her arms over her head. "I don't know. I don't know what's going on."

Jill felt the mattress move as Tom moved back into a seated position, and after several seconds, she peeked out from under the safety of her arms and saw him staring out the darkened window with a thoughtful look on his face.

She rolled upward, sitting beside him. Nudged his knee with hers. "What are you thinking?"

He sighed and stood, looking like he wanted to pace, but instead merely looked down at her, hands shoved in his pocket.

"I think you should be careful."

Her eyebrows lifted. "Of...?"

"Vincent."

"He would never hurt me," she said without hesitating.

"Not intentionally, no, but..."

Her foot snuck out, tapping against his shin gently. "You called me here to dump me. Don't hold back now."

His smile was humorless. "You've known Vincent for years."

"Right..."

His blue eyes were steady on hers. "How many of those years have you been in love with him?"

Jill's heart leaped in her chest. "I'm not—it's not—"

"Regardless," he said, his voice gentle, "the timing of his attentions seems off to me. I'm not saying he doesn't care for you, but if you move forward with him, be very sure this isn't a case of him wanting what he can't have. He's had plenty of time to make his move, and he waits until you have a ring on your finger."

His words struck a nerve. Sharply.

The truth between Tom's words was unavoidable.

If Vincent had feelings for her—and the "if" was incredibly real—why now?

What if all the hot looks lately were classic territorial male? Uninterested in a woman right in front of him until another man wanted her.

She swallowed.

She'd think of that later. Much later.

But for now...

Jill stood as she twisted the diamond ring off her finger and held it out to Tom.

He hesitated a moment before extending his palm. "It doesn't feel right that I take this back."

Jill smiled a little as she dropped it into his waiting hand. "Trust me. It's much more wrong for me to keep it."

They both looked at the glittering ring for several seconds before his fingers closed around it.

Their eyes met, and then incredibly—they laughed. A real, honest-to-God belly laugh of two people consumed with a heady sense of relief.

"We don't have to figure this out right this second, but logistically, how does this work?"

Jill blew out a breath. "I'll take care of canceling the caterer and the venue, but in terms of telling people..."

"You let me know when you're ready," he said quietly.

Jill smiled in gratitude. By telling people, she had meant telling Vin, and she suspected Tom knew it. Was letting her handle things her way.

"Actually..." Tom dug his hand into his pocket and came out with the ring. "Keep it for now. Until you're ready to tell the world. Then you can give it back."

"Tom—"

He gently pulled her left hand toward him, slipping the ring on. It was a very different gesture than when he'd done it weeks ago, but no less sweet.

"You're a ridiculously good guy," she said, leaning her cheek against the door as he opened it for her.

He winked. "I know it. And trust me, there are moments when I wish that light I mentioned—I wish it were meant for me, but..." He shrugged.

Jill gave him a sad smile before she lifted to her toes and pressed her lips to his cheek.

"Good-bye, Tom."

He smiled, managing to look completely unperturbed after just being dumped. "See ya, Henley."

It was exactly what she would have done.

She shook her head and smiled as she turned away, realizing now what she should have known all along: that she and Tom were practically the same person.

And it had taken her far too long to realize that she didn't want a male version of herself. She wanted...

She wanted her opposite.

She wanted *Vin*.

CHAPTER TWENTY-FOUR

Traveling with another person could cause turmoil in the most stable of relationships.

And Vincent and Jill were anything but stable.

Still, Jill was looking forward to their California trip. Maybe the new environment was the change she needed to clear her head.

Jill drained the last of her coffee, washed the cup, and dried it. For the first time ever, she wasn't the one rushing around, and the extra time felt decadent.

Vincent had texted her earlier saying that he was running late. Not really his thing, but the guy was allowed to oversleep now and then. God knew she'd done it a handful of times.

When he pulled up outside her apartment, she was ready, wheeling her bag down the drive.

"Morning!" she said as he came around the back of the car and practically threw her bag in the trunk.

He grunted.

Jill sighed. "Have you had your coffee yet?"

"Yes, I've had my coffee," he snapped.

"Okay, so the bad mood is just..."

He slammed the trunk and returned to his side of the car without responding.

"Well, this should be fun," Jill muttered as she got into the passenger seat.

There were several tense moments of silence before Jill turned to face him. "I thought we were done with this."

"Done with what?"

"The silent treatment."

"I'm not being silent," he snapped.

"You're also not using more than, like, five words in a sentence."

"Never bothered you before."

Well, it bothers me now! she wanted to scream. *It bothers me now because I need to tell you something important.*

Like the fact that I ended my engagement, and...

He crossed the console and flipped on the radio. Loudly.

Guess they were done talking.

Maybe he'd just woken up on the wrong side of the bed, but she was getting tired of this.

They'd been making slow progress toward getting back to their normal selves since the sort-of fight after the disastrous Holly Adams interrogation, but now it felt like they were back to square one:

Lying to each other.

Jill glanced down at her left hand. The ring felt like a mockery now. It was a mockery. She was no longer engaged.

For a moment, she dreamed about tugging it off. Chucking it out the window and telling Vincent the truth. The whole truth.

Instead, she pressed her lips together and looked out the window.

She let him have his silence. Hell, she wanted it. Maybe the big grouch was finally starting to rub off on her after all these years.

Vincent's bad mood persisted all the way to the airport.

All the way through the security line.

Continued even when she waited in a ridiculously long Starbucks queue to fetch him a coffee.

By the time she was buckling her seat belt, Jill was starting to wonder if Anth had been completely wrong about Vin's feelings for her. Because the man sitting beside her was hardly a man in love. Or even like.

She glanced over. He was a man who . . .

He was stiff as a board, his knuckles actually white where they clenched the armrests.

Concerned, she set her stuff on the still-vacant window seat to her right and put a hand on his arm. "Vin? You okay?"

He gave her a stiff nod, but his eyes never stopped darting around the plane.

"You are not," she accused. "What's going on? Did you see something?" she asked, subtly glancing around in case it was his cop instincts on high alert.

Another shake of his head, this time in the negative. Jill opened her mouth again, but he uttered a curt "Drop it."

"Fine," she snapped.

Jill put her headphones on and pulled out her e-reader to open the romance novel she'd been waiting for weeks to find time to read. Just let him dwell on whatever had crawled up his butt.

It wasn't until the plane pulled away from the gate that Jill had the happy realization that in an almost unheard-of stroke of aviation luck, the window seat next to her had never been occupied.

Not that she minded the middle seat, but it was a long flight. A little space wouldn't hurt, especially since her only company was a suddenly-grumpier-than-usual Vincent.

Jill glanced around to make sure the flight attendants wouldn't gripe at her if she switched seats as they were doing their slow taxi, only to freeze when she saw Vincent's face.

He wasn't pissed. Wasn't grumpy.

He was *scared*.

Oh. *Oh!*

Immediately, Jill tugged off her headphones, dropped her e-reader into the seat pocket in front of her, and tucked her arm into his.

He didn't even glance down.

"Hey," she whispered. "Why didn't you tell me?"

No response.

"Vin." She shook his arm. "You're scared to fly? Is this why you were so grumpy all morning?"

"Shut up, Henley."

She smiled then, careful to keep the smile gentle and not mocking.

The man was really, truly scared, and as someone with a not-so-minor spider phobia, she understood what it was like to be crippled by an irrational but unavoidable terror.

Jill forgot all about moving to the other seat, and

instead let her fingers run along his forearm where it gripped the armrest like a lifeline.

She vaguely remembered a couple years ago when the Moretti family had flown to California in the days after Christmas to visit Marc.

Vin had stayed behind, and she'd given him so much crap.

She regretted that now, because clearly it hadn't been a callous move so much as a terrified one. She should have known that only something major would have kept him from his family.

The plane slowed to a stop, and she could hear his breathing, slow and controlled. The plane stayed still for several moments as the pilots waited permission from air traffic control, or however that worked.

Then it moved forward. She felt Vin's muscles jerk under her fingertips, his previously slow and controlled breath now coming hot and panicked where it ruffled against her hair.

Jill knew the moment the plane left the ground because Vin went all the way rigid, and her next move was purely reflexive.

She slid her fingers over his forearm, trailed over his wrist until they reached his palm. The second their fingers were aligned, his bigger hand crushed over hers. They were holding hands.

It wasn't a romantic handhold. Or a sexy one.

He was practically crushing her fingers, and sweat was beading on his forehead.

But it was important, all the same. Important that she be there for him.

"It'll get better in a moment," she said, just as a particularly rough bit of air jerked the plane.

"How do you figure? We're a couple thousand feet in the air," he said through gritted teeth.

"It'll smooth out once we reach cruising altitude. Take-off's always the worst."

So was landing. But she didn't mention this.

Jill silently prayed that it wouldn't be a particularly turbulent flight, and her prayers were answered when the plane eventually leveled off and the jerking stopped.

Eventually the flight attendants made their "coming through the cabin with drinks" announcement, and even better, the seat belt light went off.

"Do you need to go to the bathroom?" Jill asked.

"I'm not a child, Henley."

"I'm just saying, you might want to go while the seat belt light is off."

He gave her the side-eye. "It comes back on some-times?"

Vincent still hadn't released her hand.

"If it gets bumpy," she said patiently. "Vin, have you never flown before?"

"I have," he grunted. "A couple times."

"And this um, fear—"

"It's *so* much more than fear."

She smiled. Good for him for not trying to puff up his chest about it. "Has it always been there?"

"Pretty much. Never figured out how to reconcile willingly putting one's self inside a tin can hurled through the air with a couple sticks attached."

"Sticks?" she asked. "Oh. You mean the wings?"

They hit another bump, and he exhaled, clenching her hand even more firmly.

"Let's talk about the case," she suggested, trying to get

his mind off the tin-can-with-sticks scenario. "Did you get that e-mail I forwarded to you with the article about Kathryn DeBorio...?"

Slowly, slowly, Vincent's breathing evened out as he answered her questions. His grip on her fingers eased somewhere over the Midwest, the pad of his thumb lightly stroking along her forefinger as they talked.

Eventually they exhausted the case and moved on to his family. They discussed Anth's overprotective almost-father tendencies, Elena's recent moodiness, his parents upcoming anniversary, and what the kids should to do celebrate...he asked about her mom, which she answered. Asked about the wedding, which she didn't.

Jill found herself surprised when she felt the subtle downward dip of the plane's nose signaling their initial descent. She was fairly certain Vincent in all his sweaty tension wouldn't agree, but it was one of the shorter flights she could remember.

Six hours had felt more like two.

Jill told herself it was just because she'd let herself get wrapped up in conversation. She was a talker after all.

Vincent's grip tightened slightly during the bumpy descent, although he seemed less on the verge of death than he had during takeoff.

She felt the rough bump of the wheels hitting the runway. Felt the familiar pressure of being pulled forward.

She grinned at Vincent and squeezed his fingers. "We did it."

Well, *they* hadn't done anything.

But he'd survived, and that was something.

He didn't smile back.

Nor did he release her hand.

Not until they reached the jetway and the Fasten Seat Belt sign clicked off did he finally, finally let go.

And before he did, he briefly, roughly jerked her hand to his mouth. Pressed his lips against the back of her hand just briefly.

"Thank you," he whispered.

Vincent stood then, easily maneuvering their bags out of the overhead compartment, but Jill stayed seated a bit longer under the guise of putting her stuff back in her bag.

In reality, she paused because she wasn't quite ready to stand, too worried that her legs would be shaky.

Not from the flight.

But from the realization that she could still feel Vincent Moretti's lips burning against the back of her hand.

CHAPTER TWENTY-FIVE

Vincent and Jill were still operating under the assumption that Lenora Birch had been killed over professional jealousies or vendettas, rather than personal ones.

Their bosses, however, wanted no stone left unturned, particularly given the cost of sending two of their homicide detectives to California for three days.

Which was how Vincent and Jill came to find themselves on the back patio sipping iced tea with James Killroy, an aging but still relevant action star.

And Vin would never admit it—not in a million years...

But he was starstruck.

Vincent wasn't a movie buff by any stretch of the imagination, but like most guys, he enjoyed a good espionage movie. Enjoyed the car chase movies. Enjoyed blow-'em-up movies.

James Killroy had been the king of those types of movies a decade earlier, and just last year had topped the box offices with a blockbuster about an aging spy brought back into active duty.

Of course, his brooding stare and perfect delivery of one-liners wasn't why they were here.

"You're sure I can't offer you anything stronger?" James asked, lifting his own whiskey in question.

Jill smiled politely. "Normally I'd love that pinot grigio you offered, but alas... working."

The older man studied her. "Working on the murder of Lenora Birch."

"Yes sir," Jill said, giving that perky smile that turned most men to mush.

If James Killroy turned to mush, he was too good of an actor to show it. The man wasn't cold, or even chilly, but he was definitely holding himself at a distance. He was trying to figure them out as much as they were trying to figure him out.

"You and Lenora were... romantically involved?" Jill asked.

"Hmmm," James said in confirmation, leaning back in his chair and staring down at the amber liquid in his glass. "Long time ago. Long time."

"Thirty-eight years ago," Vincent supplied.

James laughed. "A bit long to have me on the short list of murder suspects, wouldn't you say?"

Jill gave another one of those sweet smiles. "We're looking into everyone from Lenora's past who was in New York at the time of her murder."

"Well... I can assure you that I wasn't in New York to see Lenora Birch. It was my son's twenty-first birthday.

He attends Fordham. I flew in to take him to a ridiculously expensive dinner, then paid for him and his friends to go out and celebrate—safely."

"Your son's birthday just happens to be the same night that Lenora was killed?" Vin asked skeptically.

James stared at Vincent over his glass, and Vin felt an honest-to-God urge to fidget. "Yes."

"I assume you've checked the hotel security cameras at the Westin where I was staying. I got back to the hotel before ten."

Lenora had been killed sometime around ten thirty.

"At this point it's just a couple of questions—due diligence," Jill said. "You and Ms. Birch...there's an eleven-year age difference there."

At this, James smiled. "Yes. And trust me, if there's ever an older woman for a twenty-two-year-old kid to become enamored with, it's Lenora Birch."

"She was quite beautiful," Jill said.

"Yes, but that's not what I mean."

"Oh?" Jill asked.

James sat forward, setting his glass on the table. "I met Lenora at a film premiere. It was one of my first movies, and my role was barely large enough to warrant an invitation. Lenora had nothing to do with the project, but back then premieres were fewer...all the big names in Hollywood leaped at the chance to attend. To stay relevant."

"Who made the first move?" Vin asked.

"I did," James said with a small smile. "The studio hosted a party after the viewing. I'd had one more drink than was smart—enough to make me stupidly bold. I saw her standing near the bar, and I just...talked to her."

There was no softness in the way James told the story;

he might as well have been talking about his experience at the car wash.

"And she responded," Jill said.

James shrugged. "I think she was amused. Perhaps flattered. At thirty-three she was still beautiful, but she was always incredibly aware of her advancing years. Always worried about the hot young starlets on the scene who would steal her throne."

"But nobody ever did," Jill said. "Not really."

"No," he said, picking up his whiskey again. "Lenora was one of the true greats. Her looks started to change, certainly—the ingenue shifted to the sophisticate shifted to the powerful dame. But her acting only improved with each change."

"You dated for three years," Vincent said. "What was the relationship like?"

The actor rolled his eyes. "This can't possibly be relevant to the case."

"It is if you killed her," Vincent said, hardly believing he uttered that sentence to James Killroy.

The older man studied him for several moments, then tipped his glass in Vin's direction. "You're direct. I like you. And even though the question is bullshit...The relationship was...stable, at least compared to some of the more volatile relationships I was involved in before and after."

"Stable?" Jill prompted.

"Lenora was a calm woman. Difficult to rattle even when I left water rings on her expensive coffee table, cigarette burns on her vintage couch. She'd express displeasure, certainly, but she never really got angry. Not with me. Not even when I deserved it, which was often back then."

"You were happy."

James rolled the glass between his two palms. "Happy enough. I learned from her. She seemed to enjoy me. I wasn't always faithful, and I suspect she wasn't either, but it worked for us."

Vin's eyes narrowed just slightly, his hero worship of James Killroy taking a sharp hit just then.

Vincent might not believe in true love and happily-ever-after, but he absolutely believed in fidelity. It was part of the reason he steered clear of traditional relationships. If he wasn't one hundred percent sure he wouldn't be tempted by another woman, he didn't pretend to commit.

"How'd the relationship end?" Vincent asked James.

"Honestly? I barely remember. There was no fight. No big blowup. My career started to pick up, and hers had never slowed down. Our paths crossed less and less. Our schedules rarely overlapped. I'm not even sure I remember having the conversation that things were over. They just . . . were."

"How'd you feel about that?" Jill asked.

James smiled grimly. "Not murderous, if that's what you're getting at. Seriously, I understand you two are just doing your job—I do. Hell, I've played a homicide detective once or twice . . ."

Yeah, because that's the same thing, Vin thought.

" . . . but honestly, check with the hotel. I was back in my room by ten. Ordered a movie—one of those boring, award-winning types. Was asleep by midnight."

"We'll check the cameras," Vin said, setting his iced tea on the table, sensing that they were done here. Admittedly the man didn't seem particularly torn up about the violent death of an old lover, but there was no spark of any kind when James spoke of Lenora.

Not passion, not anger...barely even interest.

"Mr. Killroy," Jill said, scooting forward in her chair as they all prepared to stand. "We're currently operating under the assumption that whoever wanted Lenora dead was perhaps motivated by a professional slight, rather than a personal one."

The actor nodded thoughtfully. "Makes sense. The only time the woman got fired up was if she thought something would negatively impact her career."

Vincent and Jill exchanged a look. It was almost comical how often that phrase was being uttered.

"Does anyone come to mind? Anyone who who might have had some sort of professional vendetta toward Lenora."

He lifted a shoulder. "Sure, tons. Hollywood's a competitive, sometimes vicious place. But everything I could think of...they're old. Decades old. Lenora's screen time has been limited to minor, grandmotherly roles in the past couple years, and anything before that..."

Again with the shoulder lift. "Who has the energy to hold on to anger for that long?"

Who indeed?

If they knew that, perhaps they'd have their killer.

CHAPTER TWENTY-SIX

Six hours later, three suspects down, and they weren't any closer to knowing...anything.

"It's like Lenora Birch was a robot," Jill said, dunking a tortilla chip into an enormous bowl of guacamole. "How many times can we hear that the woman rarely showed emotion?"

Vincent said nothing as he took another sip of his tequila.

They were done for the day. *Way* done. He supposed that they could have—should have—gone back to the airport hotel that the NYPD had booked for them. Gone over their case notes again.

Strictly speaking, debriefing over tequila and guacamole while watching the sun set over the Pacific Ocean probably wasn't exactly what the bosses had in mind.

But fuck, they'd earned this. Him, because Vincent

somehow managed to get himself on the plane despite the fact that every fiber of his being had rebelled.

Jill, because she'd held his hand the whole damn way, and God bless her, hadn't once laughed at him.

It's not like he wanted to be afraid of flying.

That's what his brothers—the only ones who knew of his "condition"—thought. That he just needed to suck it up and get over it.

Did they really think he hadn't *tried*?

He'd read the books. Tried all the mental tricks.

Nothing helped. He just really, really fucking hated flying. He was always reading that it was the "lack of control" that made people afraid of flying, but that never felt quite right.

For him it was more the realization that if he was going to be in the tiny statistical sliver that died in a plane crash—it was going to be one shitty-ass, terrifying death.

But admittedly this flight had been...well, still awful.

But better too.

Better because of her.

He glanced over to where Jill was licking salt off the rim of her margarita. His eyes latched on to that pink tongue for a heartbeat too long before he forced them back to the gorgeous sunset in front of them.

She pushed at his shoulder. "See. Told ya California wasn't so bad."

He helped himself to a chip. "Okay, so it has a couple things working in its favor."

"Speaking of which, bummer Marc couldn't get out of his shift tonight, but I'm excited to see him tomorrow!"

Vin nodded. So was he. He only wished that Mandy had been conveniently unavailable, but alas, the four of them were doing dinner the following evening. It had been too damn long since he'd seen his brother.

Marc made the plane flight worth it.

Mostly.

But excited as he was to see Marc, he didn't want to let his brain latch on to the fun part of the trip until they'd worked through a bit more of the work part.

"You said Lenora Birch was a machine," he said, looking across the table at Jill.

"Robot," she said, dunking another chip. "I said 'robot.'"

"I don't think so," he said, shaking his head.

Jill wiped her mouth. "No?"

"Not wearing your heart on your sleeve doesn't mean that you don't have one."

Jill's eyes locked on his, narrowing slightly. "Speaking from experience?"

He let his gaze hold hers, even though he knew it was dangerous. Even though he'd been telling himself all week that this—whatever this was—had to stop.

He took a sip of tequila. For courage. "Just because someone doesn't talk about feelings doesn't mean they aren't there."

"Fair enough," Jill said slowly. "But you have to understand that another person won't know what to do with those feelings if they're not aware of them."

"What if the other person *is* aware of them—but is just scared to death," he challenged.

"Why would she—or he—be scared?" Jill said as they both scrambled to hold on to the illusion that they were still talking about the case.

He searched her face. "Maybe because that person isn't

quite as open—or in touch—with her feelings as she'd like to believe."

Jill's eyes narrowed. "So you're saying that all of these people who act like Lenora Birch is a robot are incorrect? Lying to themselves?"

"I'm saying that maybe they tell themselves that she was cold and unfeeling because they can't face their own fear that maybe she was just unfeeling toward *them*."

Jill leaned back in her chair, taking a sip of margarita. "If Lenora felt strongly about anyone, she didn't show it."

He leaned back as well, mimicking her easy posture, even as his body was held rigid with tension. "Perhaps she tried. Perhaps they missed it."

Jill licked her lips, but whatever she was about to say next was interrupted by the return of their server asking if they wanted another round.

"Actually, we were just on our way to dinner," Vincent said before Jill could reply.

She snapped her mouth shut but waited until after the server walked away to get their bill before asking, "Dinner?"

He pulled his wallet out of his back pocket. "Got the name of a place from Marco. Great food, buzzing atmosphere, but not annoyingly trendy."

Jill didn't even try to contain her excitement. "Any chance of celebrity sightings?"

He smiled. He knew she was going to ask that. "Marco said it's not out of the question."

Jill slapped at the table and made a little squeal of excitement.

"Okay, but first to the hotel," she said, still drumming her fingers against the table and all but bouncing in her chair.

"Why?" he asked, handing the server his credit card the moment she came back to the table.

Jill gave him an exasperated look and plucked at the white blouse that was her standard "interrogation" uniform. "Um, to change. Obviously."

Vin rolled his eyes toward the orange and red California sky. *Obviously.*

CHAPTER TWENTY-SEVEN

It was unfair, really, just how exceptional the Moretti gene pool was. A fact Jill sometimes forgot, given one was her partner, one was her best friend, and the others were like brothers.

But seeing Marco Moretti for the first time in years, Jill had to admit that it was one damn fine-looking family.

Vincent's brother had the same dark hair as the rest of them, and brown eyes like Vin and Anthony, rather than the blue of Luc and Elena. And while there was certainly no mistaking that all the brothers, well, were brothers, they each had own unique appeal going on.

Anthony was the stoic, serious one. Classic tall, dark, and handsome.

Luc was the charming heartthrob. Quick with a smile and a wink.

Vin had the gruff, rough edges of a bad boy, which was played up significantly by the ever-present leather jacket.

And Marco…Jill tilted her head as she studied him over her glass of delicious pinot grigio…Marco was the reliable one. The one you'd want as the bodyguard or your emergency contact.

He was tall—nearly as tall as Anth's six-four, perhaps—and had the same broad shoulders of his brothers. Clean-shaven jaw, crisp white shirt…

Marc caught her staring and winked.

Jill smiled. Apparently Luc wasn't the only brother quick with a wink.

They'd been at the restaurant for all of fifteen minutes, and two things were abundantly clear.

(1) Marc had missed his brother. And vice versa.

(2) Mandy Breslin absolutely did not deserve Marc—or any Moretti.

Granted, the woman was beautiful. Exceptionally so. Jill remembered her as being a blonde, but her hair was currently a gorgeous dark chocolate shade that fell in long, shiny layers down to rather perfect boobs. Her waist was tiny, her butt toned and tight, her legs long. She was also one of those women who managed to look perfectly made up, yet not at all. The type that probably spent an hour putting on her makeup in such a way that made it look like she was wearing none.

Everything about her screamed effortlessly gorgeous.

"So, Mandy, how are things with you?" Jill asked, once it became abundantly clear that Marc's girlfriend was wildly bored with Marc and Vin's nonstop "cop-talk."

She glanced up from where she'd been nibbling at the bru-schetta on her plate—no bread, mind you, just the tomatoes.

It was as though she came alive right before Jill's eyes. The bored, vaguely sulky look disappeared.

"Really good!" Mandy said, tucking a strand of hair behind her ear as she let her eyes go all animated and sparkling. "My agent thinks I'm on the verge of a big break, but I'm trying not to get cocky, you know?"

Jill had to give the other woman credit; she may not have hit her big break yet, but she was a better actress than the Morettis gave her credit for. She was currently nailing the role of girlish and modest.

Jill felt Vincent shift in his chair beside her, and she sent him a silent message to bite his tongue.

"That's great," Jill asked. "So how does that work, you just tell him or her the types of roles you're interested in?"

"Yup! My agent's one of the big names, so she's the first to know about all the prime roles."

"Does your next role require you to be a brunette?" Vincent asked, taking a sip of his beer before gesturing to her newly dark hair.

"Oh, no, I don't have anything specific lined up. I just got so sick of everyone trying to cast me as the clueless bimbo. Brunettes get taken more seriously. No offense," she said with a glance at Jill.

"None taken," Jill said with a thin smile. She was totally willing to bet that Mandy's previous platinum shade of blond hadn't been any more natural than the dark chocolate tresses she was rocking now.

Mandy leaned forward. "So, have you talked to, like, a ton of famous people on your trip?"

"Sweetie," Marc said, resting a hand on the back of Mandy's chair. "You know they can't talk about the case."

She pouted prettily. "But the case is all over the news.

And they wouldn't have flown all the way to LA if they weren't interviewing somebody famous."

Jill and Vincent were saved from having to evade her question by the server who came to take their dinner order. Truth be told, they sometimes fudged the rules when they were within the Moretti circle of trust. Vincent's father all but demanded to be kept apprised of updates, as though he were still the police commissioner. And Luc and Anth were part of the force, which meant they were privy to more information than most.

And Jill was pretty sure that had it not been for the presence of Mandy, they'd probably be filling Marc in. He wasn't NYPD, but he was a cop. They could trust him.

But every instinct told Jill that they absolutely, in *no* way, could trust Mandy Breslin to keep her glossy mouth shut.

Not that there was anything to report.

She and Vincent had spent the entire day going from gorgeous mansion to gorgeous mansion. She'd been offered more iced tea and flavored cucumber water than she could stand.

Every meeting had been a virtual repeat of yesterday's meeting with James Killroy.

Yes, I was in New York the night Lenora Birch was killed. No, I didn't see her. No, didn't want to see her. No, why would I?

It was sad, almost. As famous as Lenora Birch had been, she seemed to have virtually no friends. No enemies either.

The woman seemed to inspire virtually no emotion in the people around her, which was as strange as it was frustrating.

Vin touched her arm and she glanced up, startled to

realize that it was her turn to order and she'd completely zoned out.

"Oh, sorry!" She glanced down at the menu, completely forgetting what she'd planned to order.

The restaurant was one of the New American–cuisine dining places, which offered everything from fancy house-made pasta, to elaborate salads, to squab—whatever that was.

"I'll try the butternut squash lasagna," she said. "And another glass of wine."

Mandy was staring at Jill in wonder as the server took their menus. "Oh my gosh, I love that about you!"

"What?" Jill asked.

"You didn't even flinch when ordering carbs!"

"She's a homicide detective," Vincent said irritably. "If she doesn't flinch at the sight of a decapitated drug dealer, I don't think pasta's going to do her in."

"Vin," Marc said mildly.

"What?"

Jill patted Vin's arm. "I'm guessing maybe it's the decapitation talk your brother's objecting to."

He shrugged, and Marco quickly steered the conversation toward safer topics. The family. The latest movies. Mandy and Marc's renovation project.

Even with Mandy's slightly inane contributions to the conversation, it was, in some ways, the perfect evening.

The weather was ideal—they'd opted to sit on the heated patio, and there was just the slightest breeze coming off the water. The wine was amazing. The food some of the best she'd ever had.

But mostly, she was happy because *Vincent* was happy and relaxed.

She knew that he was probably frustrated about their lack of progress in the case, as she was, but for once, he seemed to be able to put it aside. To enjoy himself.

His posture was easy, his smiles more frequent than usual.

As though sensing her thoughts on him, he glanced at her as Mandy lectured Marc on the differences in tile they'd been selecting for their bathroom remodel and lifted his eyebrows.

"Okay?" he asked quietly.

She smiled. "Yeah."

"Then you won't mind if I do this..."

He reached over and helped himself to a generous portion of her lasagna. Jill watched as he chewed, then glared at her plate. "That is *not* lasagna."

She patted his arm. "Don't worry. I won't tell your mother that you liked it."

"In that case..."

He took another bite, which Jill then countered by taking a bite of his braised short ribs, which was decadent and meaty and absolutely amazing.

"Oh my God," she muttered, taking another bite, this time washing it down with a sip of his red wine, which as the server had promised was the perfect match for the heavenly dish.

She caught him watching her and she gave a sheepish smile as she took another sip of his wine. "Sorry, not sorry?"

His smile was slow and warm, which in turn made her warm, which made her realize...

She hadn't thought about Tom. Not once, all day.

Jill had been perfectly, utterly unaware of her former fiancé.

Vincent purposefully held her gaze—as though knowing exactly what she was thinking and daring her to look away.

His smile had faded, but the warmth in his eyes hadn't. If anything, his gaze heated, and then it dropped to her mouth.

Before Jill realized what was happening, Vincent's hand lifted, and with his napkin he wiped gently just below her lip.

She reared back and he gave a rueful smile. "Red wine."

Jill licked at the spot he'd just touched—regretting that it had been with his napkin instead of his finger.

Her eyes closed in dismay at the realization.

Because she knew then.

She wanted Vincent Moretti.

She'd *always* wanted him.

She sucked in a shuddering breath and looked away from him, staring down at her plate.

Jill started to take another bite of her lasagna, only to realize her appetite had fled, and worse...her hand was shaking.

She dropped her hands to her lap, and because she couldn't look at Vin, she lifted her attention to Marc and Mandy, whose argument had finally subsided.

Marc was watching her, his expression both thoughtful and sympathetic, as though he knew exactly what she was thinking.

And Jill resisted the urge to howl, because this Moretti—the one who knew her least—seemed to realize in moments what Jill had taken years to acknowledge.

That Vincent Moretti was more than her partner.

So much more.

What Vincent was to her, she didn't know how to name. Or wasn't ready to.

But it didn't change the fact that she'd been out of a relationship for all of a week.

No. Out of an *engagement*.

She shouldn't be having these feelings, much less acting on them.

Jill barely remembered the rest of the meal. She remembered ordering dessert, although that had been more to provoke the *small salad, no dressing* Mandy than it had been about actual hunger.

And she only managed a tiny portion. Her stomach was too wound up in knots to manage more than a couple bites of the amazing bananas foster.

Outside the restaurant, Jill hugged Mandy good-bye with a promise to check out some sitcom where Mandy had six lines as a "prominent guest star."

Marco gave Jill a warm hug and kissed her cheek, lingering just long enough to whisper, "You're good for him."

She pulled back and gave him a long look.

Both of them knew who "him" was, and Jill wasn't at all sure she and Vincent were good together. They couldn't even seem to have a straight conversation unless it dealt with a grisly murder.

Vincent had refused to do valet, which meant that the walk back to their car was long . . . and quiet.

Unfortunately for Jill, she hadn't bothered to check the nighttime temperatures in LA when she'd been packing, and she was learning firsthand that California in late winter wasn't quite as warm during the evening hours as her short-sleeve shirt would have wished for.

"Cold?" he asked.

"Yes."

"Want my jacket?" he asked.

She glanced at him, surprised. In all the years they'd been working together, he'd never offered her his jacket. Held doors for her, put furniture together, even patiently held up artwork for her in her apartment so she could find the precise place to hang it...

But he'd never offered the jacket.

Granted, she usually had her own jacket.

But still, the offer felt personal somehow. And because of that...

"No, I'm okay," she said.

She felt his eyes on her profile.

He stopped and she stopped with him, holding up a hand as he started to shrug out of his jacket.

"No, really, it's okay—"

He moved closer, pulling his coat around her shoulders, and Jill's objection scattered because the coat was warm and heavy and familiar.

She glanced up at him, but he refused to look at her, already walking away, his pace faster than before.

"If you're going to be grumpy about it, I don't want it!" she said, scampering after him.

He didn't bother to look back.

She kept it on, even on the car ride back to their hotel, studying the well-worn sleeves. "Where'd you get this, anyway?" she asked. "You've had it as long as I've known you."

"It was a gift."

She rolled her eyes. "Okay. I get it. The talkative mood is gone."

It wasn't until they pulled into the parking lot of their hotel that he spoke again. "My dad bought it for me. A graduation gift from college."

She glanced at him. Vincent *never* talked about college. All of the Morettis had gone—a degree wasn't necessary to join the NYPD, but Maria Moretti had insisted that all her children attend. She'd told Jill once that she wanted them to know that being a cop was a choice, not a family obligation.

The Moretti matriarch had wanted her babies to have options.

And then one by one, her sons had attended college. Graduated. And then promptly entered the police academy.

"Penn State?" she asked, searching her memory for Vin's alma mater.

He nodded. "My family came down the weekend of graduation. My mother started squeaking about how I didn't have anything appropriate to wear under the stupid cap and gown. My dad took me shopping with strict instructions from Mom to get a respectable suit. I saw this jacket and just…wanted it. It was badass, and *man* did I want to be badass."

Jill smiled at the boyish admission.

"Your dad got it for you?"

"Not right away." Vincent pulled into the parking spot. "It was ridiculously expensive. There was no way I was about to ask him for it, and I had exactly zero money of my own."

He stopped the car, but neither moved. "I didn't even realize he saw me looking at it until later that night when my parents gave me my graduation gift."

Jill smiled at the sweetness of the memory. Tony Moretti was a gruff, but caring, man—much like Vincent. She was betting the moment was all the sweeter from the awkwardness of it.

"Well I appreciate you lending me such a beloved item," she said as they walked into the lobby.

"Don't be weird about it," he muttered.

Jill smiled.

Yup. Gruff and caring all right.

The elevator ride up to their floor was quiet.

Vin paused outside his room, and Jill shrugged off the coat. She didn't look up at him as she handed it back.

But then his fingers touched hers as he accepted it, and her eyes flicked up of their own volition.

It was a mistake.

Because whatever was written on his face made her want to lean into him—to toss that coat, beloved or not, to the side and wrap herself around...

She took a step back and swallowed.

Tom's warning went through her head.

He wants what he can't have.

She took another step back.

"Well, 'night."

"'Night," he said, his voice a little rough.

She nodded once, and started to move toward her own room next door when he caught her arm.

Jill froze, even as common sense made its first appearance of the evening and told her *for the love of God, walk away.*

"Jill."

She bit her lip. She didn't say anything. Couldn't. She only stared at his face, both begging him to let her go and begging him to say—whatever it was he needed to say.

His hand lifted slowly. His thumb brushed her cheek, just for the briefest of moments before this thumb and forefinger closed around a strand of hair that had escaped her ponytail.

"I wish—" He cleared his throat. "I wish…"

Not yet, Vin. First I have to tell you I'm not engaged. I need you to know…

"Wait," she whispered. "I don't—"

His eyes seemed to shutter close, blocking all emotion, but not before she saw a flash of pain cross his face that felt like a vice around her heart.

But before Jill could correct him—before she could add the crucial words "not yet" to her rejection, he'd released her hair.

He turned toward his door, opening it and stepping inside before she'd had a chance to gather her thoughts.

"Vin—"

The door closed in her face.

CHAPTER TWENTY-EIGHT

Vincent supposed he should have addressed it the morning after, but he hadn't known how.

How does one apologize for making a sort-of move on an engaged woman?

Vincent wasn't good at apologies. Wasn't good at emotion.

Hell, he wasn't good at talking.

So he'd taken the coward's way out. And said nothing.

Neither had she.

They hadn't sat together on the plane ride from LA back to New York.

Vincent had let Jill think that the airlines had just messed up, but in reality, he'd slipped away to call customer service the moment he'd seen the rock on her finger, still firmly in place, and the sinking feeling in his stomach had been almost unbearable.

Whatever he'd thought had been between them in that moment had either been one-sided, or hadn't been enough for her to end things with the Pretty Boy.

Jill was still getting married, and he was still...

Lonely.

The thought of sitting beside her for six hours...

Somehow the thought of holding her hand was a hell of a lot more painful than not holding it.

He'd paid for it with every bump of the incredibly turbulent flight home, but he told himself he'd earned it.

It was no less than a man lusting after another man's fiancée deserved.

It was now three days after they returned from their LA trip, and Vincent was beginning to think that he'd imagined that entire disastrous scenario outside his hotel room that night.

They were speaking—the silent treatment wasn't really an option given their working relationship.

But the easy camaraderie was once again gone, as was the sexual tension.

Vincent leaned back in his standard-issue desk chair as he watched her talk on the phone at the desk across from his.

She'd been on and off the phone all day, although most of the calls had been from her cell phone, and she'd slipped outside to make them.

Wedding stuff, he'd guess.

He tried really hard not to care. Really he did.

But this particular phone call was from her desk phone and definitely related to the Lenora Birch case.

A case that was all too close to being labeled a cold case.

It would be the first of Vincent's career and thankfully, it gave him something to think about other than her.

It wasn't just that it was a blow to his ego. Or to his perfect record.

It was that someone was getting away with *murder*. And he didn't have the faintest idea who.

"Yes, thank you, Ms. Lee. If you could send over everything you have, that'd be so appreciated. No, copies are fine. Thank you, we really appreciate it…yes. Yes, I was a fan of hers too. So sad…yes, we're doing everything we can…"

Jill finally hung up the phone and Vincent leaned forward. "Who was that?"

Jill plunged her fingers into her hair before tugging the blond strands outward slightly in frustration.

She looked as exhausted as he looked. "Janice Lee from the library. I've asked her to pull every newspaper article she has on Lenora Birch and send it over."

"You think there's something we haven't seen?"

She lifted her shoulders. "We've checked LA papers and New York papers, but smaller presses…I dunno, there could be something."

He blew out a breath. "Papers from what time frame?"

"*All* time frames."

"That could take forever."

"I know it could take forever, Vin. Do you have any better ideas?"

He studied her for a moment. "Let's take a walk."

"I don't want to take a walk."

He smiled at that because her voice was snippy, and very un-Jill-like. "I'll buy."

"You only ever want to buy the cheap stuff."

He was already on his feet, moving behind her chair and then lifting it so he all but dumped her out of it. "C'mon. Starbucks. You can get one of your sugary-with-sprinkles sugar fests."

Jill grabbed her jacket and followed him outside, although judging from the dark circles under her eyes and her shorter-than-usual temper, her cooperation had more to do with her need for caffeine than it did interest in spending time with him.

Jill chattered the entire way to the coffee shop.

About the case.

About her new shoes giving her blisters.

About how it was maybe going to rain and how she should have brought a different jacket and why wasn't it spring already?

Then she chattered as they stood in line at the coffee shop.

About the terrible movie she'd seen last night with the totally ambiguous ending because what's even the point if they don't tell you what happens?

And about how her hair stylist had to reschedule.

She chattered all the way home.

Did he think they should go see Holly Adams again?

Did he think it was true that they were finally getting a new car?

And finally, when they were just a few steps away from the precinct and he'd said little more than his coffee order and *mm hmm*, Vin couldn't take it anymore.

He stopped. Touched her arm.

"Jill."

She glanced up at him, her smile as wide as ever, but her eyes were nervous and that broke his heart. They couldn't go on like this.

"Can we talk?" he asked.

Her smile, incredibly, went wider. Even more false. "*You're* asking to talk?"

Her laugh was even more brittle than the smile, and Vin said a silent prayer that they'd be able to repair whatever it was that he'd broken.

He merely stood, fiddling with the white plastic lid of his coffee, feeling unbearable as hell as he waited for his partner to decide whether or not to hear him out.

"Okay," she finally said on a long breath, as though she'd managed to talk herself into a completely wretched task.

Vincent should have felt relief, but mostly he felt a sudden stab of panic when he realized for all his desperation to fix things between them, he didn't know how.

Silently they walked to a small park a block away from the precinct. It wasn't one of the city's better. It smelled mostly like dog piss and pot, and this potent mixture of odors ensured that they had relative privacy as they sat on a chipped, wobbly bench.

For several seconds they said nothing. Jill sat perfectly straight, her small hands cupping her enormous coffee, not moving.

Vin blew out a long breath, leaning forward and resting his forearms on his knees before deciding to get it over with.

"You and Tom," he said, his eyes locked on a discarded cigarette butt in the dirt at his feet. "You're okay?"

"We're . . . on good terms," Jill replied.

"That's good," he said woodenly. His thumbnail flicked at the plastic lid.

"Vin—"

"I owe you an apology," he said, interrupting. "I don't know what the hell I was thinking that night in the hotel, but it was out of line."

Her shoulders hunched. "You seemed like you wanted to say something that night—something important."

Vin said nothing. Stared straight ahead as a pair of pigeons hacked their way through a discarded hot dog bun.

"Actually," Jill said softly, "it seems like there's been a *lot* of times lately that you've wanted to say something. I feel like we keep going in circles of unfinished conversation."

He nodded, still not looking away from the fucking pigeons.

"So let's finish it," she said quietly.

Jill leaned forward then so they were shoulder-to-shoulder, although she too stared straight ahead at the birds.

It was as though it was too much for them to talk meaningfully and make eye contact.

He swore softly and dipped his head.

What was he supposed to say?

Don't marry Tom?

Give me a chance?

Give us *a chance?*

What did he want from her?

Did he really expect her to call off her wedding on the off chance that there could be something more between them?

What kind of first-rate asshole was he, to ask her to postpone a for-sure thing (Tom) for an unstable, noncommittal flight risk (him)?

He'd had *years* to ask her out. Why now? Why wait until she was no longer available?

It was a question she'd ask—one she *should* ask.

And one he didn't have an answer for. All he knew was that he died a little inside every time he thought about her leaving him.

But he'd be damned if he chose his happiness over her own.

It had to stop.

"I've been an ass, Henley," he said, giving her a brief glance.

"Well—I'm used to that."

He smiled grimly as he realized what he had to do.

He had to lie.

Vin swallowed, forced himself to turn and look at her. The lie would be all the more convincing if he could pull it off while making eye contact. He waited until she'd shifted, matching his position so they were face-to-face.

She took a sip of her coffee, and waited. Her eyes round and blue and...completely unreadable. Since when had she become a mystery to him?

Since she came home with a ring on her finger. That's when.

"You know that old cliché—wanting what you can't have?" he asked gruffly.

She blinked. "Sure?"

"Well," he said. "That."

Jill blinked again. "Usually I'm pretty good at deciphering the words you're not saying, but I need a bit more."

Fine. She wanted it all laid out there? Fast and furious? *Fine.*

"The thought of you marrying another man has been

making me crazy," Vincent said, the words terrifying, because this much, at least, was true.

Her breath caught a little. "Why?"

Good Christ, how did regular men do this? Lay it all out there?

"Because I thought—I guess it never really occurred to me that you...that..."

"That someone else would find me attractive? Want to marry me?" Her voice was quiet, not as caustic as it could have been. But she was on edge, definitely.

"No," he said. "I mean—*fuck*. I just thought—it never occurred to me that I might lose you."

"You won't—"

He held up a hand. "I need to finish. And I thought that somehow if I could get you not to marry the other guy, that things could keep going on as they were. And I thought the way to get you not to marry Tom was to convince you that we could maybe be...something."

They stared at each other in mute silence for an uncomfortably long time, until he finally cleared his throat. "You can say something now."

There was a little whisper of a smile around her lips, although not a happy one. "Okay." She sucked in a long breath. "Okay, I'll just ask. Have you been messing with my emotions the past several months because you want me? Or because you don't want Tom to have me?"

He cleared his throat and glanced at his coffee. "I want you to be happy."

"That's not an answer, Vin. No more evasions. Do you have feelings for me—beyond partner, beyond friend? Yes or no."

Vincent felt both incredibly hot and unbearably cold at

the same time. As though his body was physically incapable of telling the lie he needed to tell.

But her answer left him no wiggle room—no space for half truths.

He lifted his head and told the biggest lie of his life.

"No."

CHAPTER TWENTY-NINE

There wasn't enough ice cream in the world.

Not enough wine.

Not enough terrible, mindless television.

Jill had tried it all, but nothing helped.

She hurt.

That one word from Vincent—that succinct, no bullshit *no*—had hurt a million times worse than walking away from Tom.

Which told Jill more about her own heart than she could bring herself to admit.

It will get better, she told herself for the millionth time as she stared blindly into the fridge. *It's only been three days. The sting will fade, and it will be like all of this never happened.*

Her phone buzzed, and Jill closed the fridge. Nothing in there but pudding and a fast-wilting bag of mixed greens for that salad that she kept meaning to eat but never wanted.

The text was from Elena. Missed you at brunch. Want to grab a movie?

Jill grunted. Sunday brunch with the Morettis. Damn right she'd skipped it. Sitting across from Vincent while he shoveled in biscuits and sausage, completely oblivious to her pain?

Pass.

Not in a movie mood, she texted Elena back. Sorry to miss everyone at brunch!

Texting was amazing. Lies were so easily disguised with an exclamation point.

Everything okay?

Or not.

Yeah, why?

Elena texted back. You're being weird. Vin's being weird. You guys get in a fight?

Jill swallowed. You'd have to care about the other person enough to fight. Something Vin wouldn't know shit about.

Just tension on the case—still no break, Jill replied.

Hmm. K. We could go wedding dress shopping? A girl from work told me about a brand-new boutique. Up and coming designers, unique, not crazy expensive.

"God." Jill dropped the phone beside her on the couch, leaning back and digging the heels of her hands into her eyes.

She needed to tell Elena about the wedding. Needed to tell everyone about the wedding.

Correction: the *lack* of wedding.

She glanced down at the ring on her finger that seemed

to get heavier every day. Last night she'd dreamed that the band had grown smaller and smaller until it had cut off all circulation and she'd had to have her finger amputated—by a clown.

Jill hated clowns (who didn't, really?).

It was so time to get rid of this ring.

But first—the announcement.

Jill stared for a long time at her phone, then picked it up. No time like the present.

And who better to start with than one's mother?

Especially since her mom, while certainly excited on Jill's behalf, had been only marginally interested in the wedding planning. Jill's parents had been married on a beach in Malibu with only their best friends present, and she must have asked Jill a million times if she was "sure she wanted all the fuss."

Oh, to have listened to her mother.

A knock at the door interrupted Jill's resolve to spice up everybody's Sunday with a bomb of an announcement.

She rolled off the couch.

It was probably Elena. Jill knew it was only a matter of time before her best friend realized something major was going on and demanded that Jill spill all of the gory details.

At least it had better be Elena.

The alternative was Vin, and she was so not ready to see him. She'd had a hard enough time faking that everything was fine at work. Without the protective barrier of homicide discussions . . . she couldn't. Just couldn't.

It wasn't Elena.

Nor was it Vincent.

"Maria!"

Reflectively, Jill ran a hand over her pajamas, wishing that she'd have put on real clothes. Or, you know... showered.

Vincent's mother smiled kindly, looking as put together as ever in her usual Sunday attire. A green dress today that perfectly suited her complexion, making her look forty-something instead of the sixty-something Jill knew she was.

"May I come in?"

"Of course!"

Jill followed Maria into the kitchen, doing a quick scan to make sure it didn't scream *single-woman*. Other than the open bag of potato chips on the coffee table, it could be worse.

"May I get you coffee? Tea?"

Maria smiled. "You have tea?"

"Ah—" Jill mentally scanned her cupboard inventory. "Yeah, that's a no."

"Just a glass of water would be fine. That food at the diner is so salty, but I find I love it anyway."

"So brunch was good?" Jill asked, pouring them both a glass of water from the Brita filter in the fridge.

"It was... fine," Maria said. "We missed you."

Jill said nothing to this. In all honesty, Jill only joined the family at brunch once a month or so.

Partially because she didn't want to overstep the delicate line between family and non-family, and partially because she was afraid if she went more than that, it would hurt all the more that she *wasn't* family.

"So, how are—"

"Jill." Maria's voice was kind, but firm. The same voice Jill had heard Maria turn on her own children a million times in the past, but being on the receiving end was a whole other ball game.

"Yeah?" Her voice was too high. Squeaky.

Vincent's mother moved to the kitchen table, sitting down as she placed her water glass in front of her. Then she tapped the finger gently with one finger. "Sit."

Jill sat.

"Tell me."

It was a command, but a gentle one.

Jill didn't have to ask what Maria meant—instinctively she knew that the older woman meant tell her everything.

And incredibly . . . she wanted to.

Jill pushed her glass aside, folded her hands, and placed them gently on the table in front of her. "I'm not marrying Tom."

Maria merely nodded. *Go on.*

"We called it off before the California trip. It was mutual—I mean truly mutual, not just one-of-us-is-trying-to-save-face mutual."

Jill's thumb rubbed against the underside of the ring. Tight. So uncomfortably tight. But not for much longer.

She told Maria about how things had been weird with her and Vincent, but not in a way she could describe. She told her about the half conversations, and the bickering that felt more personal than usual.

She told her about that moment in the hall when Vincent had touched her cheek.

Maria watched Jill carefully, but Jill watched Maria just as carefully.

If anyone knew what was going on—really going on—with Vincent, it would be his mother.

But the Moretti matriarch had a wicked good poker face.

And then Jill got to the part about the park bench the other day.

"I asked him straight out if he wanted me," Jill said, looking at her thumbs. "I was tired of all the weird dancing around each other. I just wanted it out there."

She squeezed her eyes shut. "But now I wish it wasn't out there."

"Nonsense."

She opened her eyes and looked at Maria. "Nonsense?"

"It was good of you to put an end to the games," she said, reaching across the table. "You two have been playing them for far, far too long."

"Only a few weeks," Jill grumbled.

Maria laughed softly. "My dear. Don't start lying to yourself now."

Jill's lips rolled inward in denial of what Maria was getting at. This thing with her and Vin—it was new.

Wasn't it?

Deep down, Jill suspected she knew better. Knew that whatever was between her and Vin had always been, well...*more*.

But that didn't mean she knew how to define it.

And she certainly didn't know what to do about it.

"I worry about all my children," Maria said, somewhat absently. "Luc and his secret ghosts. Anthony and his pressure to be everything to everyone. Elena—I worry that she's spent so much time toughening her outer layers that her inner layers are unreachable. Marc, I worry that he's too good—too trusting of people—and that he'll get burned. But Vincent...I worry about Vincent most of all."

Jill looked up in surprise. "Why? He's so—"

She broke off, unsure of the word that she was looking for. Self-sufficient? Independent?

"He knows how to take care of himself," Jill finished. "He doesn't need anyone."

Maria's smile was a little sad. "I believe that's what he wants everyone to think. Perhaps even believes it himself."

Jill was skeptical. "With all due respect...I've been chipping away at Vincent's crusty layers for years, trying to figure out if there was some traumatic incident that made him so—"

"Guarded?" Maria replied.

"Ah, sure, we'll go with that," Jill said. "But as far as I can find, there are no deaths in his past, no schoolyard bullying, no dramatic heartbreak, no secret lack of confidence born of feeling inadequate in a family of champions. Nothing that would explain why he's so closed off."

Maria traced a finger up and down her water glass, but she said nothing.

Don't pry. Do not pry, Jill. He'll never forgive you if you ask his mother—

"Is there something?" Jill heard herself ask Maria. "Something that happened to make him...*guarded*?"

Jill went with Maria's word choice, since her default of *antisocial jerk* wasn't quite how every mother hoped to hear her son described.

"I don't know," Maria said finally. "I don't think so. I suppose it's always possible that he'd be keeping some hidden hurt from all of us, but I think maybe it's subtler than that. No one event that we can put a Band-Aid on."

"So there's nothing," Jill said, shoulders slumping. "No way to fix it? Not that he needs fixing, it's just—"

Maria sighed and stood, picking up her water glass and taking it to the counter. She turned around and crossed her arms, looking strangely hesitant, as though she wanted to say something but wasn't sure she should.

"Maria," Jill said quietly. "Please—I care about him."

The older woman's face softened considerably. "I know you do, sweetie. It's why I'm here. To ask if you were sure—really sure—about this Tom fellow. But I see you got that sorted out on your own, so the last thing I'll say..."

She took a deep breath. "Vincent was shy as a child. Not horribly so. Not enough to be picked on, but his quietness could be off-putting, I think. He's always been an observer. The boy that watched before joining in. But you know how children are..."

"They move fast," Jill said with a smile.

"They certainly do. They misconstrued his hesitancy for lack of interest and stopped trying to include him. He was left out of things more than my others. It became more noticeable in high school. Eventually I suspect it became a vicious cycle. He would be quiet because he was excluded—he was excluded because he was quiet."

Jill's throat hurt at the picture Maria was painting. Vincent had always been an outsider, but Jill'd always figured it was because he wanted to be. The thought that she could have been wrong—that he was guarded because he'd never learned to be different...

"I guess what I'm saying," Maria said, sounding tired, "is that I don't know that Vincent knows how to accept love—or even affection. But what really breaks my heart—I don't know that it's ever been offered. I don't know that anyone's ever tried to love him."

Jill ignored the tear in her heart at that last sentence. "But...he's had girlfriends..."

Maria waved this away. "I know my son. If he felt strongly about any of them, he'd have brought her home to meet me. Meet the family."

"Wait, you've never met a single one of his women?"

Maria's smile was gentle. "That's what I'm trying to tell you."

Jill shook her head, confused.

"You, Jill. You're the only one he's ever brought home."

Jill's first instinct was denial. "Yeah, but not as a girl-friend. As a partner."

Maria's eyebrow went up. "All of my sons have had partners at some point in their career. How many of them do you see as part of the family like you?"

Jill warmed a little at the mention of being part of the family, even as panic settled a little as what Maria was saying was starting to set in.

She was still trying to process it as Maria washed and dried her water glass and then put it away as though she owned the place.

Vincent's mother then gave a self-satisfied nod as if to say, "my work here is done," and then headed toward the front door.

Jill scampered after her. "Wait—Maria. If what you're saying...if he does think of me as more than a partner. Why did he say otherwise when I asked him?"

Maria took a step closer, placed her warm wrinkled hands on Jill's cheeks. "Sweetie, if you'd spent your entire life silently wanting—desperately wanting—someone to love you, and never having that gift even offered—would you know how to *give* it?"

Jill closed her eyes. "What am I supposed to do?"

Maria patted her cheek softly. "I think, if you want him...I think you'll have to be the brave one."

CHAPTER THIRTY

As it turned out, Jill's chance to be brave came around that very evening.

After Maria left, Jill had sat on the couch for a good forty minutes replaying the entire conversation in her head, trying to figure out what Maria Moretti expected her to do.

Trying to figure out if she even *wanted* to do it.

In the end, she'd binge-watched old episodes of *CSI* before taking a long-overdue, scalding-hot shower.

She'd barely wrapped herself in her warm fuzzy robe when a knock sounded at the door.

Jill ignored it.

It wasn't like her to be antisocial, but one unexpected guest was about all she could handle for the day.

Honestly, didn't people call anymore? What if she was at the grocery store? Or a movie. Or having sex. As far as everyone in her life knew she was engaged, for God's sake.

The knocks grew louder as she towel-dried her hair.

She was about to flick on the hair dryer when she heard his voice.

"I swear to God, Henley, if you don't open this damn door I'm armed and I will—"

Vincent.

Of anyone standing on her front porch he was perhaps the one she was the least ready to see.

And also the only one she'd open the door for.

It was a decision she regretted the second she saw his face.

She'd seen Vincent angry, oh, about a million times. The man had a short fuse, and it burned hot and fast and often.

But she wasn't quite sure she'd ever seen him like this.

"Hey," she said as he brushed past her into the house. "What's going on?"

"What's going on?" he mimicked.

He spun around in her direction just as she started to follow him into the kitchen. The abrupt change brought them face-to-face before he thrust out his right hand in front of her.

His knuckles were bleeding.

Instinctively she reached for his hand, about to insist that they put something on it, but he jerked back and put several feet behind him.

"What happened?" she asked.

He continued to stare at her. "You're a fucking cop. You're supposed to *deduce*. What do you *think* happened?"

Okay so he was mad *and* cranky.

"You got in a fight," she said patiently.

"I did."

"With Anth?" she guessed. The two of them were constantly going at it, although rarely with fists.

"Nope."

"Luc?"

"Let me tell you about my night," he said, his voice deceptively calm now. "See, I went over to Anth and Maggie's for dinner. Had a nice time, got to look at the latest sonogram, all of that—"

He turned and stalked into the kitchen, continuing his story as he did so. "Got a craving for whiskey. All that talk about nurseries and baby names will do that to a single man. So on the way home, I stopped by a bar. One of the fancy hotel bars off Broadway where you can be anonymous, you know?" he asked, pulling an open wine bottle off her counter and tugging off the cork.

"Okay..." she said, urging him on.

He poured himself a liberal glass. Didn't offer her one.

"Except I *wasn't* anonymous, Henley. Saw someone I knew. Any guesses?"

Jill went through her mental catalog of people Vin might have run into that would result in a fight. The list was...long. Past suspects, past witnesses, other cops. Whatever his tragic reasons, the man wasn't exactly in the business of making friends.

She shook her head. "Tell me."

"Tom," he said, a wide, horrible smile on his face.

Jill's stomach dropped.

"Yup, that's right," he said, lifting his glass to her. "But wait, that's not all. I saw Tom...and another woman. A blonde that was not you. And he was far, far more friendly than an engaged man has any right to be with another woman."

Jill closed her eyes and tensed as he moved closer.

"But then Tom's not engaged now, is he, Jill?" His voice was soft. Dangerous.

She shook her head mutely.

"Sure would have been nice to know that before *I punched the guy for cheating on you*."

Jill let out a little whimper of dismay that was entirely self-directed.

How could she have been so selfish?

So stupid?

"Jill."

She didn't move.

"Goddamn it, Jill, look at me."

She did, only to suck in a breath when she saw how close he was. Too close.

"When?" he growled.

"When what?"

His fingers wrapped around her shoulders, digging in just slightly. "Don't play dumb. When did you and Tom end your engagement?"

Jill swallowed.

He kept their gazes fused, and had there only been anger there, she might have stepped away. Might have suggested they have this conversation when he'd calmed down.

But there was something beyond the anger. Something far more dangerous to both of them. Hope.

"When?" His voice was hoarser now.

"A week before LA. The day after the dinner party at my house."

Something unreadable flashed across his face—something that looked almost like guilt, but that didn't make sense.

Then his head tipped back as he sucked in a long breath, and she couldn't tell if it was the answer he'd wanted, or the answer he'd feared.

"Why?" he asked. "Why'd you guys break it off?"

"You know why," she said quietly, silently begging him not to make her say this. Not after he'd told her he didn't want her just a few short days ago.

He shook her a little. "Tell me why, Goddamn it. Why aren't you marrying him?"

His eyes were frantic now. Desperate. And maybe a little scared.

Maria's words from earlier came rushing over Jill. *I don't know that anyone's ever tried to love him.*

And then she remembered Vincent's mother's parting words.

If you want him... you'll have to be the brave one.

And Jill knew in that instant, that she *did* want him. She wanted Vincent Moretti desperately, consequences be damned.

And so Jill did the bravest thing she could think of.

She went on her toes.

And kissed him.

CHAPTER THIRTY-ONE

Jill's lips touched his, and Vincent went still with shock.

They'd kissed before. Meaningless pecks, quick kisses of triumph over a break in a case. That one time he'd pretended to be her boyfriend to ward off a creepy ex.

But those had been casual kisses. Friendly kisses.

But this?

The way her lips trembled under his, the way her fingers gripped the lapel of his jacket, holding him close...

It didn't feel casual.

And it sure as hell felt a lot more than friendly.

The question was...

What did Vin do about it?

Did he hold on to his anger? Because Vincent was angry. Almost unbearably so.

Or did he...

In the end, there was no question.

Not really.

It was *Jill*.

Slowly, his hands lifted until they found her waist. He didn't return the kiss. Not just yet. His palms molded to her sides, learning the shape of her before sliding back until his fingers met at the middle of her back, allowing his fingertips to trace her spine.

And then Jill bit his lip.

A fierce, sweet little nip of her teeth against his bottom lip that shattered the last of Vincent's self-control.

Vin's hands flattened against her, one arm sliding around her hips to jerk her forward. No more space separating them.

His other hand slid up. His fingers tangled in her blond hair.

Vincent pulled back just slightly as he tilted her face up, relishing her gasp of shock, her look of pleasure . . .

And then he closed his mouth over hers and took.

Jill's kiss had been gentle. Tentative. Vincent's was not. His mouth slammed down on hers with all the want—the unidentified longing of the past six years. His tongue swiped against her bottom lip. She opened, and when their tongues met—tangled—they both moaned.

Jill squirmed, but he tightened his grip, keeping her hips anchored against his.

Truth be told, he'd never really understood the appeal of kissing before now. It was nice, certainly, but merely the precursor to bigger and better things.

But kissing Jill—kissing Jill felt like the main event. Not that he *wanted* it to be the main event—he wanted other things, definitely.

Wanted to peel off her robe, wanted to hear what kind

of sounds she made when he touched her. Wanted to know if she liked it gentle or rough, playful or intense.

But for right now—right now, it was enough to feel her tongue against his, taste her lips, to feel the way their breath mingled together as they fought for the same air.

Jill's fingers released their grip on his jacket, only to wiggle underneath as she tried to pull it off. She let out a little sound of frustration when it got caught on his shoulders, and he smiled at the realization that her urgency matched his.

He released her, pulling back just enough to yank the jacket off, their mouths never losing contact as he tossed it blindly aside.

Vin felt Jill's fingers go for the sash of her robe, but his fingers manacled her wrists, winding them around behind her as he walked her backward into the wall.

"Not yet," he whispered against her mouth.

He wanted to see her. All of her. But he'd waited a fucking long time for this. No way was she going to rush him through it.

She tugged at her wrists, but he held firm as he deepened the kiss until they were both breathless and writhing.

Jill's wrists were small enough for him to hold with one hand as the other slid up her side, his palm just barely skimming the outer curve of her breast before very lightly wrapping around the base of her neck as he pulled his mouth back from hers.

"Tell me you want this," he said roughly.

She let out a little laugh, her eyes cloudy. "Isn't it obvious?"

His fingertips pressed against her lightly and he saw her eyes flare with passion. Interesting.

"Don't play games with me, Henley."

In response she went on her toes and licked his bottom lip. Vincent growled, stamping a hard kiss over her mouth before pulling back once more.

"Tell me. Tell me you're done with him. Tell me you're not marrying someone else."

It came out as a gruff command, and he was grateful for the raspy quality of his voice. Kept him from what he really felt like doing...

Begging.

He wanted to beg Jill to be his and only his.

His tongue trailed down the soft, smooth column of her neck as she tilted back with a soft sigh.

"Tell me," he said again, his lips moving back up her neck and coming to rest at a sensitive spot under her ear. "Tell me you're mine."

It was more, perhaps, than he should have revealed, and for a heart-lurching moment of silence he thought he'd pushed it too far—pushed her too hard.

She pulled her face away from his, and Vin swallowed his disappointment, his fingers slowly releasing her wrists as he started to step back.

Jill pulled him back.

Her fingers came to his waist, fisting in the fabric of his T-shirt, waiting until he met her eyes.

And then she smiled. "I'm yours."

Vincent's breath came out on a rush as his mouth slammed down on hers once more, lifting her off her feet and slamming her backward once more toward the wall.

Jill met his urgency gasp for gasp, her strong legs wrapping around his waist as her arms locked behind his head, fusing their mouths.

He greedily explored her legs, fully exposed now by the robe that had hiked its way up around her hips.

His hands moved over her calves, fingertips brushing against the soft skin behind her knee as she made small begging noises.

His palms ran along the back of her thighs until he cupped her ass in his hands, angling her body so that the fly of his jeans rubbed against her in just the right way to make her moan.

"Please," she whispered against his mouth as she wiggled.

It was all the invitation he needed.

He pulled her against him more fully, her small frame making it easy for him to walk them both those few crucial steps to her bedroom.

Her bedroom was a fussy, feminine affair. Lots of purple and white and flowers.

Vincent barely noticed as he dropped her none too gently on the bed and then crawled over her, caging her with his body as he stared down at her.

Her chest rose and fell rapidly. The sash of her robe was nearly all the way undone now, her breast inches from exposure. He'd only have to hook one finger beneath the fabric to reveal the soft skin...

Vincent lifted one hand. But instead of drifting down, his hand went up to where her hair was fanned out on the bedspread. He rubbed the blond strands between his fingertips. It felt like silk.

Her eyes drifted closed, and before he realized what he was doing, he'd leaned down and gently, reverently kissed both her closed eyelids before trailing along her high cheekbones, down over her pointy little chin, before brushing against her lips.

"Vincent."

It was a sigh—his name was a sigh on her lips, and that's all it took. That one simple sound, and he was lost.

His hand slid down her neck, his fingertips brushing gently against the hollow of her neck, until one finger was hooked under the lapel of her robe.

He eased slightly to his left until he was on his side, his leg still draped over both of hers, pinning her as his finger slowly pulled her robe down millimeter by millimeter, exposing her pale skin to his gaze.

Vincent paused when he neared the peak, his eyes locking on hers. Holding her gaze as he slowly, deliberately pulled the robe that last crucial inch, letting the back of his index finger graze her nipple as he exposed her all the way.

Jill cried out at the touch, and Vin's cock got even harder at the sound.

Curious if she was always that sensitive, he repeated the motion, moving his finger back up, brushing her again.

She gasped.

He grinned evilly then. Six years trying to figure out how to get the upper hand on this woman, and this was all it took.

Vincent rested the pad of his thumb on the tip of her breast, barely touching her—torturing her.

She arched her back up into him and he pulled his hand away. Again and again they repeated the motion, her desperate to have his hand on her, him just as determined to make her wait.

Only when she was cursing him, sounding very much like, well, *her*, did he give her what she wanted.

He captured her nipple between this thumb and

forefinger, idly rolling it as he watched her pant. Vincent let the edge of his thumbnail scrape her just slightly and she nearly came off the bed.

"Ah, Jill," he said reverently. And then when he couldn't help himself any longer, his own control at the brink, he scooted down and brought his mouth to her breast.

He started with the tip of his tongue, flicking her nipple just lightly, before lapping at her in rhythmic strokes.

Her fingers tangled in his hair, clasping her to him as he drew her into his mouth, sucking the sweet puckered tip into his mouth.

His hand slid across her chest, shoving the robe aside to reveal her other breast, repeating the same torturous process on that side until she was sobbing with need.

Vincent's hand slid down her belly, his fingertips tracing over the soft curve of her lower belly until sliding down farther and finding the elastic band of her panties.

He used one finger to trace all around the elastic, starting with the tip before lifting his hand and repeating the slow process at the sensitive crease of her inner thighs.

Jill's hips arched up and he pulled his hand away.

"I hate you," she gasped.

He merely grinned and repeated the motion all over again, this time accidentally on purpose letting his finger slip beneath the fabric.

Vincent moved upward slightly, waiting until she turned her face to his before kissing her, long and deep.

He let one finger roam over the front of her underwear then, and he groaned in satisfaction when he found her wet.

"Damn it, Jill."

In response she pulled his mouth more firmly against hers with one hand as the other drifted down to the front of his jeans. He growled in response, his hand pulling hers away and pinning it above her head.

"Think you're in control, do you?" she asked.

In response, Vincent slipped one finger under the elastic of her panties.

She gasped.

"I don't know," he said as he gently explored her folds. "Am I in control?"

"I hate you," she said again, this time around a moan.

"Hmm, that doesn't sound like hate, darling."

"It is. It definitely is," she said, her voice a little rough.

"Well then, I guess you want me to stop," he said, sliding his hand away from her, smiling when she whimpered in protest.

"Please," she said, her wrists twisting under his grip.

"Please what?" he said, his lips fastening once more on her nipple.

He glanced up at her as his mouth played at her breast, finding her watching him with cloudy blue eyes.

"Still feeling the hate?" he asked roughly.

Wordlessly, she shook her head.

Rewarding her, Vincent slid down her body, releasing her hands as he did so, gratified when her fingers instantly found his head, running through his hair.

He kissed each of her ribs, taking his time, listening to her panting breaths, before he pulled back and glared at her robe, which was still hooked on her arms and kept getting in his way every time she moved.

"Off," he commanded.

For once, she didn't argue. She sat up, slightly tugging

her arms free of the bulky fabric before yanking it away and tossing it aside.

"Better?" she asked, lifting an eyebrow.

In response, his hand flattened across her chest, pushing her back to the bed as his mouth continued its downward descent, his fingers trailing over her rib cage until they reached the top of her panties.

He watched her eyes as he pulled her underwear down and off. There was no shyness in her eyes—only hunger.

And then she was naked, and Vincent's own hunger ratcheted up a notch or two. His fingers trailed over the inside of her ankles, and it occurred to him that one of them should feel worried about the line they were about to cross.

But Vincent didn't want to think about tomorrow. Didn't want to think about anything other than running his lips up the inside of her calves.

So he did.

His lips lingered on her skin, trailing up and down her lean legs, learning her taste. His hands wrapped around her ankles, pushing them up so he had access to the soft, sweet skin behind her knees.

By the time he reached her inner thighs, letting his mouth plant wet kisses to the supple skin there, she was right where he wanted her—panting and eager.

His teeth scraped her inner thigh and she arched off the bed, his name a plea on her lips.

Only then did he give her what she wanted.

Vincent waited until she'd once more met his eyes.

Then he licked her.

Slow and slick, his tongue worked over her, learning what she liked and where she liked it.

Jill's hands found his hair, her nails scraping lightly against his scalp, and Vincent swore softly against her wet flesh.

His cock pressed hard and angry against the fly of his jeans, and he reached down to adjust himself even as his tongue fluttered over her.

"Vin." Her voice was breathier now. Panicked.

In response he slid his hands beneath her ass, pulling her all the way against his mouth as she exploded in a torrent of sharp cries and maybe a few naughty words.

Vincent kissed his way up her body. He'd planned to give her a few minutes to recover, but her hands were already at his waistband, her fingers making quick work of the buttons on his jeans before sliding those and his briefs over his ass.

He started to pull back to pull them off, but her hands held his hips.

"Now."

Vincent let out a harsh, tortured laugh. "Condom. Tell me you have condoms."

"I do." Her thumb ran over his lip. "I'm also on the pill, and just got tested for all the fun stuff."

He groaned against her neck, because he too checked out these things on a regular basis, and the thought of sliding inside her, skin on skin . . .

Vin rolled on top of her, hands sliding beneath her hips as he angled her just right . . .

He thrust inside her with one firm, smooth stroke that had her arching off the bed.

So. Fucking. Tight.

And perfect. She was perfect.

When he was all the way buried inside her, he stayed

perfectly still, feeling her clamp around him, his breath hot and urgent against her neck.

He pulled his hips back slowly before thrusting forward again. Repeated the process again, pulling out slowly, thrusting in hard. And again. Jill picked up his rhythm immediately.

Vincent tried to keep the pace slow and deliberate, but when Jill's legs lifted, her ankles locked around his ass, arching up to him, he lost it.

His hands held her hips, pinned her lower body to the bed as he buried himself again and again in her small, hot body.

He came harder than he ever had before, erupting with an inhuman roar as he exploded inside her.

Perfect. Fucking perfect.

His mind went blank with pleasure then, and when consciousness finally returned, he was slumped on top of her and she was moving uncomfortably beneath him.

He pulled back. "Sorry." His voice was gruff. "Too heavy?"

"No," she said, her own voice raspy. "It's just…your buttons."

Vincent glanced down and let out a little laugh as he realized that he was still completely clothed, his pants down around his knees like a high school virgin who couldn't wait even five seconds longer.

He rolled off her, starting to pull his pants back up, but her small fingers wrapped around his wrist.

"What are you doing?"

His eyebrows lifted. "Getting dressed?"

Hers lifted right back. "Take it off, Moretti. All of it."

The command was casual—joking, but the sentiment behind it…

"You want me to . . . stay?"

Goddamn, but he hated how hopeful his voice sounded.

Still, he braced himself for her to kick him out. To tell him that this had been a mistake, a onetime fling to scratch the itch . . .

She smiled, slow and intimate.

"Yeah. I want you to stay."

CHAPTER THIRTY-TWO

Jill was resting lazily on Vincent's chest when her phone on the nightstand buzzed.

She reached for it, feeling both a flicker of guilt and amusement at the text message on her screen.

"Tom said he forgives you for almost breaking his nose."

Vincent's hand clamped around her wrist as he lifted the hand holding her cell phone up to his face. "Tell me you're not texting your ex while you're lying naked beside me."

"Of course not," she said, pressing her lips to his shoulder. Then she did it again, just because she could. "He's texting me."

Vincent made a growling noise and plucked the phone out of her hand, tossing it back on the nightstand before he rolled over her.

She ran her fingers over his shoulders, surprising herself with the greedy need to touch him. Jill wiggled beneath him suggestively, noting the unmistakable flare of heat in his eyes.

But instead of taking the hint, he stared...no, glared... down at her.

"Jill."

She froze at the serious note in his voice, her hands falling back weakly to the bed. She had a pretty good idea what was coming, and even though it was a conversation that needed to happen, she was dreading it.

Still, his voice was gentle, and his gaze softened slightly as he looked down at her, so that helped.

Vincent propped his elbows on either side of her head. "Tell me."

She brought her hands to rest on his forearms. "Tell you..."

He toyed with a strand of her hair. "What happened with Tom?"

Jill licked her lips. "It...it didn't work out."

"Obviously. But I need a bit more than that. I just slept with a woman who up until a few hours ago I thought was engaged. Hell, up until two weeks ago you *were* engaged."

Jill slapped her hands over her eyes and groaned. "Oh my God. When you say it like that, I sound like such...such..."

"A hussy?"

"Yes!" she exclaimed, even though his voice was teasing. "I feel icky. Like a man-eater who jumps from one man's bed to the next. Although you should know, it had been awhile with—"

He laid a finger over her lips. "I don't want to know. Not about that."

"So what *do* you want to know?"

He looked down at her then, his expression hesitant and Jill had a pretty good idea why. Communicating with their bodies was one thing—gasps and moans and really good sex ... well that was easy, in a way.

But this—the emotional stuff—was harder. Especially for a man like Vincent.

And not particularly easy for her either. She knew how people saw her. As an open, heart-on-her-sleeve kind of woman.

And she sort of was.

But that didn't mean she wasn't every bit as afraid of heartache as other people.

Throwing her love—if it had even been that—at Tom had been easy. He'd been open and wanting to receive it. And even had he rejected it, Jill supposed she'd always known on some level that getting rejected by Tom wouldn't crush her.

She dropped her gaze to Vincent's Adam's apple.

Throwing something as powerful as love at Vincent ...

That was risky. Scary.

She knew that he'd never intentionally hurt her, but that didn't change the fact that Vincent Moretti was perhaps the only man on earth who could crush her.

Jill returned her eyes to his gaze, found him watching her.

"Why didn't you tell me? When it ended ... you could have ..." He swallowed nervously. "It would have meant a lot to know."

Jill's heart squeezed at the admission, and guilt racked through her. "I was scared."

He frowned. "About what?"

She took a deep breath, wondering how much to tell him. She started to look away, but his palm cupped her face. Brought it around to face him. "Jill."

"There were two parts to it," she said slowly. "The first was about me...I wanted to be damn sure that you weren't just a rebound. I wanted time to think before, well...this. And the second was about you. I wasn't...I wasn't sure if you'd only wanted what you couldn't have."

His gaze darkened. "Explain."

"I've been right in front of you for six years," she said softly. "Right there, this whole damn time. But it wasn't until after I got serious—really serious—about someone else that you seemed to want me back."

He was silent for several moments, then dipped his head with a soft oath before he rolled off of her so they were lying on their backs, side-by-side.

Vincent lifted a hand to his face, his thumb and forefinger pinching the bridge of his nose tiredly. "Here's the thing, Henley...if I tell you the truth...you'll have no reason to believe me."

"Try me," she said, rolling onto her side and looking down at him.

He dropped his hand and met her eyes. "When you were gone for three months, I was...I felt..."

Vin blew out a breath, then tried again. "That day you got back from your mom's, I was going to ask you out. On a date."

Her jaw dropped, and he rolled over so they were face-to-face. "I swear to God, Henley, my wanting you has nothing to do with you getting engaged to Tom. It took me a while, yes. It took me far too damn long to realize that I wanted to be more than your partner, but I *did* realize it."

She reached out and lightly touched the back of his hand. "And then I came back...engaged."

He swallowed. "Yeah."

"What about now?" she asked softly. "Do you still want to ask me on a date?"

"I do, but—"

Her heart dropped.

"I'm not a hearts-and-flowers kind of guy. I don't...I don't know that I can be what you need. Or want."

"Well what can you be?" She forced her voice to stay light. To keep from pushing him too hard in a direction she wasn't sure either of them wanted or knew how to handle.

His gaze turned warm as his hand moved forward, settling on her bare waist. "Well, for starters, I can be your partner."

"Oh yeah?" she asked as his hand moved down slightly, resting on the curve of her hip before moving back up again. "Is that all?"

He moved closer, his mouth settling into the hollow of her throat, and she sighed. "I can also be a decent friend—beat up your fiancé when he goes to dinner with other women, things like that?"

His lips moved over her neck and she arched toward him even as she let out a little laugh. "I guess I could use a friend."

"What about a lover?"

"Nah," she said flippantly. "I'm good."

Vincent's hand moved up, covering her breast. His thumb drifted over a nipple and she moaned.

"You're sure?"

"Mmm hmm," she managed.

Vincent moved down her body until his mouth was even with her chest, his thumb continuing to toy with her before he let his hand fall away, so she felt only his warm breath.

"I guess you don't want my mouth here then," he said, moving imperceptibly closer.

Jill arched toward him, but he moved back, just out of reach. "What's this? Changing your mind?"

"Vin," she whined.

He looked up at her, his eyes hungry. "Thought you didn't want a lover."

"I lied," she whispered as her back arched again so that her nipple brushed his lips. He rewarded her with a soft lick before he pulled back again.

"See, I don't know that I can work with a liar, Henley. Seems to me—"

Jill shoved him onto his back, rolling on top of him. She maneuvered his big arms to his side, her hands pinning him to the bed and he let her, just for a moment, his eyes gleaming mischievously up at her.

"Ah, so you *did* change your mind."

Jill didn't bother responding. She was too busy moving her lips over his shoulder. His pecs. Her teeth grazed his nipple and he hissed.

"What about you," she said, her mouth moving slowly down his torso. "Do you want a lover?"

Her hand closed around his cock as he groaned. "Ah—"

"What was that?" she asked innocently, stroking him.

"Yes," he said.

"Yes what?" she moved farther down, her lips brushing against the tip of him, relishing his guttural groan.

"Yes," he said, his fingers tangling in her hair. "Yes, I definitely need a lover."

She couldn't resist the small smile of victory before her lips closed around him.

Lover was good enough.

For now.

CHAPTER THIRTY-THREE

It was typical that the moment one thing went right in Vincent Moretti's life, another would go horribly wrong.

"I can't believe they're closing the case," Jill said for the hundredth time around a bite of her turkey sandwich. "We were so close!"

He gave her a look as he took a drink of Coke.

"Okay, so we weren't *close*," she said, mouth mostly full. "But we were getting there. We always get there."

He dragged his fry through ketchup, barely registering that the fry was cold and that he didn't even like ketchup.

Vin threw the fry back on the plate and took a deep breath. He was trying not to be pissed. He really was.

But it was the first case that his superiors had ever pulled him from.

And the worst part was, he didn't even blame them.

Not only had they not solved the case—they hadn't

gotten fucking close. If you held a gun to Vin's head and told him to name the killer—he couldn't.

He didn't have a fucking clue who'd killed Lenora Birch, and the lack of control made him irritable. Itchy.

Pissed.

Jill took a sip of her iced tea, only to pull it back when she realized her glass was empty. She looked around for a server, then sighed. "I miss when Maggie used to work here."

"You're just saying that because of the free pie," he said.

She had a point though.

Much as he was happy that his new sister-in-law had gotten out of her dead-end job as an under-appreciated waitress at the Darby Diner, the weekday lunchtime gal who'd taken Maggie's place had proven to be a good deal more interested in her iPhone than her customers.

Jill set her empty iced tea glass aside and reached for his Coke, taking a long sip before digging back into her sandwich. "How come you're not more mad about this?" she asked.

"It's diner food, Henley. Our bill's not going to be more than twenty dollars."

She rolled her eyes. "Not about the diner. About the case."

He reached across the table to take her fry. It was every bit as cold and soggy as his.

"I am upset," he muttered. "I just don't know what ranting about it's going to do."

"You rant all the time."

"Exactly," he said. "Usually *I* rant and you sprinkle glitter on everything. But since you're ranting on this one, I figure it's time for a role reversal."

"Oh, got it," she said. "So if I'm the grumpy one today, and you're going to take on the positive one"—she glanced around dramatically—"I see no glitter. Or even a smile."

He forced his mouth into a farce of a smile, which coaxed a giggle from her.

Her giggle then coaxed an *actual* smile from him, and before he knew what was happening, they were staring across the table grinning at each other.

It had been like that in the week since they'd started sleeping together.

One minute they were their usual old bickering selves, and the next minute, it was, well...*happy*.

Vincent's smile slipped a bit as the thought that had been quietly nagging him for days crept up once again.

What if this thing between him and Jill was part of the reason they hadn't solved the case.

Technically, they separated their personal and professional life.

He didn't cop a feel when they were on the job, much as he wanted to. They didn't kiss in between coffee breaks, didn't talk about *them* while they were on duty.

But if he was honest—really brutally honest—his head hadn't been in the game since Jill had returned from Florida with that damn ring on her finger.

And now that the ring was *off* her finger—

Well let's just say it was even harder to concentrate on the job when half the time he wanted nothing more than to toss her in the backseat and screw like teenagers.

He blew out a breath as he faced the truth looming in the back of his mind.

What if Lenora Birch's killer was going to go free

because Vincent had spent the past two months thinking with his dick instead of his brain?

"Uh-oh," Jill said, pushing her plate away and crossing both arms on the table. "I know that look. What's going on?"

"Nothing," he muttered.

"No, we don't get to do *nothing*," she said. "Not as partners, not as lovers."

He glanced around. "Jesus, keep your voice down."

She lifted her eyebrow. "First of all, there are only six customers in here right now. None are in hearing range. Second of all, why so jumpy?"

He pulled his wallet out of his pocket. "Are you done?"

"No, I want more iced tea."

"We don't have time for Joyce to get back from her smoke break."

"Really?" Jill crossed her arms. "We don't have time? Where exactly are we running off to? Last I checked, we don't have a case—"

"Because we fucked up," he said, standing and heading toward the door.

Jill caught up with him when they were outside, grabbing his arm and pulling him around. "Why do I feel like that was a loaded statement?"

He ran his hand through his hair. "We lost this case, Jill—we let a killer go free because we couldn't find the clues."

"It happens, Vin. I don't like it any more than you do. I'm beating myself up too, but it had to happen to us sooner or later—"

"And isn't it interesting that we got dropped from the case the very week we started screwing."

His words were harsh. He didn't mean them to be, they just slipped out.

She said nothing, and he reached out a hand, relieved when she didn't step back.

If anything she looked...amused?

Jill's lips twitched a little as she took a step closer. "Is that what this is about? You're *actually* doing that cliché guy thing where you think your brain didn't solve the case because it was sex-addled?"

"Maybe," he muttered.

Jill smiled softly, her fingers briefly touching the tips of his before he let his hand drop. Before someone saw them.

"It's not like that, Vin. Whatever was going on with us didn't change the fact that the killer hasn't left us a single clue."

"Or we missed something," he said as they walked to the car and climbed in.

"Or that," she said. "But we have to let it go. Not only for our sanity, but because it's an order. Another case will come up tomorrow, or the next, and—"

Both of their phones buzzed just as the police radio crackled.

Five minutes later, Jill and Vincent looked at each other and grinned.

"Well, whadya know, Henley—looks like we just got ourselves another case."

She clicked her seat belt into the buckle. "We do indeed. Maybe your famous instinct will actually work on this one."

"Maybe. Assuming I'm not distracted by a cute blonde with a mouth like a—"

Jill turned her head and gave him a look.

"Lady," he finished. "A mouth like a lady."

"What does that mean?"

"Hell if I know," he muttered as he turned the ignition. "But it's better than what I was going to say."

But Jill wasn't listening. Her phone was already up to her ear as she called in to their superiors to tell them they were on their way.

Five minutes later, they were pulling up to the curb of a mid-rise apartment building in Spanish Harlem. Jill jumped out of the car, notebook already in hand.

Vin paused a moment, taking in the swarm of cops, the yellow tape—the curious onlookers, the just-now-arriving media.

And then there was Jill.

His eyes sought and found his partner. She was wearing a simple black suit, her hair pulled back in its usual ponytail.

She'd already scooted under the caution tape, deep in conversation with one of the uniforms. Her pen was moving across the page of her notebook as she nodded along to whatever the officer was telling her.

Then she flipped her notebook shut and glanced around until she saw him. Their eyes met, and she held out her hands in a *what's the holdup, get your ass over here, Moretti* kind of way.

Vincent couldn't help it. He smiled.

Yes, there was a dead body inside that building, yes, he'd just had his first unsolved murder go on record, but right now, those didn't seem to matter as much as the woman in front of him did.

Jill was his.

The only question was ...

For how long?

How long until she realized that he needed her light a hell of a lot more than she needed his darkness?

"Dude, Moretti. Get a move on it," she called. "Even you can't solve a case by standing in the street."

Instinct told him he didn't have much time with her.

And since his instincts were never wrong, he fully intended to make the most of the time he did have.

CHAPTER THIRTY-FOUR

Jill knew she was gloating. Big-time.

She *also* knew she didn't feel even the tiniest bit bad about it. The cork of the cheap champagne finally gave in to all her tugging and twisting and went shooting across the room with a satisfying pop.

She glanced at Vincent, who stood behind the stove stirring some sort of meat sauce that looked amazing. He gave a skeptical look as she poured two glasses of champagne and handed one to him.

"Meat sauce requires red wine."

"So, when we eat your precious meat sauce, we'll have a glass of red," she said, lifting up his hand and then shoving the champagne flute into it. "But first, we toast."

Jill held up her glass, waiting patiently until he finally rolled his eyes and complied.

"To us," she said.

His eyes shuttered, and Jill stifled her sigh at how jumpy he was about anything related to them.

"To the best damn homicide detectives in the NYPD," she clarified, more for his sake than hers.

As expected, the clouds in his brown eyes lifted and he clinked his glass to hers. "That was pretty fucking exceptional today. Even for us."

"If we can continue to get a confession on the same day that the bodies are found, we'll restore our reputation in no time," she said, taking a sip of the wine, loving the way the bubbles matched her mood.

It's not that she was okay with the fact that they hadn't found Lenora Birch's killer. She wasn't. At all. In fact, she was sure that the lack of closure on the case would continue to haunt both of them for some time.

But that didn't change the fact that she and Vincent had done damn good work this afternoon.

Granted, it hadn't exactly been a stumper.

A twenty-one-year-old girl named Maria Salvez, found dead of multiple stab wounds on her blood-soaked mattress…

But wait, *twist*!

Only *half* of the blood was hers.

Quick calls to local hospitals and they'd found themselves victim number two. A twenty-four-year-old male with multiple stab wounds, in serious but stable condition.

It had taken Jill about ten minutes of sweet talk before she found out that the guy had been sleeping with his best friend's girlfriend.

The boyfriend found them in bed and lost his mind, grabbed a knife…

A classic, tragic tale. One that made Jill positively sick to her stomach, and all the more gratified when she and

Vin had found Maria's killer within two hours of discovering the body. The bastard had been skulking at his sister's house, drinking a beer and eating a corn dog, looking cocky as hell.

It had taken less than five minutes of Jill and Vincent's trusty good cop/bad cop routine before the guy confessed.

Open.

Shut.

Awesome.

"I'd forgotten how good it feels," Jill mused, taking a sip of her champagne.

"Sure," Vin said, tasting the sauce on the stove. "Until the damn lawyers strike some sort of bullshit deal and the guy gets off easy."

"Uh-uh," Jill said. "Don't rain on my parade right now. We did good, Vin. It was a win."

A win they'd sorely needed after the Lenora Birch disaster.

Jill watched as Vincent added salt to the sauce, envying his confidence in the kitchen. She knew her way around the stove, but only with the help of a very, very detailed cookbook. She'd never quite mastered the "pinch of this, a dash of that" approach that the Morettis all seemed so comfortable with.

"You're staring," Vin said, not looking up as he tasted the sauce once more.

"Because you look good," Jill said, taking a sip of her champagne and leaning against the counter.

And he did. He'd been wearing a white button-down but had discarded it almost the minute they'd walked in the door, and he was now dressed only in dark slacks and a white undershirt that did nice things for his amazing arms.

"Keep the compliments coming," he said, holding a spoon out to her so she could do her own taste test of the goodness he had happening on the stove. "It'll help keep me from being peeved at you."

"Why would you be peeved at me?" she said, blowing on the steaming sauce before taking a tentative bite.

"Today when we found Garcia—anything seem wrong with that?"

She replayed it in her mind. They'd shown up...found him plopped on his sister's couch with that damn corn dog. They'd asked where he was at the time of the murder and gotten a *fuck-off*, followed by *bitch-deserved-it*...

They'd hauled him off the couch, read him his rights as she'd cuffed him—

"*Oh*," she said, eyes going wide.

Vin lifted an eyebrow. "Yeah. 'Oh.' "

"Was it your turn?" she asked sweetly.

"That voice doesn't work on me, sweetheart. Neither do the baby blues."

She batted her eyelashes. "How about this?"

"Nope," he said, advancing on her. "It was my turn. Fair and square."

"Well now, hold on," she said. "What about the entire three months that I was gone? You got to cuff plenty of people, and I got to cuff none."

"Doesn't count. You weren't there," he said. "You know the deal. We take turns with the cuffing. And this one was mine."

Jill pursed her lips. "Are you sure—"

He moved closer, pinning her to the counter with his weight. "Shall I get the log?"

Jill ran a finger along the V-neck of his shirt. "Maybe

we retire the old take-turns-cuffing thing. I mean, it's a little childish—"

His eyes narrowed. "It's the best part of our job, and you know it."

Jill took a sip of her champagne. He was right. It was the best part of their job. There was something so satisfying about the click of the cuffs when you knew you had the right guy.

"What if I told you I forgot?" she said, lifting her eyes to his. "It's been a while, after all. I've been on sabbatical."

"I'd believe you, baby," he said. His voice was calm. Lulling. Dangerous.

"You would?"

"Mmm hmm." He moved even closer, slowly pulling the champagne flute out of her hand and setting it aside behind her. "But it doesn't change the fact that you were out of turn, Henley."

Jill was finding it harder and harder to concentrate with his warmth pressed against her, his big arms caging her in, his mouth so damn close—

So addled was her brain with lust that even when his hands found her hips, turning her around to face the counter with the perfect amount of roughness and gentleness, she didn't realize his intention.

So full of want was every cell in her body as he gently raked his teeth over her neck, that she didn't quite comprehend that he'd maneuvered her hands behind her back.

Not until the unfamiliar feel of cold metal against her wrists, followed by the very familiar sound of a soft click, did Jill realize what had just happened...

Her partner had just cuffed her.

She tried to whirl around, but he caught her waist with a gentle scolding noise, then pressed against her, molding his chest to her back.

"Vin—"

His hands ran up her sides, then back down until they rested on her hips.

"Yes, detective?" he said roughly against her ear.

She twisted her wrists futilely. "Let me go."

"Maybe next time you'll think about the consequences of your actions," he said, sliding a hand around to press a hand against her stomach and pulling her more firmly against him.

"My actions—*ahh*." She broke off when he started kissing her neck.

"What was that?" he asked, his lips never breaking contact with her skin.

She tried once more to turn, but his grip tightened.

"Don't. Move," he growled.

Jill tried not to move. She did. But when his hands ran up over the front of her breasts, palms teasing her, she arched, wanting more.

His fingers slowly undid the buttons of her blouse, his mouth never stopping its hot teasing of her neck.

Vin flicked open the front clasp of her bra, shoving both that and her shirt roughly to the sides before putting his hands on her.

Jill's own hands jerked against the handcuffs as his fingers found her nipples, tweaking her in just the right way to find that exquisite place between pain and pleasure.

By the time his hands moved down to her skirt, his fingers pulling the fabric upward, inch by slow inch, Jill was panting.

"If I say sorry, do I get these off now?" she asked.

In response, he placed a hand on her back, pushing her gently but firmly forward so she was bent over the counter.

He slid down the back of her body until he was crouched behind her, roughly pushing her skirt the rest of the way up over her hips.

Jill squeezed her eyes shut, torn between embarrassment and arousal. Then arousal won over, because his fingers hooked into her panties, yanking them down so she was completely exposed.

"Shall I read you your rights, Henley?" His breath was hot on her skin, his fingers dragging slowly along her inner thighs.

"Wha—what?" She was definitely panting now.

He pushed her thighs wider apart. "You have the right to remain silent..."

Vincent slid his hand upward, one finger sliding slightly into her.

Jill moaned.

"Apparently you're forgoing that right," he said, his teeth nipping at her left butt cheek as his fingers continued to play with her.

"Vin, you—"

"Careful, baby. Anything you say can and will be used against you in a court of law."

He eased his finger all the way inside her then, his other hand sliding around to her front to rub her in slow, torturous circles.

"You're a bastard," she said, pressing her cheek against the cool surface of the counter, even as the place between her legs grew wetter, hotter.

"Yeah? Tell it to your attorney. Because you have a right to talk to a lawyer—" He broke off at Jill's cry of pleasure as he slid another finger inside her.

Vincent was still in control, but he was unraveling fast. She could hear it in his breath. Feel it in the way his hands were shifting from teasing to greedy.

She parted her legs as far as she could with her panties still around her ankles, silently encouraging him to continue his wicked touch.

His forefinger centered on her core, rubbing in tight, perfect circles, and Jill's entire body tensed—begging for release.

Release he didn't give her.

He withdrew his hands, standing behind her. Jill heard the clank of his belt buckle, the rasp of his zipper.

Felt the brush of his fingers against her as he positioned his cock at her opening. But not entering.

She pushed her hips back, and he pulled away slightly. "Tell me what you want," he said, tracing the sensitive finger just above where the handcuffs held her hostage.

Jill refused to answer. He already had her handcuffed and bent over her kitchen counter. Damned if she'd give him everything.

She looked over her shoulder, lifted her eyebrows in challenge as she remained stubbornly silent.

His eyes narrowed, and his hand slid down to her butt, slapping it just hard enough to cause a delicious little sting. "Jill."

She pushed her ass toward him in response, arching her back, and relished his little groan.

"Sorry, babe. Not good enough," he said, planting a kiss between her shoulder blades.

Then he spun her around, dropped to his knees, and tongued her.

Jill gave a sharp cry, pulling at the handcuffs in a desperate, futile attempt to hold his head against her. But she didn't need to. His hands found her hips, holding her still as his mouth devoured her in a hungry caress.

Only when Jill sobbed his name did he stand, nipping her nipple once before spinning her around once more and plunging into her with one firm smooth stroke.

He paused then, resting his forehead against her shoulder, his breath ragged. He kissed her once on the top of her shoulder. It was a sweet gesture completely at odds with the fierceness of the rest of their encounter, and she turned her head, her lips finding his. Their tongues tangled in a hot kiss until he finally pulled away, his eyes latching onto hers. When she turned around he pulled back before pushing into her, slowly.

This time when Jill leaned forward, it was of her own volition, and Vincent groaned in gratification. His fingers dug into her hips as he took her hard.

There was nothing soft about the way he drilled her into the counter. Nothing tender about the sounds their bodies made as they slapped together. Nothing delicate about the way she came apart the second he slid a hand around to her clit.

But when Vincent found his own release, the way her name sounded on his lips sounded like a prayer.

And that was *everything*.

CHAPTER THIRTY-FIVE

Vincent wasn't prone to embarrassment. He didn't think he was hardwired for it.

But when his vision stopped spinning enough to pull himself away from Jill and unlock the handcuffs, he was damn glad her back was still to him, because he felt oddly shy at the way he'd taken her like an animal.

Shyness transitioned to regret as he saw the faint red lines around her wrist. "Ah, Jill—"

She turned toward him, kneeling to pull her panties up before wiggling her skirt back down and giving him a coy look.

"Don't you dare," she said, lifting to her toes and pressing her lips to his. "Don't you apologize."

"But—"

Her arms wound around his neck and she deepened the kiss.

Vincent kissed her back, mainly because it was a chance to hold her.

When they pulled back, he surprised himself by kissing both her cheeks, then set to righting her bra, rebuttoning her shirt.

When he glanced up, she was watching him with such amused surprise that the embarrassment crashed over him again.

What was wrong with him? It was just sex. It was just—

Except it wasn't *just* anything.

Sex with Jill wasn't just mind blowing. It wasn't just an intoxicating combination of raunchy and playful.

Sex with Jill felt a hell of a lot like coming home.

And even more scary, it felt a lot like *it'll never be this good with anyone else, ever.*

Fuck.

He moved toward his sauce, unsurprised to see that the bottom had burned a little thanks to their interlude.

He scraped at it with the wooden spoon, then picked up the champagne he didn't really like and tossed back the entirety.

"You okay?" she asked.

He glanced at her, saw the wariness on her face—realized that she wasn't just expecting him to pull away. She was counting on it.

But for tonight, he didn't want to be that guy. He didn't want to be the guy that clammed up and was emotionally unreachable.

He was that guy—he knew that. Knew that he didn't have whatever other people had that made them good for another person forever and ever. There was no way he'd subject Jill to a lifetime of his frequent need for solitude, or his inability to make the proper chatter at social functions.

Even if he remembered to occasionally bring her flowers, he didn't know how to put together all the pretty phrases that women seemed to want.

But maybe for tonight, he could pretend that he was her man. That she was his.

He reached out and grabbed the front of her shirt, pulling her toward him for a quick kiss, his hand sliding over her back and down to her ass, which he gave a playful tap. "Anyone ever tell you you're a dirty girl?"

She let out a little laugh. "I'm the dirty one? Didn't seem to me I had a lot of say considering I was handcuffed and bent over the counter."

His cock stirred at the memory, as well as the steamy look in her eyes. She could say whatever she wanted, but she'd fucking enjoyed every moment of it.

So had he.

He bent his head again, and she laughed lightly, dodging his kiss. "No way, Detective. I know that look. You're feeding me first."

"*Then* we can do a repeat?" he asked, opening the box of pasta and dropping a handful into the water he'd had boiling on a back burner.

Jill pulled down plates and water glasses. "I'm thinking repeat, with a twist."

He lifted an eyebrow. "Twist?"

She nipped his shoulder with her teeth as she passed. "Yup. Say, maybe...I'm the one with the handcuffs."

He turned to look at her. "Jillian Henley."

She shrugged as she set the table. "What? Now that

I've seen what's beneath the clothes, I wouldn't mind having all that solid muscle pinned down for my personal pleasure."

To Vin's surprise, the idea was arousing. He was game for just about anything that would involve her putting her hands on him. All over him.

Vincent served them both a hefty portion of the pasta, and Jill kept her promise of red wine with dinner, pouring him a glass and topping off champagne for herself.

As they settled down to eat, Jill's usual happy chatter mingling in with companionable silence, Vincent was struck with an unfamiliar sense of contentment.

No...that wasn't quite right.

He'd been *content* before Jill had left for Florida. Back before she'd rocked the boat. What he was feeling now was much bigger.

He shoveled the last bite of pasta in his mouth and sat back to find her watching him. "What's up?"

She pressed her lips together briefly in the way she always did right before she said something he wasn't going to like, and he instinctively braced himself.

"Do you want to stay?" she asked.

He looked at her in surprise. "I thought we cleared that up right about the time I agreed to let you handcuff me."

"No, I mean—well yes, I want that. But I mean, do you want to stay and...hang out? Watch a movie? Or TV? Or we could read—"

Her words came out in a rush, and he frowned. "What's got you so nervous?"

She fiddled with her napkin. "It's just...have you noticed that we're usually either talking about work, or having sex?"

"Sure," he said. "But those are two of my favorite things. And yours too, if I'm not mistaken."

"I know. And you're right; I love those things too. And I'm not suggesting less, of either, it's just—"

She blew out a breath and met his eyes. "I want to try normal with you, Vin."

He swallowed. As far as requests from a woman went, it was about as innocuous as it got. She wasn't looking for a ring, or to take him to meet her mother, or to go shopping for drapes.

She wanted to watch a movie with him.

Hell, it's not like they hadn't done it before. There'd been plenty of times where they'd defaulted to watching a movie when their brains were spent after working on a case.

But this was different, and they both knew it.

It was on the tip of his tongue to remind Jill that he didn't do normal. He didn't do boyfriend.

But then the thought hit him...

Why?

Why didn't he do normal?

Why didn't he do boyfriend?

He'd never even tried.

And if he was going to try with anyone, it would be Jill.

She was worth at least that. She deserved so much more than *normal*.

"You're freaking out," she said on a sigh, pushing her plate away. "I just wish I knew why—"

He reached across the table and grabbed her hand before he could lose his nerve. He kept his touch gentle, his thumb gently rubbing against her palm until she calmed and looked at him.

"I'd like to stay," he said quietly. "And as for normal . . . I can give you normal for *me* . . ."

She smiled. "That's all I want. You don't have to pretend with me. You know that, right? I know who you are. What you are. Warts and all. And that's who I want to stay and watch a movie with me."

Vincent felt his chest tighten a little. He wanted to take the words and cling to them. Wanted to ask if they'd still be true a week from now when he was in one of those rotten moods where he wanted to be left alone and snapped at her.

He wasn't good enough. He wasn't even close.

But the way she was looking at him now . . . as though he were everything she'd ever wanted—

He couldn't give it up. Not yet.

Vincent turned her hand over and lifted it to his lips.

"I'll stay on one condition," he said, running a thumb over her knuckles and holding her eyes. "You got any popcorn?"

CHAPTER THIRTY-SIX

Vincent felt like a chump. An utter, foolish ass.

He took a step back and surveyed the table. It looked...
Ridiculous.

It might be better with a tablecloth, or whatever, to
cover up the dented wood table he'd gotten at a garage
sale a decade ago.

But the day Vincent bought a fucking tablecloth would
also be the day he died, so that was out.

Maybe she wouldn't notice with the candles. They
weren't fancy—just white stubby things he'd picked up for
the odd windstorm that knocked the power out.

But combined with the flowers. Yeah. He felt like a
chump.

He thought about putting them away, but she'd texted
saying she was on her way over. If he got caught in the act
of *un*-setting the table, he'd look even more foolish.

He'd just have to ride it out and hope that she didn't:

(a) laugh

(b) get the wrong idea that this was the type of guy he was going to be.

He wasn't the hearts and flowers guy.

And yet… Vincent sipped his wine and considered the table. Apparently he *was* that kind of guy.

Correction:

Jill Henley made him want to be that kind of guy.

At least dinner he could pull off without feeling like a complete ass.

Vincent seasoned the steaks, poked at the potato baking in the oven for doneness, and then refilled his wine.

There was a knock at the door, and Vin glanced at the table in panic. Did he light the candles *now*? That seemed cheesy. But if he didn't light them, it seemed too random…just two unlit candles chilling on his table with those Goddamn flowers.

In the end, it was decided for him.

Jill let herself in and was in the kitchen before he even had a chance to think about where he might have stashed his matches.

He waited with trepidation to see if she'd laugh in his face at the table, but she was glancing down at her phone and didn't seem to even see the flowers.

Vincent told himself it was just as well that she wasn't into that kind of thing. It's not like there'd be a repeat.

And yet, he felt…

Deflated.

Then she glanced up, met his eyes, and smiled—one of those happy smiles that lit up her whole face, and Vincent was gone.

It didn't matter if she saw the flowers or laughed at the candles, because she saw him.

And that was what mattered. All that had ever mattered.

"Wine?" he asked.

"Later," she said, moving toward him and winding her arms around his neck before pulling his head down to hers for a long, lingering kiss.

"I was thinking…" she said, when she pulled back and gave him a sexy look.

He kissed the tip of her nose, refusing to feel embarrassed by the dopey gesture. "Yes?"

She kissed him again, briefly. "Take me out."

He pulled back. "Huh?"

"I know, I know, you hate that stuff, but hear me out. We could get all dressed up, I could put on lipstick, high heels. Go into the city, somewhere fancy, a little overpriced…"

"I was thinking we could eat in," he said slowly.

Jill pushed back. Her smile was still in place but she looked…disappointed. "We *always* eat in, Vin."

"I know, but—"

"No, I mean literally *always*. We've been seeing each other for two weeks now, and we haven't gone out once other than crappy diner lunches."

It stung. Just a little.

"Wine?" he asked, pushing the unexpected disappointment aside.

"Um, sure," she said, sounding bored.

"So how was—"

"Are you ever going to take me out?" she interrupted. "I mean, I don't need it all the time. I know it's expensive, and not your thing, but Vin...I don't want Chinese food and crappy pizza for the rest of my life."

Just tell her. Tell her that you're trying. That you spent an obscene amount of money on the best steaks you could afford, and somehow draw her attention to her flowers...

But it felt wrong now. This wasn't how it was supposed to happen.

He felt a little lost and a lot defensive.

"I thought you knew what you were getting into. Fancy restaurants and romantic gestures have never been part of the equation."

"So what, we just put on our sweatpants and call it a night, every night?"

He started to lift his hand to the table, but he let it drop to his side. "You know what, Henley? If you wanted oysters and Dom and red roses, maybe you should have stuck with Tom and his arsenal of tuxedos and his yacht that's always on fucking standby."

He waited for her to deny it. Waited for her to tell Vin that it was him that she wanted.

Instead she looked miserable.

As miserable as he felt.

"What is it that we're doing here, Vin? Are we just partners with benefits?"

He opened his mouth, but she wasn't done.

"I know, you don't like labels, you don't think you're a romantic guy, you're skittish, I get that. I've been patient. I'm dealing with it. I don't need promises of forever, but I just...I need more."

Her voice was a little wobbly and he swallowed, his mouth dry.

He racked his brain for the right thing to say. Words

had never been easy for him, but they'd never been this hard.

Nor this important.

And yet, he still didn't know what to tell her.

He stayed silent, and in true Jill fashion she just kept talking. "I've been thinking that this relationship...that this relationship has been a long time coming. Fate, or whatever, but what we have is nothing more than you deciding you wanted something you couldn't have but aren't at all sure you want to keep it."

He stepped closer. "That's bullshit. This is more than that, and you know it."

She looked away, and he cupped her jaw. "I'm not going to apologize for fighting for you, Jill."

She put both hands on his shoulders, shoving him away, and his heart cracked just a little.

"I want more, Vin."

He shook his head to indicate he didn't understand.

She pressed her hands together. "Tom wasn't the one that I wanted, but he was offering me what I wanted. Marriage. A future."

Vin's head tilted back, realizing he wasn't going to like where this was going.

"And you," she continued. "You *are* the one that I want, Vin. I think you're maybe *the* one, but—"

"No buts," he said, moving toward her again, caging her in. "Let that just be enough."

She lifted her hands, set them against his chest, gently. Regretfully. "I don't think it *is* enough." She lifted her eyes to his. "Not for me. I want more. I want it all."

They stared at each other miserably for several seconds, and she licked her lips nervously.

"Vin, can you tell me—do you just need time? Is it just taking things slow? Because I can do that. But you put up warning signs on almost a daily basis. Like there's a bunch of yellow caution tape around your heart, and I just need to know if it will always be like that."

"Jill—"

"I need to know if you think you could ever love me," she said, her voice a little bit urgent now.

He'd never felt so miserable. He wanted to tell her yes. He wanted to say whatever would bring her smile back and take them back to where they were before.

But he wouldn't lie to her. She'd been right before when she'd said that trust was the one thing they'd always been able to count on in each other.

So he told her the truth. Knowing it meant losing her.

"I don't know," he said quietly. "I don't know what that feels like."

I don't know that I can take that kind of risk.

She nodded, not looking the least bit surprised, and that somehow made it worse.

He lifted a hand to her cheek. "Can't we just stay as we are? That's been pretty good, right?"

She slipped away from him. "I need a little time to think about things."

He swallowed. "How much time?"

"I don't know. It's just that I've gone from being engaged, to being single, to jumping into *this*, whatever this is, and it's been great, it's just…"

She rubbed her eyes. "I think I need a minute."

"Okay," he said quietly. "Do you want a glass of wine? I can put on music, or—"

"I think I'm going to head home."

It hurt. He was prepared for it, but it still hurt.

He nodded slowly. "I'll be around when you need me."

"I know," she said, not looking at him.

"Jill—"

She turned away, giving him her back, and he sucked in a quick breath.

In that moment, Vincent knew precisely the reason he avoided falling in love.

Because it meant feeling like this. It meant feeling half-alive.

"I'll be here," he said again. Quietly. Weakly.

She turned then, walked slowly toward his front door, and he willed himself to call out to her.

But he was also mad. Mad that she was so wrapped up in her little dream bubble of what romance looked like that she couldn't even see that he was *trying*.

He waited for her to turn back around. To come back and tell him that she wanted him, flaws and all. That staying *in* with him was better than going *out* with someone else.

She didn't.

CHAPTER THIRTY-SEVEN

Lying about being sick did not exactly rank in Jill's Top Moments to be Proud Of.

But since facing Vin was so not an option just yet, Jill was on day four of "the flu."

Vincent, of course, would know better.

But her bosses wouldn't.

Still, Jill had found a way to assuage her guilt, slightly: by working.

Granted, she wasn't working on a case she was supposed to be working on.

But in a desperate move to stop the ache that happened every time she thought about Vincent, she'd thrown herself into the Lenora Birch case.

Sure, she had explicit orders to let that one go—but she was willing to bet that if the higher-ups had their choice between her sitting and watching soaps while eating Ben

& Jerry's, or her going through decades-old news articles in an attempt to find something they'd missed, they'd choose the latter.

Still, the task was daunting. Lenora Birch had been famous and old. The result? Hundreds of articles mentioning her name.

There were casting announcements, casting rumors, film reviews, film screenings. And that's before you even got to the gossip rags, where there were feuds and catfights and tantrums and divorce.

Jill's cell phone buzzed as she was reading a particularly juicy account of Lenora's on-screen chemistry with James Killroy.

A quick glance showed it was Elena for, oh, the millionth time.

Jill put the phone back down without answering. Was she avoiding her best friend? Yes. Was she proud of it? Certainly not.

She wasn't mad at Elena. Not at all.

But Elena had the misfortune of being related to the one person Jill couldn't even *think* about right now.

Her phone buzzed once more. Elena again.

Jill was just about to put the dang thing on silent when there was a knock at her door, timed in perfect rhythm to the phone. Almost as though the person knocking was also listening to the phone ring.

Jill gave a rueful smile as she pushed herself off the floor where she'd been sitting cross-legged in a pile of paper and went to the door.

Unsurprisingly, it was Elena.

Her best friend was dressed in a knee-length sweater dress and killer boots, and was holding a grocery bag.

Elena held out the bag. "I would have brought chicken soup, but I hazarded a guess that chips and wine were a better remedy."

For a moment, Jill had an odd flashback to that first night back from Florida when Vin had held out that smashed doughnut for her.

She pushed the thought aside.

Jill smiled as she took the bag. "You'd be right. I'm not sick so much as—"

"Being a bit of an idiot?" Elena asked, pushing her sunglasses up on top of her head.

Jill set the grocery bag on the floor with a thump and threw her arms around Elena and squeezed. "I'm sorry. I'm so sorry for avoiding you."

Elena wasted no time hugging Jill back. They were both huggers by nature. Always had been. "I don't blame you. Not one little bit. Vin can be an utter monster—"

Jill pulled back. "Wait. For God's sake, let's do this while sitting down, preferably with junk food and an adult beverage."

Elena's eyebrow lifted. "It's three o'clock on a weekday."

Jill shrugged. "That's cool. We can talk about the dirty handcuff sex I had with your brother *sober* if you want…"

Elena groaned and grabbed at the grocery bag as she headed toward the kitchen. "On second thought, do you have any really long straws? I'm thinking of just going straight from the bottle."

Five minutes later, they were seated on Jill's couch, armed with a glass of pinot grigio and a bowl of salt and vinegar chips.

"You making a creepy scrapbook?" Elena asked, gesturing toward the papers strewn about their feet.

Jill pulled her knees toward her chest. "I've been try-ing to distract myself."

Elena nodded. "I suppose that's one of the perks of your job. Homicide's about as good of a distraction from relationship issues as any."

"Right?" Jill said. "Although it all feels like a waste of time. Vincent and I had weeks to turn up a suspect, and nothing stuck. Nothing clicked. I'm missing something, but I just don't know where to look."

Elena gave her a steady look. "Perhaps the problem is all the 'I' in that past statement. Isn't the entire point of having a partner, to well, partner on these things?"

Jill dug her hand into the chip bowl and stayed silent.

Elena put an elbow on the back of the couch and rested her face on her hand. "Talk."

"Nothing to talk about," Jill said around a mouthful of chips.

"But you guys *did* cross the sexy-line, did you not?"

Jill gave her a look. "It's your brother. You really want to be having this conversation?"

"I'll confess it's not my favorite. But when it comes to choosing between you and Vin…well let's just say he's not even my favorite brother."

Elena's voice was teasing—Jill knew her friend was only referring to the fact that Elena and Vincent were prone to squabbling. But the offhand comment squeezed her heart a little bit.

It made her wonder if Vincent wasn't always slightly aware of his status as the family loner. If it wasn't part of the reason he held himself back from everyone.

The reason he held himself back from her.

He wasn't accustomed to being anyone's favorite. Wasn't used to being first in anyone's life.

"We had a thing," Jill said quietly.

"A thing."

"Yeah, like a...fling."

"A fling is something you have with a guy you meet in a bar, not the guy who's been your other half for *years*."

"Well, it was. Um. It was..." Jill took a sip of wine.

"C'mon. Spill. You guys sexed it up, and then...?"

"And then..." Jill waved her hand. "Nothing."

"It was bad?"

"No! It was—" Jill paused, remembering she was talking to Vincent's sister. "The physical part wasn't the problem."

"Ah."

"Yeah," Jill said, relieved that Elena got it. "Ah."

"Let me guess, the dude won't open up. Won't talk to you. Won't let you in?"

"All of the above."

Elena took a sip of wine. "But you love him anyway."

Love.

A tricky word, that.

Jill had never been one of those people who'd had trouble saying it. She'd always given and received love fairly easily.

But loving Vincent...

Loving Vincent was scary. Risky.

Horribly, alarmingly *big*.

Loving Vin wasn't easy. He was stubborn and prickly and difficult.

And loving him was also...inevitable.

As though it were inconceivable for anyone but him to hold her heart.

"Crap," she muttered.

Elena made a sympathetic noise and reached to tug a piece of Jill's hair.

"What happened?"

"I don't even know. It's like one second I asked him to take me out to dinner. Just once. And the next we were, like, breaking up."

Elena's eyes narrowed slightly. "What day was this. *Exactly.*"

Jill thought back. "Um...Friday?"

Elena closed her eyes. "Oh no."

Jill stilled. "Oh no what?"

Elena bit her lip. "When you went over there, was there anything...different?"

"Different?" Jill thought back. "No, it seemed exactly the same. That was sort of the problem."

"So you didn't look around?"

"I guess not." Jill said, totally confused.

Her friend blew out a breath. "Okay, I'm going to show you something, but promise not to freak out, okay?"

"Okay..."

Elena pulled out her phone and scrolled through her photos before holding out the iPhone to Jill. "This is what he sent me on Friday."

Jill glanced down. "Um, a couple of utilitarian candles and some ugly flowers?"

"Look closer."

She did. It took her a half second to recognize it. "That's Vin's table."

Elena nodded slowly.

Jill's heart seemed to stop. "No. He did this? He got... flowers?"

"He sent me this, wanting to know if it worked without a tablecloth."

Her heart started beating again, but this time it squeezed. Hard. "Oh my God."

"He was trying to do, like, a thing," Elena said miserably. "He had steaks and..."

"Oh my God," Jill repeated. "Crap. And then I come in there, all, I want to go out..."

She tossed the phone back at Elena before throwing her hands over her face, her eyes watering. "I want to die."

"You didn't know," Elena said smoothly, rubbing her back.

Jill dropped her hands. "But I should have. I'm a cop. I should have looked around, I should have..."

I should have read him.

"Oh my God. This is the worst. What do I do? Apologize? Grovel?"

"What do you want to do?" her friend asked carefully.

She met her friend's eyes steadily. "I want him back. But... we had this fight, and I couldn't even get him to admit... *anything.*"

"He cares about you. You know that. Everyone knows that."

"I know." Jill stared at her wineglass. "And for the longest time, that's been enough. But I want *big* love, Elena. I want the fairy tale. There's a reason I said yes, and it wasn't the right reason, but it's still there. I want the big wedding. I want the giddy anticipation of Valentine's Day. I want date nights, and a big, messy family—"

Jill blew out a long breath.

"And you know, even as much as I want that—I'd give it up... all of it... if he loved me, you know? It would be enough to be loved by him."

"And you don't think he does?"

Jill grabbed a handful of chips and crunched irritably. "I flat-out asked if he thought he might, some day. He looked ready to puke and didn't say a word."

"Oh, Vin," Elena said quietly.

"The worst part is, I *miss* him. It's been only a few days, but I miss everything about him. About us."

"We need more wine," Elena muttered. "And a plan."

Elena came to sit beside her and grabbed her hands. "Jill, Vin may not know how to tell you with words, but take it from someone who grew up with the big oaf . . . *this* is Vincent in love."

Jill drew in a sharp breath, and Elena squeezed her hand harder. "He may not even know it yet. He has no idea what he's doing. I'm guessing he's terrified. But he's trying, Jill. His ugly flowers . . . that was him trying. That was him *loving you*."

Jill squeezed her eyes shut.

"Oh God," she said quietly. Her chest felt tight. Swallowing was suddenly difficult. "He must have felt so . . . rejected."

Elena's face was sympathetic. "If it's any consolation, I'm sure he didn't handle it well. And I'm not trying to tell you how to feel, or what to do. I'm just asking—well, okay, begging actually—give him a chance, Jilly. You matter to him. And I know it's hard, because you and Vin have been soul mates for like half a decade, but don't forget that this element of your relationship is new."

Jill groaned and dipped her forehead toward her knees. "Oh jeez. I basically asked him to propose after two weeks of dating."

Elena laughed and patted her head. "Well, yours is an unconventional love story, sweetie."

Jill sat back up. "So what do I do?"

Elena stood and took both of their wineglasses to the kitchen. "Call him. Tell him to come over. And then be naked. But for the love of God, wait until I leave."

Jill stood, dodging the newspaper articles scattered around her floor as she went to join Elena in the kitchen. "You're not staying?"

"Got things to do, places to be, love. And none of them involve being around while my best friend and brother hook up."

Jill walked Elena to the door.

"We're good, right?" Elena asked, shrugging on her jacket.

Jill smiled. "We're great. Way too good of friends to let something as silly as your dumb brother come between us."

Elena smiled. "So you'll implement the naked plan we talked about?"

Jill rested her cheek against the open door. "I've got to figure out what to say first."

"Don't overthink it. And *definitely* consider the naked plan I laid out for you."

Jill rolled her eyes and hugged her friend good-bye.

She stood still for several moments after shutting the door.

"I'm such an idiot," she muttered.

Jill headed toward her cell phone, but the paper all over her floor caught her eye.

The mess seemed to have grown since last time she looked, and since Jill knew herself well enough to know that the longer she waited the more burdensome the task would become, she forced herself to clean it up now.

She wasn't particularly organized by nature, but when it came to work, she *had* to be, so she carefully sorted the mess of papers by order of date, in case she'd need to quickly find something later.

Not that it would likely make much of a difference for Lenora Birch. This case seemed determined to stay cold—ice cold.

Finally Jill got to the last scanned article. It was over fifty years old, and the original must have been so faded that the scanned image was barely legible.

In fact, it was so hard to read, and so old, that Jill had barely glanced at it the first time. It was a local story from Lenora's hometown of Lorrence, a tiny town in Ohio barely big enough to be on most maps. Understandably, a local girl getting cast as the lead in a major Hollywood film was a big deal.

A Love Song for Cora went on to garner an Academy Award nomination and was the movie that launched Lenora's career.

Jill placed the article on top of the pile and sat back on her heels. She couldn't help the wistful smile as she glanced down at the article. She wondered if its columnist—a Bill Shapiro—had had any idea that his little article would be the first of hundreds on a Hollywood legend.

Her eyes skimmed the hard-to-read print. Bill Shapiro's writing was amateurish, at best, and his irritation at being unable to get a statement from the producer, the director, or Lenora herself was thinly veiled.

Ultimately the only "insider" willing to speak with

Bill had been an assistant casting director, Miles Kennedy, and Bill had obviously done his best to add a bit of drama, despite the lack of big-name references.

According to Mr. Kennedy, Ms. Birch's casting as Cora Mulroney was a bit of a happy accident—an accident that had yet another tie to the little town. As it would turn out, it was actually the *younger* Birch sister who originally caught the attention of the director during the auditions. Upon learning that Miss Dorothy Birch was no longer available, the elder Lenora was cast, as she'd been a close second choice for the role of Cora...

Jill frowned.

Dorothy Birch was an actress?

And a good one, apparently, if she'd been the first choice for the now iconic role of Cora.

What in the world would have come up to make a seventeen-year-old girl pass up the opportunity of a lifetime?

And how must it have felt that that very film had made her older sister a household name?

Jill didn't have siblings, but she couldn't help but think that must have left a scar.

A very deep, very long-lasting scar.

Her mind whirring into overdrive, Jill quickly rifled through the pages toward the other end of the stack until she found the article she'd been reading just hours earlier.

It was from the Entertainment section of the *LA Times*—celebrating the fiftieth anniversary of *A Love Song for Cora*.

The anniversary had been just three days before Lenora's death—timely coincidence Jill and Vin had disregarded as unimportant before. The film, while famous, was old, most of its principal actors and behind-the-scenes legends long dead.

A Love Song for Cora was free of the controversy and scandal that followed Lenora in her later films. The fact that its anniversary had overlapped so closely with Lenora's death had seemed a bittersweet send-off for one of Hollywood's sweethearts.

Jill picked up the other article—the older one, from Ohio—and chewed her lip. Reread the part about the role of Lenora being the director's second choice.

It was probably nothing.

It certainly didn't feel like a breakthrough. Whenever Vin had one of his premonitions, or a surge of Spidey sense, it seemed to rip through him with vicious certainty. When Vin knew something, he knew it. One hundred percent.

Jill didn't know anything.

Didn't feel anything except a faint tingling.

Was a quote from an ancient news article really worth pursuing? Hell, it wasn't even an *actual* quote. For all she knew Bill Shapiro had gotten Miles Kennedy's answering machine and decided to make something up to add a little flair to his otherwise dull recitation of the facts.

Jill stood and stretched, her eyes flicking back and forth between the two articles.

It was probably nothing. She was pretty sure it was nothing.

But then again, this sort of assessment was usually Vincent's part of the job. Her role came after.

Jill picked up the phone to call Vincent, although with a very different agenda than she'd had just a few minutes before. This time she needed her partner.

"Dang it," she muttered when he didn't pick up. He was still at work. She could call into dispatch, get him on the radio...

But that seemed excessive. It wasn't even an open case, and she didn't have proof beyond the blurry scan of a small-town newspaper publication that was a half-century old.

It could wait.

She texted him to call her, then put the phone back down.

Her stomach rumbled, telling her the only thing she'd eaten was a handful of chips.

Jill went back to the kitchen and started to go through the motions of making a sandwich. Bread. Mayo. Mustard. Ham.

She cut the sandwich into neat triangles and then stared down at it without taking a bite.

The tingle she'd felt earlier was more of a buzz now. Distracting enough that she couldn't seem to think about anything except Lenora Birch being pushed over the railing of her home. Probably by someone she knew. Trusted.

Someone who had a grudge...

"Oh, for Pete's sake."

She poured a glass of the wine Elena had brought over, wanting to calm her nerves. But that too sat untouched next to the sandwich.

The buzzing was getting louder.

"Okay, fine," Jill muttered to herself. "It can't hurt to have the conversation."

She headed to the bedroom, pulling out a pair of slacks and a blue button-down. She pulled her hair into a ponytail before grabbing her badge.

And her gun. She wasn't an idiot, after all.

She checked her phone as she headed toward the front door. Nothing from Vincent. Jill hesitated for a moment, wondering if she should have him meet her.

Then she remembered that she was supposed to be sick, but Vincent was still working. For all she knew, he was knee-deep in the middle of an active homicide case, and if she pulled him out of that for a not-quite-hunch on a cold case that they weren't supposed to be working on...

She patted her gun reassuringly as she opened the door. She was a damn good cop with a firearm. She could *certainly* handle talking to a frail sixty-six-year-old lady on her own.

CHAPTER THIRTY-EIGHT

Vincent was about four minutes away from catching Jill's "flu" in order to avoid a huge backlog of paperwork, when his father called.

"Pops," Vin said, answering his cell.

"You busy?"

Vincent glanced down at his computer, then at the Post-it note that served as his to-do list.

Flipped over the Post-it note, looked at the list that extended to the other side.

Looked back at the computer and that patient, blinking cursor.

"Nope," he replied.

"Good. Got time for a late lunch? I'm close to Darby's."

Vincent raised his eyebrows at that. Partially because it was nearly four o'clock. That was a really late lunch.

And also because his father rarely left Staten Island these days except to go to church.

In fact, Tony Moretti was increasingly becoming a homebody as he gradually adjusted to retirement. If he could be coaxed from the comfort of his house, it would have been for a good cause.

And in the case of Vincent's father, the only thing that qualified as a good cause was meddling in his children's business.

Vincent was apparently the offspring du jour.

"Sure, what time?" Vin asked. If nothing else, he was curious to see what he'd done this time to warrant the lecture.

"How about...now? I'm a couple blocks away."

Vincent rolled his eyes. Of course he was. "Sure. Meet you there."

Vin was nearly out the door when Captain Rodriguez called his name. Swearing softly, Vin turned around.

"Going somewhere, Moretti?"

"Lunch."

His boss frowned. "Didn't you just go on a coffee run, like, twenty minutes ago?"

"That was for coffee. Now I need food."

The captain crossed his arms. "You know, I've always been tolerant of your methods since you're damn good at getting results, but between Henley's leave of absence, and then the Lenora Birch case, and now Henley being out sick again—"

"I know," Vincent said, trying to make his face look apologetic. "It's actually for that very reason that I'm headed out to grab a bite to eat with my father. He's determined to talk some sense into me, and I'm all too ready to listen."

Rodriguez's frown lifted slightly at that. "Your father? The police commissioner?"

Former, actually, but Vin wasn't about to make that distinction just now.

"Well, all right," his boss said slowly. "Don't take too long. And what's the story with your partner; is everything—"

Vincent was out the door before his boss could finish the question.

Vincent was pretty damn good at bullshitting about just about everything, but any mention of Jill still rubbed like salt on an open wound. He'd been doing his best not to even *think* about Jill. He sure as hell didn't want to talk about her.

Didn't want to talk about the way he couldn't go to sleep because she wasn't beside him. About how he'd handed any cases to other detectives the past couple days because he couldn't bear to work without her.

Hell, even coffee didn't taste good anymore because she wasn't there to drink it with him.

Vin didn't know how to explain any of that to himself.

He wasn't going to start running his mouth about it to other people.

His dad, apparently, had other ideas. Vin knew it the moment he walked into the Darby Diner and saw his father...

And his two brothers.

"Shit," Vincent said, looping onto the booth beside Luc as he glared across the table at his dad and Anth. "This is an ambush, huh?"

"Dad's idea," Luc said, taking a sip of coffee.

That was probably true. Both of his brothers were

dressed in uniform, which meant they too had likely gotten an unexpected "late lunch" summons.

"I'm sure you put up a huge protest," Vin grumbled.

"Hell no. I've been waiting a good long while for it to be your turn, Big Brother."

"Same here," Anth chimed in.

"My turn for what?" Vin asked.

"Oh, you know, just the usual 'you're being an idiot' speech," Luc said.

Anth's grin was evil. "I love those."

"Really?" Vin snapped. "Because I was there when *you* got said speech, and you didn't seem to love anything about it. And you," he said, shifting his attention to Luc, "remember that time Mom and Dad cornered you about—"

"Enough." The quiet command came from their father. "We're not here to ambush you."

Anthony coughed.

"We just want to know what's going on."

"Nothing," Vin snapped.

"Well, see, I'm having a hard time buying that," Anthony said, leaning forward and folding his fingers on the table. "Because the cat's out of the bag about Jill's engagement being long over."

"Cat's also out of the bag that you two have been sleeping together," Luc said.

Vincent jerked slightly in response. "Who told you that?"

Anth's smile was sly. "You just did."

"Fuck," Vincent muttered. He was better than this.

"We just want to know what's going on," his father said again.

Vincent picked up the menu as a way of avoiding the question, but his father knocked it back down again. "We ordered you a cheeseburger."

Vincent opened his mouth, looking for an argument, only to realize that a cheeseburger was exactly what he wanted.

A waitress appeared at that moment and placed a Coke in front of him, and his scowl deepened because that too was exactly what he wanted.

"Good," his father said, correctly reading him as always. "Now tell us—"

"What's going on," Vin finished. "I know the question, I just don't know the answer."

He braced himself for them to start badgering him, but to his surprise, the men of his family looked sympathetic. As though they knew what he was going through.

And perhaps they did. Vincent didn't know the details of his parents' early courtship, but his mother was strong willed, and his father was, well...difficult.

As for his brothers, Vin had recently seen firsthand how uphill their battle had been. Luc, because of his dark secrets and the not-so-minor fact that Ava had once been out to expose them. Anth, because of some ridiculously misplaced notion that his career ambitions precluded him from being in a relationship.

Vincent appreciated the sense of camaraderie. He did. But it wasn't the same. For both Luc and Anth, there'd been very specific demons that needed slaying. Luc and Anth had been broken, yes, but the problems had been *precise*. Problems, which, with the right woman and the right circumstance, could be solved.

But with Vin—Vin didn't have any demons to be

played. Didn't have toxic secrets that only needed to be coaxed to the surface. Like them, he was broken, yes, but not because anyone or anything had broken him.

He'd always just been... apart, somehow.

There was a moment of silence as their food came, and paper napkins were placed in laps, and Anthony muttered irritably about the injustices of pickles, and Vincent started to think he might get off easy.

And then Luc dropped his spoon back into his bowl of chili and turned to face Vincent. "I know what you're thinking, and your case isn't different. You're not special."

Vincent's cheeseburger turned dry in his mouth, and he had to wash it down with Coke.

"How did you—"

"Know what you were thinking?" Anth finished for him. "Because we've been there. We all think that our special brand of emotional hang-ups is special."

"Don't know how I raised three idiots," their father said, jabbing a fry around the table at this sons.

"Oh good, a pep talk," Anth muttered.

"I'm serious," Vin's dad said. "You're exceptional cops, but you're a bunch of goobers when it comes to personal lives."

Luc took a bite of chili. "And I suppose you got it right with Mom the first time? No bouts of stubbornness or saying the wrong thing?"

Tony's eyes narrowed on Luc. "What did your mother tell you?"

Luc shrugged. "Nothing."

"Good," their father muttered.

"But Nonna said you were an absolute moron," Anthony chimed in quietly.

Tony dropped his Reuben. "Now see here, what my mother never understood was that I had to do things my own way, on my own timetable—"

Vincent set his glass down hard enough to rattle the table. "Exactly," he said. "Which is why I'll ask that my family let me and Jill do things our way, at our speed."

The three of them stared at Vincent for a moment before exchanging a glance.

"Nah," Luc said finally, reaching over and stealing a fry. "That would have flown, say, five years ago."

"Bambino's right," his father said gruffly. "That woman is the best thing that ever happened to you. It's time that you stop pussyfooting around and—"

"Make an honest woman of her," Anth said in a rather impressive imitation of their father.

Tony jerked an elbow at Anth, unperturbed by the subtle mockery. "Yeah. That."

"I'm trying," Vincent said quietly. "You think I'm not fucking trying? I bought her flowers. I set out candles. I cooked."

"Damn," Luc said, looking impressed. "And she's still pissed at you?"

Vin pushed his plate away, mostly untouched. "She didn't know."

"What do you mean she didn't know?"

"She just … she came over wanting to go out, muttered something about not wanting Chinese food—"

"You cooked Chinese food?" Luc interrupted.

"No! Steaks. But she didn't know that, and—"

"What about the flowers?" Anth asked, puzzled. "She didn't put the pieces together?"

"Well, I don't know that she even saw the flowers."

"Okay, this is bullshit," his father said with a shake of his head. "Total bullshit."

Vin lifted his eyebrows at his dad's input. "Perhaps. But I didn't go about it the right way, so maybe she's right to be pissed. But then she got all...girly."

"Oh, dear God. You didn't tell her that, did you?"

Vincent ran a hand over his face, feeling tired. "No, but she started rambling about how I have caution tape around my heart, and would I ever love her, and how she wants marriage."

Luc whistled. "Our Jill doesn't pull her punches."

"But she's got a point," Tony said. "It's been what, five, six years?"

"It's been three weeks!" Vincent said, slamming his palm on the table.

Anth squinted and made a face. "Eh. It's been more like six years."

"Jesus," Vin said, putting his elbows on the table and dropping his face into his hands. "What is it you'd have me do? Hire an opera singer to serenade her? Hold a boombox over my head outside her window? Set up a scavenger hunt that leads to all her favorite kinds of tacos just to show I care?"

"Wait. She has multiple favorite kinds of tacos?" Luc asked. "That's either hot, or weird, I can't decide."

"I don't think Jill cares so much about what you do," Anth said quietly. "I think she cares about how you feel."

Vincent lifted his head. "I've never been good at that stuff."

"Nobody is," his father said gruffly.

"No, I mean—"

"I know what you mean," Tony interrupted. "You think

that because you're quiet and a loner, that because you don't wear your heart on your sleeve, and that because you sometimes overthink things to death—"

"I'm next in the naming Vin's flaws game," Luc whispered to Anth.

Tony ignored his youngest son and pressed on. "You think that because you're hyper-rational and prefer facts to fancy and data to whimsy that you're not capable of love. That you don't deserve it."

Out of the corner of his eye, Vin saw his brothers exchange a glance, but Vincent never looked away from his father, torn between wanting to argue and desperately, *desperately* wanting to believe what his father was saying.

"Dude, is that what this is all about?" Anth asked, his voice kinder than Vincent was accustomed to. "You think that just because you don't show feelings that you don't have them?"

"This conversation is ridiculous." His voice was gruff. He started to push out of the booth, but Luc grabbed his forearm.

"Stay."

Luc had abruptly shifted from Luc, charming younger brother, to Luc, badass cop, and Vincent found himself doing exactly as he was told.

Vin swallowed, oddly nervous. "I guess I've always just figured that something was missing. That some part of me was dead. Or was never alive, or something."

"Why the *hell* would you think that?" his father asked.

"I don't know how to connect with people. People don't... I don't know how to make people like me."

What Vin really meant was that he didn't know how to make people *love* him. It was an uncomfortably vulnerable moment, and judging from the way his father and brothers looked away for a moment, as though to give privacy, he suspected they knew what he meant.

Luc cleared his throat. "So just to be clear...you don't think you can love Jill, because you don't think she'll ever love you?"

They'd shifted verbs. *Like* to *love*. But Vin didn't bother to correct his brother. Nor did he confirm his brother's assessment.

But it was spot-on.

It was the reason he froze when she'd asked if he could love her. If he could ever do *forever* with her.

He wanted that. Of *course* he wanted it. Had always wanted it just about as long as she'd been a part of his life.

But he didn't know how to put it out there. Because he knew that if it was one-sided...if she didn't love him back, or changed her mind...

He didn't think he could bear it.

"Vin, listen—" Anth said, sitting forward.

Vincent groaned. "You're going to go Big Brother on me, aren't you?"

Anthony ignored this and shifted attention to Luc. "Luca. When you told Ava how you felt about her. How'd it feel?"

"I nearly shit my pants," Luc said cheerfully, shoveling in another bite of chili.

Anth nodded. "Same with me and Maggie. It was the hardest thing I've ever done in my life, putting myself out there like that. And the best. *Easily* the best. Dad. What about with you and Mom?"

Tony blew out a breath and looked away. All three of his sons looked at him, waiting.

"It was a long time ago," he said with a wave of his hand.

"Dad," Luc said in a coaxing tone. "Do it for our emotionally stunted Vinnie here…"

His father's eyes flicked to Vincent's for a fraction of a second. "I threw up. Before I told her how I felt. And after."

"There you go, big guy," Anth said with a clap on his dad's shoulder. "You see, Vin, there's no such thing as easy. You're not damaged. You're not broken. You're just male."

Vincent scratched his cheek. They made it sound so easy.

Also, terrifying. *Lots* of body functions involved.

"If you can't tell her, how about you start by telling us?" Luc said. "Do you love Jill?"

Vin forced himself to look his brother in the eyes. "Of course."

Luc smiled. "See? Easy."

Vin glared.

"Look," Anth said, "the worst that can happen is she guts your insides. Leaves you a hollow shell of a man, but according to you, you're already there, so—"

"Okay," Vin said, standing before Luc could stop him. "Good talk, guys."

"You going after her?" Luc called after him.

Had his father not been there, Vincent would have shot the finger over his shoulder, but instead he just kept walking.

"I better see that girl at brunch on Sunday!" Tony bellowed.

Vin didn't respond to that either.

They'd given him plenty to think about. And a part of him knew they were right.

But the other part of him was itchy. Tense. As though something were wrong, but that he couldn't place his finger on.

He rolled his shoulders, tried to shake it off as he walked back toward the precinct, but the feeling got worse.

Maybe it was all this talk about Jill, and the way that they'd left things. The things he needed to tell her...

He pulled out his cell phone and slowed to a stop in the middle of the busy sidewalk as he saw that he had two missed calls from her.

Vin hadn't heard from her in days, and she'd called him twice in a twenty-minute span.

The itchy feeling grew worse. The way it did when he knew he was close to the killer, but didn't know the *who*.

He resumed walking and called Jill back.

It rang a handful of times before voice mail picked up.

He walked faster and called again.

Voice mail.

"Damn it," he said so sharply that a handful of people glared at him.

He ignored them. Called Jill again. "Come on, Henley—"

Nothing. No answer.

Vincent made it back to the precinct in record time, ignoring the handful of colleagues that spoke to him either in greeting or with a request.

He went to his desk only long enough to grab his car keys out of the top drawer and then he was off again, all but running toward his car.

He had no *good* reason to think something was wrong. She could be in the shower. Or on a walk. Or more likely, screening his calls.

But he sped all the way to her place.

Just in case.

CHAPTER THIRTY-NINE

The second Dorothy Birch greeted Jill at the door of her lovely, if modest, apartment, Jill felt like an idiot.

The woman was wearing white slacks, a pale purple blouse, and old-fashioned pearls. Her shoes were the orthopedic kind Jill's grandparents had both used to wear.

Her expression was polite, but also bewildered.

It was *so* not the face of a killer.

"Hello, Detective Henley. How lovely to see you again. Won't you please come in?"

"Thanks for agreeing to see me," Jill said, feeling awkward as she let herself in.

"I was just making some tea. Would you care for some?"

"That'd be nice, thanks," Jill said with a small smile.

Dorothy made a small gesture toward the living room, and Jill went to sit in the same spot she had last time she'd been here.

Only this time there was no Vincent.

She was extra glad she hadn't called him now. Vin would never have mocked her for being wrong—but it would have been embarrassing all the same.

"I'm surprised to see you," Dorothy called from the kitchen. "I was under the impression the police had closed the case."

"We've had to expand our focus to other things," Jill called back, fiddling with a fussy flower arrangement on the table. It made her think of the flowers Vin had bought her, and she stopped. "But all of us wish we could get a break."

Dorothy emerged from the kitchen, holding the tray with the easy walk of someone much younger.

"And have you gotten a break? Is that why you're here?"

Jill took a breath. "I...I don't know. But I was doing some reading today and wanted to get your opinion on something."

"Of course," Dorothy said. "Sugar, if I remember correctly?"

Jill nodded, smiling in thanks as Dorothy dropped in a sugar cube and handed Jill the delicate teacup.

Jill used the adorably tiny spoon to dissolve the sugar cube as she considered her next approach.

"Where's that handsome partner of yours?" Dorothy asked.

Jill took a sip of tea and tried to hide her wince, wondering if it would be inappropriate to ask for another sugar cube. One definitely wasn't enough to cut the bitterness.

"Working another case," Jill replied.

It was a risky move. If she at all thought Dorothy a

suspect, she should have told her Vincent was on the way. Hell, that the whole NYPD was on the way.

But then she'd run the risk of Dorothy feeling threatened. And if she did know something...if she'd done something...Jill needed the other woman relaxed.

She took another sip of tea, bigger this time, hoping that if she drank this one fast enough, it would be easier to ask for extra sugar in the next round.

"Ms. Birch—"

"Dorothy."

Jill smiled. "Dorothy. I was going through old articles today—hoping to uncover an old feud we may have missed before, and I came across something curious."

"More tea?"

"Oh—sure," Jill said, holding out her cup. "And an extra sugar cube wouldn't go amiss. I've got a sweet tooth."

Dorothy laughed. "Me too, dear. Me too."

Jill noticed the other woman's hands shaking a bit as they took Jill's cup, and she looked away, wanting to spare the other woman the indignity that old age sometimes had on the joints.

"You and Lenora were from Torrence, Ohio?"

"Yes, that's right. Just about the tiniest town you can imagine. One butcher, one salon, one market...that sort of place."

"It sounds lovely," Jill said with a smile.

"It had its charms," Dorothy said, handing Jill's cup to her. Her hands were steadier now. "But both Lenora and I found we preferred the big city. So much energy here."

Jill nodded and took a sip of tea. Better. Much better. Honestly, why did people pretend that bitter tasted good?

Coffee tasted better with sugar. Chocolate tasted better with sugar. Tea *definitely* tasted better with sugar.

"Ms. Birch—Dorothy—did you know a Bill Shapiro back in your hometown?"

Dorothy tilted her head. "I suppose it sounds familiar, but goodness, it's been a long time. You have to remember, Lenora and I left Ohio for Los Angeles when I was only seventeen."

It was exactly the opening Jill needed. A way for her to close out this lead without ruffling feathers if she was wrong.

"Because you both wanted to get into acting?"

There was the tiniest of pauses. "Yes. We used to talk about it all the time."

Jill nodded. Then nodded again. For some reason her thoughts felt fuzzy. As though they were coming from the very, *very* back of her head.

She took another sip of her tea and forced herself to concentrate. "You both auditioned for the role of Cora Mulroney, is that right?"

Dorothy's face had gone a bit taut. At least it seemed that way through Jill's blurry vision.

Wait... why was her vision blurry?

"Yes, that's right," Dorothy was saying.

"And you..." Jill's teacup rattled to the table as she pressed a hand to her now-spinning head. "You...Bill Shapiro wrote an article—"

Why couldn't she keep any of this straight?

"I used to have a golden Lab," Dorothy said.

A golden Lab? Like a dog? Why were they talking about a dog? Jill struggled to keep up, but couldn't. Thinking felt hard. Like after too much tequila.

"Jensen was his name. The sweetest dog you can imagine. But...he got old. I suppose we all do. They found cancer. Slow-growing, so I didn't put him down right away, but toward the end he started to hurt a little, and I wasn't ready to say good-bye."

Jill tried to make a noise. Tried to think. She couldn't. She felt herself slump back against the couch and fixed her eyes on Dorothy, trying to put the pieces together.

"They gave me some medication for him. Sedatives, to help him sleep. To make him comfortable."

Sedatives.

That's why she was foggy.

Dorothy Birch had drugged her with *dog medicine*. It was so unbelievably *inglorious* that Jill wanted to rage, except that would take energy she didn't have.

"I didn't mean to do it," Dorothy was saying as she took another sip of her own tea. "I was just so darn angry, Detective. That was my role. *I* was supposed to be Cora Mulroney. *I* was supposed to be the star. But then she convinced me that she should get her break first. Because she was older. And that she'd help me get another role. A bigger, better one."

Dorothy's laugh was brittle. "We all know how that goes, don't we? I let it go. For *years*, I let it go. Let her have the spotlight. Told myself I didn't want it. But then... then I couldn't."

Dorothy's voice faded to quiet, in a sort of crazy-person way. Or maybe that was Jill's head, which wouldn't stop spinning.

She couldn't see Dorothy anymore, and Jill had a moment of panic until she realized that she'd closed her eyes. Just for a moment. She was so *tired*.

"Why?" Jill wasn't sure she'd actually managed to speak the word, or if it just rattled around in her brain, but either Dorothy had heard her, or she was still rambling on, because she answered.

"Lenora promised that we would go to the anniversary showing of *A Love Song for Cora* together. She was supposed to accept an award—some iconic woman in Hollywood nonsense—and she said she'd call me up on the stage. To give me the recognition I deserved. To acknowledge my sacrifice…"

Jill heard Dorothy stand. Heard the soft pad of orthopedic shoes come closer, before a hand gently touched her head. "She decided not to go, Detective Henley. Jill. She said it sounded *boring*, and that she was just going to have her agent accept the award…"

Stupid, was all Jill could think. What a stupid, petty reason to kill someone.

"I hope you'll be okay, Detective. I don't really know what effect poor Jensen's sedatives will have on you, but I *certainly* don't want you to die. But…either way, honey, I'll be long gone when you wake up, and I doubt you'll be finding me. You'd be surprised how easily old people fly under the radar. People don't see us."

Jill tried to make her mouth move. Tried to tell Dorothy Henley that she would find her. That she would make her pay for her crimes. That she would—

She would—

And then there was nothing.

Only darkness.

CHAPTER FORTY

By the time Vincent bounded up the front steps to Jill's apartment, he was completely beyond knocking.

He'd called her at least a dozen times on the way over, and she hadn't picked up once. If he barged in and found her mad, and screening his calls, fine. If he barged in and found her naked and in the bubble bath, fine. If he barged in and found her with another man...

Not fine. Not fine at all.

But they'd deal with it. He'd win her back.

He just needed her to be *okay*.

He knocked once with his fist even as he shoved his spare key into her lock and pushed the door open. "Jill! Henley, so help me, God—"

She wasn't there. He knew the moment that he stepped inside that Jill wasn't in the apartment.

Vincent checked anyway. Checked every corner. The tub, the bedroom.

She wasn't there.

"Fuck."

He stood in the middle of her apartment, hands plowed into his hair as he tried to think. Tried to tap into the strange buzzing that was roaring through him, trying to tell him... something.

Something important.

Vincent's instincts were never wrong, and right now they were telling him that Jill was in trouble, and that she needed him, and he didn't have a fucking clue—

His eyes locked on the stack of papers on the living room floor.

Jill *always* did her case research on her living room floor. Said it was where she thought best.

Vincent fell on them like a dying man, but forced himself to pause before diving into the content. To remain perfectly still as he assessed.

A quick scan of the stack in the middle showed the name Lenora Birch several times.

No surprise there. He'd been doing some research on his own as well.

But something about the way these were arranged—one big stack in the middle, two individual sheets on either side.

As though she'd held one in each hand, separate from the pile.

Slowly, Vincent picked up the papers on the right and left, separate from the main pile. Both were scanned newspaper articles. He read the older one first, silently cursing the terrible quality of the image because it took him twice as long.

By the time he reached the end, his heart was pounding. The second article, the newer one, confirmed his fear.

His Spidey sense—the one that had refused to kick in during the entire Lenora Birch case—was now going off in large, whooping alarms.

He was on his feet and racing toward the door even as he raged out loud at an absent Jill. "Goddamn it, Henley, why didn't you wait for me?"

Vincent's car was in motion even as he reached for the radio to call for backup.

The uniforms would beat him there, but that was fine. As long as someone got to Jill, he didn't care about anything else.

Vincent's breath was ragged as he sped all the way back to Manhattan.

Please let her be okay. Please *let her be okay, and I'll do anything, everything. I'll hire a sky writer, and write poetry, and go on bended knee, and I'll eat Goddamn fondue on Valentine's Day…*

It was the longest ride of Vincent's life, and he could have sworn his heart stopped a million times along the way.

But when he finally pulled up in front of Dorothy Birch's apartment building, his heart really did stop.

There were the expected squad cars, of course. A half dozen of them.

But there was an ambulance too. And there were his brothers. His brothers who beat him, because they were already in Manhattan when shit went down.

Luc's and Anthony's faces were unusually somber as they watched a stretcher be loaded into the ambulance then.

He saw it then. The blond hair. The small frame.

"No. *No!*"

Even in the chaos, his shout had carried, and people

turned to stare as he half ran, half stumbled toward the ambulance as the stretcher disappeared from view.

His brothers caught both of his arms before he could throw himself into the back.

"Easy," Anth muttered. "Let them work."

"What happened?" his voice cracked. "What's wrong with her?"

"They found her unconscious," Luc said quietly. "They think she was drugged, but they don't know with what. They're searching the place now."

Drugged. That old bitch had drugged her.

"Where is she?" Vin snarled, glancing around at the squad cars, searching the backseats for a white head.

Both brothers were silent for a moment.

Anthony finally answered. "There was no sign of Dorothy Birch when the uniforms got here. It was just Jill slumped on the couch. Judging from the open dresser drawers and clothes strewn on the bed, we're guessing she made a run for it."

Vincent's eyes came back to Jill's body. He could barely see with the paramedics moving in every direction, but she wasn't moving.

She wasn't moving.

"I'm going to find Dorothy Birch," Vincent said, his voice harsh and grating. "I'll fucking *find* her!"

One of the paramedics started to close the back of the ambulance door, and Vin reached out to grab it before it could shut in his face.

"Sir, you can't—"

"I'm a cop," Vincent ground out as he launched himself into the back of the ambulance.

"And *this* is my partner."

CHAPTER FORTY-ONE

Jell-O.

She'd been eating Jell-O for days.

Or at least hours. Jill had definitely been eating Jell-O for hours.

And it was freaking *fantastic*.

At least until the last nurse had brought her the orange kind. She started to hand it to Elena who was sitting in the chair to her right, but Elena didn't look up from her magazine, and merely pointed across the bed to Ava.

Jill handed the orange Jell-O to Ava, who plucked it out of Jill's hand with a *tsking* noise. "Now how can they expect you to get better on orange Jell-O?"

"I know," Jill pouted. "Don't they know I was drugged with dog tranquilizers?"

"The indignity. I can't even. I'll take care of this

straightaway." Ava handed the orange Jell-O cup to Luc. "Luc, take care of this. Straightaway."

He stared at the cup in his hand before shooting a puzzled look at the women. "And by take care of this, you mean..."

"Get her red Jell-O," Maggie said from the chair in the corner. "Obviously."

Luc glanced at Anthony with a *what-the-fuck* expression, but Anth held up his hands and shook his head. "Hey, man. She's right about the dog tranquilizer. Maybe it made her weird. Weird-er."

"Heard that," Jill said, shooting a finger pistol at Anthony. "And for the record, I liked red Jell-O *before* that old lady tricked me into taking doggie sedatives."

"Everyone likes red Jell-O," Elena pointed out. "It's pretty much the only Jell-O worth eating."

"I like green Jell-O myself."

Jill glanced at the door and grinned when she saw the Moretti grandmother. "Nonna!"

"There's my girl," Nonna said, moving toward the bed and giving Jill a none-too-gentle hug. "I'm sorry I couldn't make it here earlier. I had another of those dang colds. Boogers the size of—"

"Nonna, for the love of God," Luc said. "Not after you just talked about preferring green Jell-O. Actually, not ever."

Nonna ignored her grandson as she studied Jill with a slight frown. "So where is the old biddy that landed you in this horrible place, and got you dressed in that ugly gown that makes your boobs look like pancakes?"

Anthony grabbed the Jell-O cup out of Luc's hand. "I'm going to go find the red Jell-O."

"I'll help!" Luc said, half running after his brother.

Jill glanced down at the gown. "Not my best look, huh? And as for that biddy . . . still on the run."

Nonna huffed and shoved Ava out of the chair so she could sit down. "I'm not surprised. Everyone underestimates us old farts, but we can be surprisingly crafty. A wobbly hand and a shaky voice are all it takes to do surprising misdeeds."

Yikes.

Jill plucked at the hospital blanket, remembering all too well how Dorothy had played her with the shaking hand routine. She'd replayed yesterday over and over—at least the parts she could remember—and had concluded that Dorothy must have drugged her first cup of tea while she was still in the kitchen, and then the second cup of tea when Jill had looked away to let the elderly woman save her pride.

Idiot. She'd been such an idiot.

The nurse came back into the room, carrying a tray with three red Jell-O cups (Anthony and Luc must have played the cop card) and an exaggerated smile. "I hate to keep doing this, but there's a limit on how many visitors can be in here . . ."

"Why?" Nonna asked, turning around to stare at the nurse. "You think anyone died of too much well-wishing?"

"It's hospital policy, Nonna," Maggie explained, rubbing a hand over her belly and taking pity on the poor nurse. "We're all taking turns. Mom and Dad headed out so that Luc and Anth could come in."

Nonna grunted, turning back to Jill. "Who cares about *those* grandsons? Where's the one that matters?"

The room fell silent. Even the nurse seemed to

understand that this was a Forbidden Question, and quietly set the Jell-O cups on Jill's table before leaving the room. She didn't even warn them again about visitor overload.

Jill swallowed and opened her mouth, but no words came out.

"Vincent's trying to track down Dorothy Birch," Ava explained quietly.

"Why?" Nonna demanded with her usual candor. "His partner's laid up being served orange Jell-O, and he can't find someone else to track down a ninety-year-old woman?"

"She's sixty-six," Jill corrected quietly. As though *that* was what was important right now.

Nonna stood, putting hands on her bony hips. "That boy may be my blood, but I'd *strangle* him if he were here right now. I'd sit him down and make him hear all about my boogers. And my phlegm. I'd tell him about how my phlegm was multicolored this morning. And then I'd go and find that Tom—that nice, handsome, but maybe wrong-for-you Tom, and I'd bring him here and tell him to put that pretty ring back on your finger, because at least Tom—"

"Nonna, if you bring Tom into this hospital room, or anywhere near Jill, I'll put your bony ass in a home where they don't serve any Jell-O."

Jill's heart swelled at the sound of that voice. That wonderfully beautiful, familiar voice.

Nonna's frown flipped into a happy grin as she spun around, shifting enough to give Jill an unobstructed view of the door.

An unobstructed view of *Vincent*.

He came.

He was here.

Jill drew in a long breath.

He looked...

The same.

Leather jacket? Check.

Black shirt? Check.

Dark jeans? Check.

Frown? Check.

But there were differences too.

Like the bouquet of gorgeous pink roses in his right hand. That was new.

And the warmth in his gaze when his eyes met Jill. That was new too.

"Oooh-kay then," Elena said quietly, pushing to her feet. "Anyone else find that it just got uncomfortably warm in here?"

Elena silently held out a hand to Maggie, who was already awkwardly pushing herself to her feet, aided by Ava, who came around to grab her other hand.

Jill was only dimly aware of her three friends heading toward the door.

Only at Elena's not-so-soft *Nonna!* did Jill realize what was going on...

Everyone was trying to give her and Vincent privacy.

Everyone except Nonna, who'd plopped back down in her chair and helped herself to a red Jell-O. She was frowning down at it. "What is this, cherry? Fruit punch? I'm telling you, the green is where it's at. It's very—"

Ava stuck her head out the door. "Luc! Anth!"

Luc and Anthony reappeared in moments, and without having to be told—they had both lived with Nonna, after all—descended on their grandmother and very gently, very *firmly*, lifted her from the chair and ushered her from the door.

"My Jell-O!" she shrieked.

Elena gave her an exasperated look. "You were just fussing about how it wasn't green."

"Yes, but if I had to choose between red Jell-O and *no* Jell-O—"

Vincent moved for the first time since entering the room, walking toward the Jell-O, grabbing both that and Nonna's spoon in one hand before storming back to the group waiting in the doorway.

He handed it to Ava, who was closest, and then spreading his arms out to the side, flowers and all, he literally crowded every last one of his family members out the door.

Vincent started to shut the door before he reached out and grabbed Anth's arm. "Nobody comes in here."

Anth gave him a nod, and Vin started to close the door again, but not before Nonna loudly whispered to him to remember to get down on one knee.

Finally, the door was shut.

The room was silent.

They were alone.

Vincent slowly turned around to face her, his wary expression easing slightly when he saw that she was smiling.

He approached the bed until he was beside it, his right hand just inches from her own. She itched to extend her fingers. To brush hers against his, but his face was still too damn unreadable.

Vin cleared his throat and awkwardly held out the flowers. "These are for you."

"They're pretty," she said as he lowered himself to the chair beside her, "but . . ."

His eyes narrowed. "But what?"

"Well, there's two buts, actually," Jill said, sniffing the bouquet. "The first is that considering you've been off chasing a murderer that I discovered, there's something I want a little more than these flowers . . ."

"Oh yeah?"

"Yeah."

Vincent lifted an eyebrow before pulling his cell phone out of his jacket pocket. He wiggled it at her. "I may or may not have what you're looking for on this very device."

Jill breathed out a sigh of relief. "You know me."

Vin unlocked his phone, hit a button, and then handed it to her.

It was Dorothy Birch's mug shot.

Jill laid a hand over her chest. "Vincent Moretti. Don't you ever say that you don't do romance. Where'd you find her?"

"Security cameras caught her near Port Authority, getting on a bus."

"A bus," Jill said. "You don't see that every day."

"Yeah, well." Vincent leaned back in the chair. "You also don't see a sixty-six-year-old woman committing sororocide either."

"Ooh, good word," she said.

The side of his mouth tilted up. "Only a homicide investigator would think so."

She glanced down at the flowers. "I keep thinking that we should have known earlier. That we should have caught her."

"You know what *I'm* thinking?" Vin asked, leaning

forward. "I'm thinking that regardless of when we figured out it was her that you shouldn't have gone in alone."

"Agreed," Jill said.

He opened his mouth, and then shut it at her easy agreement.

She gave a sheepish smile. "I'm not proud of the way I handled it. There are no excuses, really. I was stupid."

Jill watched as his eyes turned darker. "Do you have any idea what it was like for me?" he said, his voice quiet. "Do you have any idea what it's like to show up to a crime scene and see your partner on a stretcher?"

She reached a hand toward him but stopped almost immediately. They weren't ready for that. Not yet.

"I'm sorry," she whispered.

He cleared his throat and looked away. "What was the other thing?"

"What?" she asked, not following.

"You said there were two buts about the flowers. What was the other one?"

"Oh. Um—"

She felt foolish telling him now, when his face was all closed off and unreadable.

Then she remembered Maria Moretti's words that day Vin's mother had come to visit her. *If you want him… you'll have to be the brave one.*

Jill lifted her chin. "The second thing I was going to say is that while the roses really are quite lovely, I find that I've recently discovered a new favorite flower. Carnations. Red, to be precise. Sort of like the ones a certain man got for me, only I was too blind to actually see them."

His gaze snapped back to hers. "Is that so?"

She nodded, and this time when she reached out a hand

toward him, she didn't stop until her arm was all the way extended.

His eyes traced the motion warily, and Jill stared at him steadily in challenge. If this was going to work, he needed to be brave too.

Vin blew out a breath and then leaned forward, taking her hand in both of his and cradling it.

"Jill—"

"Wait. Me first," she said. "About that night, I shouldn't have pushed you. I shouldn't have made demands, I shouldn't have rushed you into anything, I shouldn't have—"

"I love you."

Jill's words trailed off at his interruption. "What?"

He leaned his head down to their joined hands, pressed his lips against her palm. "I love you, Jill Henley. Always have. Always will. And you don't have to say it back. And even if you *never* say it back, know that I will still want you, still love you, still die for you—"

Her free hand found its way to his cheek, and he turned his head, pressing his lips to that palm as well before finally lifting his eyes to meet hers. "My brothers said that saying it would be the hardest thing I've ever done. They were wrong. It was the easiest. Because loving you is easy."

Jill's eyes filled with tears. "Took you long enough to realize it," she whispered.

He stood, leaning over her as he pressed his mouth to her eyes, her nose, then finally to her mouth, kissing her soft and sweet.

Vin started to pull back, but Jill's fingers tangled in the fabric of his shirt, holding him close. "You interrupted my speech," she whispered.

He ran a thumb over her cheek. "So finish it now. But make it quick—I'm dying to know if this hospital gown is one of the ones that gapes open in the back, displaying your perfect ass."

She laughed. "All right then. I'll skip to the end of my pretty speech. I love you too, Detective Moretti."

The playful expression vanished from his face, and something tender and heartbreaking flitted across his harsh features. "Yeah?"

"Yeah," she whispered.

His kiss was longer this time, hotter, and when he pulled back, they were both a little breathless, and both remaining red Jell-O cups had been knocked to the ground.

"I don't understand why they don't make these beds for two," he growled.

"Um, probably because the walls are made of glass."

Vincent whipped his head around to see every last one of his family members staring at them with happy smiles.

"How long have they been standing there?"

"Oh, you know. The whole time."

"And how long have my mom and Maggie been crying?"

"Also the whole time," she answered, grinning happily as she traced a finger over his jaw.

"Uh-huh. And Nonna and her camera—"

"Yeah. Whole time." She kissed his cheek.

"Awesome," he muttered. "Have they given you any indication of when you get out of this voyeuristic hellhole?"

"They said one more day for observation, then I'm all yours."

He gave a satisfied grunt and leaned down for another kiss.

"If I get rid of my Peeping Tom family, what are the odds of me getting to see that delightful open-backed gown of yours?"

"It depends," she said, running a finger along his chest. "On?"

Her hand fisted in his shirt once more and she tugged him downward, pressing her lips to his ear.

"On whether or not you've got your handcuffs."

Vincent's groan was low and tortured as he rested his face against her neck. "You're mine forever. You know that, right?"

"I do," she said, running a hand over his cheek. "At least...I'm yours until the next time I have to go to Florida, and someone with an exceptionally pretty face offers me a diamond ring—"

Jill's tone was teasing, but when Vincent pulled back, his expression was both earnest and intense. "Detective Henley, I regret to inform you that while I definitely see a diamond ring in your future, the only one who will be putting it on your finger is me."

"Oh yeah?" she asked, lifting her eyebrows in challenge. "How long will that take?"

"I'm guessing six years. Give or take," he deadpanned.

And then he was kissing her again, his hands sneaking around to the back of her gown, and Jill grinned.

No *way* were they making it six years.

ABOUT THE AUTHOR

Lauren Layne is the *USA Today* bestselling author of contemporary romance.

Prior to becoming an author, Lauren worked in e-commerce and Web marketing. In 2011, she and her husband moved from Seattle to New York City, where Lauren decided to pursue a full-time writing career. It took six months to get her first book deal (despite ardent assurances to her husband that it would only take three). Since then, Lauren's gone on to multiple books, including the bestselling Stiletto series, with more sexy stories on the way!

Lauren currently lives in Manhattan with her husband and their spoiled Pomeranian. When not writing, you'll find her at happy hour, running at a doggedly slow pace, or trying to straighten her naturally curly hair.

The Moretti brothers are three of
New York's Finest. But when the youngest,
Luc, heroically saves a kid's life, he becomes
the most famous—and the most wanted—
by a sexy, sassy TV journalist...

Please see the next page
for an excerpt from

FRISK ME.

CHAPTER ONE

Holy crap! You're like, *that* guy! You're *the* cop!"

Luc Moretti deliberately ignored the high-pitched squeal.

He took a slow sip of his much-needed coffee and threw up a silent prayer that for once, the women would be talking about some other cop.

"Tina, it *is* him! The cop from the YouTube video!"

Shit.

Pray as he might, it was *never* some other officer who was subjected to overenthusiastic hero worship. Not these days, anyway. It was always *Luc* who couldn't do so much as get on the A train without hearing some form of, *hey, aren't you that guy...?*

Yes. Yes, he was that fucking guy. Unfortunately.

"Can we get a picture with you?" one of the women asked as they both closed in on him.

"Actually, I—"

Luc's ready protest was interrupted by the deep voice of his partner.

"Ladies, ladies, let's give Officer Moretti some space! The man likes to refresh his makeup before a photo op. Moretti, did you bring that special lip balm you like to use? The one you say makes your lips all rosy?"

Luc's eyes narrowed at his partner as he reached up and scratched his nose with his middle finger.

Both women had already pulled cell phones out of their purses, ready for a shot with New York's latest hero.

Luc shot another *fuck you* glare at his partner, but Sawyer Lopez was already reaching for the girls' phones, gesturing his hands in an "all-together-now" motion.

Two curvy blondes flanked Luc on either side. Their too-sweet perfume was ruining his caffeine buzz, but he smiled for the picture anyway. The grin was habit, if not exactly genuine.

Once, Luc's smiles for pretty women had been easy and authentic. Now they were reflexive, born out of a month's worth of misplaced hero worship.

Sawyer Lopez, on the other hand, had no such hangups, and was in full charm mode.

"So where you ladies visiting from?" Lopez asked, handing the girls back their phones.

Luc took another sip of his increasingly cold coffee and rolled his eyes. At least *someone* was profiting from Luc's brush with fame.

"Little Rock," the taller blonde said, her fingers moving rapidly over the screen of her phone.

Luc had no doubt that his face had just been plastered all over every possible social media site. Again.

"Ah, that explains the cute southern accent," Lopez told the woman with a wink.

Uh-huh. It *also* explained what the women were doing wandering around Times Square—a place no New Yorker would be caught dead in unless someone paid them to be there.

In Luc and Lopez's case, that *someone* doing the paying was the NYPD.

Crowd control in midtown wasn't exactly the sexy part of being a New York cop, but it was a necessary one, especially on days where the latest teen pop star was giving a concert at 47th and Broadway.

Times Square was every cop's least favorite gig. But when there was a concert, parade, or holiday, it was all hands on deck.

"How long you here for?" Lopez asked, still trying to get the women to notice that he was giving them his best smile. They barely responded, still busy on their phones, and Luc nearly grinned at the irritation on his partner's face.

A month ago, Sawyer Lopez could have gotten the attention of just about any woman he wanted. With the dark skin and jet-black hair of his Latino father, and the pale blue eyes of a Norwegian mother, he was never short on female company.

Then Luc had become an overnight sensation, and now Lopez had to work twice as hard for his share of female attention. Luc would be gloating if the whole situation hadn't been so damned annoying.

"Excuse me, Officer, could you help us for a second? We're trying to find the Hilton—"

Luc turned to the tired-looking couple dragging around

enormous suitcases and a cranky-looking toddler. Their expressions were more exhausted than star-struck, and he smiled when he realized they didn't recognize him.

He'd nearly forgotten how good it felt to be anonymous.

By the time Luc pointed the tourists to their hotel, his partner had finally managed to recapture the blondes' attention.

"Oh *God*, no," Lopez was saying. "Listen, you want *real* New York pizza, you're going to walk a bit. I'd recommend—"

Ah, shit. Once Lopez got started talking about pizza, he could go on for hours.

And since Lopez only shared his "pizza secrets" when he was trying to get laid, experience told Luc he was on the verge of being roped into a double date with a couple of Arkansas tourists.

"Lopez. Let's move out," Luc snapped.

The two women blinked in surprise at Luc's sharp tone, and he felt a sting of regret for being a complete and utter dick.

He used to be good around women. Back when women had liked him for *him*. Back when he'd been just regular Luc, not Super Cop Moretti.

But then everything had changed. Thanks to a couple of tourists with camera phones and impeccable timing, Luc's life had become a damned carnival.

Luc gave a slow smile to soften the blow of his irritation. "Sorry, ladies. Duty calls."

His partner grunted something that sounded like *horseshit*.

Lopez had a point. Luc's excuse *was* a load of BS. The only duty they had at the moment was making sure Broadway didn't turn into a stampede.

But the women nodded in wide-eyed understanding at Luc. "New York's so lucky to have a cop like you."

Luc heard the words like a jab to the jugular, although he forced himself to smile through the wave of darkness that rushed over him. These women didn't have a clue just how undeserving of praise he was. Nobody did.

Pushing the haunting thoughts away before they could fully take hold, he gave the women a wide smile before dragging his partner away.

"I need a disguise," Luc muttered.

"Nah. Embrace it, man. Get yourself a cape. I'm thinking velvet," Lopez said. "I bet Clark Kent knows just the place to get that shit dry-cleaned."

"Hilarious. I haven't heard a million superhero jokes from my brothers, so please, bring it on."

Lopez grinned unabashedly. "I bet the Moretti cop clan is loving their little *bambino* being all famous and shit."

"You have no idea," Luc muttered.

Luc was the youngest in a family of cops. He couldn't even get in the door to Sunday dinner without his brothers bursting out of the bushes, pretending to be the paparazzi.

Generally speaking, his *bambino* status was hell, but he'd happily go back to taking shit about being the baby over this latest brush-with-fame crap.

Lopez skidded to a halt beside Luc, his eyes boring through the crowd as he slowly extended a warning finger. Luc followed his partner's glare to a sulky teen boy in saggy jeans and greasy hair parted down the middle. The kid was seconds away from attempting to ride his skateboard down a very busy midtown sidewalk.

Lopez said it all with one finger and a look. *Not cool, kid. Don't make me come over there.*

Luckily the kid correctly interpreted the warning and had enough sense to keep his board tucked under his arm until he got to a less crowded part of the city. Or at least until he got out of sight of cops.

"Wish they were all that easy," Luc said as they resumed walking.

Lopez grunted before turning his attention back to Luc. "So how's your dad reacting to your newfound celebrity? I bet Big T's either disgusted at the circus or thrilled at the prestige."

"A little of both," Luc said, tossing his coffee cup in the trash. "He's always thought cops were supposed to be unsung heroes, but he's not above wanting the Department to look good."

"Even now?" Lopez asked. "He's retired. He's not supposed to care about anything other than sports and annoying your mom."

"*Especially* now," Luc replied.

"Ah," Lopez said, nodding in understanding. "He bored?"

Luc grunted as he surveyed the crowd out of habit. "Just last week he threatened to take up paint-by-numbers if one of us didn't go over there to watch the game with him."

"Can't be easy for the guy," Lopez replied. "One day you're head of the fucking NYPD, the next day, *bam*, you're looking at a future of mundane arts and crafts projects."

Lopez had a valid point. Just a year ago, Tony Moretti had stepped down as police commissioner. The adjustment to retirement had been a rough one, made easier only by the fact that four out of four sons were cops to carry on his legacy.

Or so Tony liked to claim.

What Luc was pretty sure his father *actually* meant was that Luc's three older brothers were carrying on the family legacy. But Luc…Luc suspected that deep down, his father didn't expect much out of Luc. Not since the Shayna Johnson case had gone to shit.

Luc's brothers may push the envelope on respect for authority, but none of them had had their partner die on the job.

No, *that* horror was Luc's private torture. Private, because nobody talked about it. Ever.

But at least the rest of the Moretti siblings were on a clear path toward securing the Moretti family name as NYPD royalty. Despite his brothers' penchant for bending the rules, all had made a name for themselves as some of the city's best.

Luc's oldest brother, Anthony, was next in line for captain in his zone.

Vincent was one of the city's best homicide DTs. *The* best, according to Vin. Modesty had never been his strong suit.

Marco had taken his fair share of crap for moving to California to follow his girlfriend, but he too was moving up the ranks of the LAPD at an obnoxious rate.

And then there was Luc. Luc was just lowly Officer Moretti. The one with a dead partner. The responding officer on the Shayna Johnson case.

Until now. Now Luc was *that* cop. The hero. The one who couldn't get a cup of coffee without the barista doing a double take and writing her phone number on the paper cup of his Americano.

For most cops, the attention would have been flattering at best, a nuisance at worst.

But for Luc, it was pure torture.

Because only he really understood that Luc Moretti was as far from *heroic* as it was possible to get.

Fall in Love with Forever Romance

CUFF ME
by Lauren Layne

USA Today bestselling author Lauren Layne brings us NYPD's Finest—
where three Moretti brothers fulfill their family's cop legacy. Seeing his
longtime partner Jill with someone else triggers feelings in Vincent he
never knew he had. Now he'll have to stop playing good cop/bad cop, and
find a way to convince her to be his partner for life…

Fall in Love with Forever Romance

A BILLIONAIRE AFTER DARK
by Katie Lane

Nash Beaumont is the hottest of the billionaire Beaumont brothers. But beneath his raw charisma is a dark side that he struggles to control, until he falls in love with Eden—the reporter determined to expose his secret. Fans of Jessica Clare will love the newest novel from *USA Today* bestselling author Katie Lane.

Fall in Love with Forever Romance

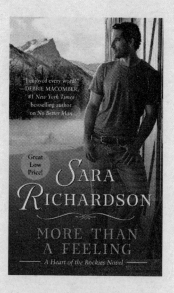

MORE THAN A FEELING
by Sara Richardson

"Charming, witty, and fun. There's no better read. I enjoyed every word!"

—DEBBIE MACOMBER, #1 *New York Times* bestselling author on *No Better Man*

Fall in Love with Forever Romance

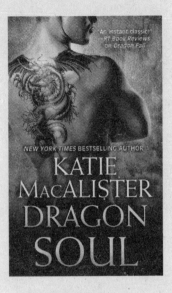

"An instant classic!"
—RT Book Reviews
on *Dragon Fall*

NEW YORK TIMES BESTSELLING AUTHOR

KATIE MacALISTER

DRAGON SOUL

DRAGON SOUL
by Katie MacAlister

In *New York Times* bestselling author Katie MacAlister's DRAGON SOUL, Rowan Dakar can't afford to be distracted by the funniest, most desirable woman he's ever set eyes on. But no prophecy in the world can ever stop true love...